Welcome to the No. 1 Ladies'
Detective Agency

The story so far ...

Following their big tent wedding party, Mma Makutsi and Phuti
Radiphuti embarked on the construction of a marital home.
Meanwhile, Mma Ramotswe found her slumbers disturbed by
dreams of a tall stranger – but she wasn't sure she was ready to
discover what this vision might portend. Soon even Mma Makutsi
had to admit that untoward things were occurring around the
No. 1 Ladies' Detective Agency, including the disappearance of
Mma Potokwani from the orphan farm, and more trouble for
Fanwell the garage apprentice ...

By Alexander McCall Smith

The
Minor Adjustment
Beauty Salon

ALEXANDER McCALL SMITH

This book is for Professor Bill Chameides
of Duke University,
in admiration of the work he has done

ABACUS

First published in Great Britain in 2013 by Little, Brown
This paperback edition published in 2014 by Abacus

A CIP catalogue record for this book
is available from the British Library.

ISBN 978-0-349-13928-9

Typeset in Galliard by M Rules
Printed and bound in Great Britain by
Clays Ltd, St Ives plc

Papers used by Abacus are from well-managed forests
and other responsible sources.

MIX
Paper from
responsible sources
FSC
www.fsc.org   FSC® C104740

Abacus
An imprint of
Little, Brown Book Group
100 Victoria Embankment
London EC4Y 0DY

An Hachette UK Company
www.hachette.co.uk

www.littlebrown.co.uk

Chapter One

Mechanics Can Cook

Precious Ramotswe, creator and owner of the No. 1 Ladies' Detective Agency, Botswana's only detective agency for the problems of ladies, and of others, had never studied business management. She knew that it was common for people who ran their own businesses to take courses on topics such as stocktaking and cash flow, but she did not feel this was necessary in her case. Mind you, the No. 1 Ladies' Detective Agency had never made a profit, although in recent years it had not made a loss either, for Mma Ramotswe had managed to juggle income and expenditure in such a way as to end up breaking even – provided that you practised what a book-keeper friend of hers called, with some admiration, *Optimistic Accounting*.

It was not that she was averse to taking advice. A few days ago she had come across a business magazine that had been left behind in the garage by one of her husband's customers, and had read it from cover to cover, over a pot of redbush tea and a large doughnut. This magazine had been full of helpful articles with titles such as: 'Making the most of your human resources' and 'How to maximise growth in difficult economic circumstances'. There was also a column called *Dr Profit's Business Clinic*, to which readers could write with their business problems and receive free advice from Dr Profit himself, a man who was pictured wearing a large square pair of glasses and a broad smile – the look of somebody, she thought, who was probably always in healthy profit.

In the issue perused by Mma Ramotswe, one concerned reader raised a problem connected with an awkward employee – 'Can one fire an employee who smells bad?' Mma Ramotswe read this question with some interest – although it had no bearing on her own business (Mma Makutsi was always well turned-out and took, she believed, two baths a day) – before turning the page and seeing an article on the maximising of growth. 'A business that isn't expanding will actually be contracting,' wrote the author. 'That rule has been shown to be true time after time. How many businessmen are there who sit and contemplate the ruins of a once-profitable business simply because they forgot to expand?'

Mma Ramotswe frowned. The No. 1 Ladies' Detective Agency was exactly the same size as it had been when she had founded it. It had one owner and one employee, one vehicle, a filing cabinet, a kettle, two teapots and three mugs. There was also one typewriter, which was operated by Mma Makutsi, and one box of stationery. These assets had been there more or less from the beginning, although the second teapot was certainly a later addition. Did that count as growth? Could you say that your business had expanded if it had gone from owning one teapot to two?

Somehow she thought that Dr Profit would answer both those questions with a shake of his head. Of course, she herself had expanded in girth since the agency was founded, but she did not think that such a form of growth was what the author of the article had in mind.

She thought of Mr J. L. B. Matekoni's business, Tlokweng Road Speedy Motors, with which she shared premises, and wondered how it would fare against this rather unsettling test. Again, it was difficult to see any significant expansion. Mr J. L. B. Matekoni still had his two apprentices, although one of them, Fanwell, was now a qualified mechanic. That might count as growth of a sort, she supposed, but it was probably cancelled out by reports that Charlie, the other young man employed in the garage, had, by all accounts, become rather worse at his job. Certainly there did not seem to be any more customers than there had been in the past; indeed, Mr J. L. B. Matekoni had complained only a few weeks previously that there seemed to be fewer and fewer cars being brought in for service.

'People have to go to those big garages these days,' he said. 'They have to do that because their cars are full of computers, and ordinary mechanics don't have all the right wires and things for these clever cars. What can you do if you look at the engine and see that it is full of electric wiring and computer chips? Where's the carburettor? Where's the distributor? Where's the starter motor?'

He had looked at Mma Ramotswe reproachfully, as if she had somehow mislaid these various parts.

She sighed. 'Everything is too complicated these days, Mr J. L. B. Matekoni. Everything is made to be thrown away rather than fixed. It is all very wasteful.'

She warmed to her theme. 'When I think of what we made do with in the past, it makes me very sad. If you found a hole in a sock, you darned it. We were taught how to do that at school. And if your collar frayed, then you had it turned. If the handle came off a cup, you glued it back on.'

'Yes,' said Mr J. L. B. Matekoni. 'You never threw things away. Nowadays, if something goes wrong, you throw it out of the window, just like that.'

'And people too,' said Mma Ramotswe. 'If you suddenly decide you don't like somebody, you throw them out of the window too. That's what wives do to their husbands these days.'

Mr J. L. B. Matekoni looked concerned. 'Out of the window, Mma?'

'Not really out of the window,' said Mma Ramotswe. 'I just use that as an expression, Rra. And it's not just wives who throw their husbands out of the window when they get bored with them; it's men too. In fact, there are more wives thrown out of the window than men, I think.'

'Either way, it's not very good,' said Mr J. L. B. Matekoni. 'Nobody should be thrown out of the window, Mma.'

They had lapsed into silence as they contemplated, in their individual ways, this decline in civility. Mma Ramotswe was not given to taking a gloomy view of things, but she felt nonetheless that there were respects in which she would find it very difficult to explain to her father, the late Obed Ramotswe, what had happened in the years since his death. It was true that Botswana had made great progress and remained a country to be proud of, but still, there were changes that it was hard to see in a positive light. She imagined walking with him through their home village, Mochudi, and showing him the improvements: the numerous public water taps, the improved sewage system, the new businesses that had sprung up. But what would she say when they were passed by a group of schoolchildren and not one of them greeted him, as it was polite, and customary, for children to do when they passed an old man? How would she explain to him that nowadays many children did not greet strangers? She saw him wearing his old hat – the hat that he had worn for year upon year and was so familiar to her, and so beloved. She wondered what he would say when he saw men walking about either with no hat on their heads – even under the midday sun – or with unusual new hats, or even caps with those curious visors in the front, but deliberately worn back-to-front. Where, he would ask, have all these new hats come from, and why did none of these hats seem to have *experience*, that indefinable quality that hats acquire after they have been worn day after day, in all weather, for year after year?

And yet, in spite of all these rather unsettling developments, there were some things that did not change. Mr J. L. B. Matekoni had not changed in the slightest – and never would, she thought. Charlie did not change either; one might have thought that he would become more mature as the years went past, but this was not the case. At the age of sixteen, when he had first started his apprenticeship, he had spent his lunch hours sitting on an upturned oil drum, ogling girls as they walked past to catch one of the minibuses plying their trade along the Tlokweng Road. Now, at the age of twenty-whatever-it-was, he still sat on an oil drum – she believed it was exactly the same oil drum – and watched young women walk past.

Of course, she thought that Charlie might try to justify this if she were to reproach him, and to argue that there was nothing wrong in spending his time in this way. She could just imagine the conversation . . .

'So, Mma? What's wrong with taking a rest over the lunch hour? I work hard all morning and then I sit and recover my energy. What's wrong with that?'

'Nothing,' she would say. 'There is nothing wrong with taking a break. But what's the point of watching girls for hour after hour?'

He would defend himself: 'But, Mma, I didn't ask them to walk along the Tlokweng Road. I didn't ask them to wear those dresses and walk like that. They are the ones you should be criticising, Mma, not me.'

It would be hopeless, and even if she turned her attention to the drum, and suggested that he sit somewhere else for a change, she would get nowhere.

'But, Mma, why change your drum if you find one that's comfortable? Why not stick to the one you like?'

No, in a world of flux and rearrangement, both Charlie and Mr J. L. B. Matekoni were as fixed in their positions as the stars in the night sky. And the same might have been said of Mma Makutsi . . . But now there was an air of uncertainty surrounding Mma Makutsi and her plans, and Mma Ramotswe was unsure how to resolve it. The problem was that Mma Makutsi was pregnant, but seemed to be quite unwilling to talk about the implications of this for the No. 1 Ladies' Detective Agency. Naturally Mma Ramotswe was pleased that her assistant was expecting a baby, but how much greater would this pleasure have been if she had plans in place for the inevitable maternity leave. But no such plans had been mentioned – not one.

Of course, Mma Ramotswe and Mr J. L. B. Matekoni had discussed the issue many times themselves, as they did that evening some months previously when he had first raised it with her. They were sitting on their veranda in that companionable manner that may come upon a married couple at the end of a day's work, when they are together again and watching the sun sink behind the acacia trees and the untidy telephone wires of their neighbour's garden. They had been talking about nothing in particular, with few matters that were likely to disturb the peace of this quiet half-hour before supper.

'I wonder when our neighbour is going to tidy up those wires,' mused Mr J. L. B. Matekoni. 'You'd think that he'd get in touch with the telephone people and get them to come round and sort things out. I shouldn't be surprised to find out that half those wires are dead – just ancient wires from the past.'

Mma Ramotswe glanced over the fence at the untidy cluster of wires attached to the wooden telephone pole. She felt that Mr J. L. B. Matekoni was probably right; the country was full of wires that might have done something important in the past but had long since stopped being used. She imagined somehow listening in to one of these wires and hearing the echoes of some forgotten exchange between people that had taken place many years before but still echoed through those old abandoned wires. One might hear a conversation that took place in 1962, perhaps, when Botswana was still the Bechuanaland Protectorate, and when cattle were the main industry and there were no diamonds. It might be a conversation between somebody in Lobatse driving up to see somebody in Gaborone and not requiring any directions because there were only a couple of roads. 'You take the right-hand road. You know the right-hand road?'

Silence, empty silence, and then a faint, tinny voice ringing down the line. 'I know that road, Rra. That is the road my grandfather lives on.'

The voice of the dead – you could hear them still, if you listened hard enough. Late people still talking, like children after lights-out: the faint, distant voices of our ancestors.

And then, as if he had already forgotten about the telephone wires, Mr J. L. B. Matekoni suddenly said, 'Mma Makutsi?'

It was a question rather than a pronouncement, and Mma

Ramotswe waited a moment or two before answering, in case the point of the question might be expanded upon. But it was not.

'Yes,' she said. 'Mma Makutsi: what of her, Rra?'

Mr J. L. B. Matekoni shrugged. 'Nothing, Mma.' But it was not nothing. 'I just happened to be wondering whether there was anything ... different about her?' He paused. 'Now that she's married, you see.'

She looked at him, and he turned away, embarrassed. 'No, I don't mean ...'

'Of course not. But it is true, Mr J. L. B. Matekoni: marriage changes people. For some people it can be quite a surprise.'

'Yes, I know that, but there is something about Mma Makutsi I would like to raise, Mma – if you don't mind.'

Mma Ramotswe looked at him expectantly. 'Please do, Rra. We have all the time in the world.'

He frowned. 'But we don't have all the time in the world, Mma Ramotswe ...'

She gently encouraged him. 'No, of course we don't, but we certainly have enough time for you to say something.'

He looked out over the garden, out towards the mopipi tree of which Mma Ramotswe was so proud. Not everyone had a mopipi tree in the garden and she had been solicitous of its welfare, giving it more water than a tree might otherwise expect.

'A question,' he said. 'When did Mma Makutsi get married? Was it seven months ago? Eight?'

Mma Ramotswe did a quick calculation. 'It was just after the first rains, wasn't it? Which makes it about ten or eleven months ago.'

Mr J. L. B. Matekoni looked thoughtful. 'Then that is the answer,' he said.

'The answer to what? To when she got married?'

8

He shook his head. 'Pregnant, Mma. Mma Makutsi must be pregnant.'

It was the simple conviction with which he spoke that struck Mma Ramotswe. It was as if Mr J. L. B. Matekoni had said something as obvious and uncomplicated as: 'This car needs new brakes' or 'Your problem is in the fuel supply'.

She was surprised that he had noticed. She had very recently seen the signs, but men often did not spot these things. 'I think she probably is,' she said. 'But I've decided that it is better to leave it up to her to tell me. I'm sure she will.'

'She may think you can't tell,' he said. 'Those dresses she wears are like tents. Anything could be happening under there. She could even have several people living under those dresses for all we know.'

Mma Ramotswe laughed. 'But it's odd that she hasn't mentioned it yet. Why would she not have told me before this?'

He shrugged. 'Sometimes people don't want other people to know because they are worried that everything might not go well. Then everybody ends up disappointed.'

Mma Ramotswe had another theory. 'I think she's worried about asking for time off to have the baby. She's very conscientious, you know. I think she may have been putting it off because of that.'

Mr J. L. B. Matekoni listened, but he wondered whether Mma Makutsi might not for some other reason be trying to hide her situation. He remembered a case of concealed pregnancy that had occurred in the family of one of his clients. 'There is a man with an old Land Cruiser,' he said. He often identified people by their cars and Mma Ramotswe was quite used to this. 'This man with the Land Cruiser – a very reliable car, you know, Mma, although it's now almost twenty-five years old – anyway, this man told me one day that his daughter had had a baby. And you know what, Mma Ramotswe?'

She waited for him to continue.

'You know what, Mma? This daughter – the daughter of the man—'

'Yes, Rra, the daughter of the man with the Land Cruiser . . .'

'Yes, that man: this daughter of his said one day that she wanted to go into town to see a friend and so she asked her father whether he could take her in his Land Cruiser.'

'Yes?'

'Well, she got into the Land Cruiser and they set off. They lived on a farm out Tlokweng way – about half an hour from town. Anyway, there they were in the Land Cruiser and suddenly she started to cry out. Her father thought it was because the road was very bumpy; their track had been washed away in places by the rains and there were big holes in it – big ones, Mma. That Land Cruiser's suspension . . .' He shook his head, whether in admiration of the suspension's capacity for endurance or sympathy for its ordeal, Mma Ramotswe was uncertain.

She knew what was coming. 'She was about to have a baby?'

She noticed his disappointment that she had guessed, and so she quickly said, 'Of course, it must have been a big surprise for him, Rra. I normally wouldn't have thought of that.'

'The baby was born in the Land Cruiser,' said Mr J. L. B. Matekoni. 'In the back.' He paused. 'They are big vehicles, of course.'

'That sort of thing is quite common among teenage girls,' said Mma Ramotswe. 'They don't want to tell their parents and everybody just thinks they are putting on a bit of weight. Then suddenly there is another mouth to feed.' She paused. 'But Mma Makutsi is not a teenager. She is a responsible woman and she has a good husband to support her and any number of babies. Her case is quite different.'

'She is definitely pregnant,' said Mr J. L. B. Matekoni, and then added, mischievously: 'I must say, Mma, I would have thought a great detective would have worked that out much earlier than this.'

She took this remark in good humour. 'Actually, I did, Rra. I have suspected it for a little while but I have not wanted to embarrass her. And then ...' She paused before continuing. 'I am not a great detective, Rra. I am a person who runs a detective agency – that is all.'

He reached out to touch her gently on the arm. 'You are the greatest detective in the history of Botswana,' he said. 'I know that. The whole world knows that.'

She thanked him. It was now time for her to go into the kitchen and prepare their meal. You could be a great detective, but you still had to cook supper.

She looked at Mr J. L. B. Matekoni. He had never cooked anything in all the time they had been married, except on one occasion when he had tried to bake a cake and had failed miserably.

'Would you like to cook supper one day, Rra?' she asked.

He stared at her with incredulity. 'What was that, Mma? I thought you asked me whether I would like to cook supper.'

'I did,' she said.

His jaw dropped. 'I am a mechanic, Mma ...'

'Mechanics can cook. Ladies can fix cars. It's different these days, Rra. Men can do things. Women can do things. There is no work that is reserved just for one sort of person. Not any more.'

He looked injured. 'But what would I cook?'

'Anything,' she said. 'The same things that I cook.'

His injured expression now turned to one of misery. 'But I do not think that it would taste very good, Mma.'

She spoke gently. 'We can talk about it some other time. I like to cook for you, Mr J. L. B. Matekoni. And for the children too.

I am teaching Motholeli to cook now and she is getting better and better. It is not a chore.'

'And I would teach Puso how to cook,' muttered Mr J. L. B. Matekoni. 'If I knew how, that is . . .'

Mma Ramotswe smiled at this. 'Yes, it is best to learn first, then teach.'

'And I like to eat the food you cook, Mma. I shall try to help you more. Maybe I could —'

She stopped him. 'You have always been very good with the washing up,' she said. 'Many men are good at that.' She paused. 'If they remember, that is.'

As it happened, Mma Makutsi did bring up the issue of her pregnancy only a few days after this conversation. She broached the subject quite casually, during a silence in the office while they were waiting for the kettle to boil.

'I should tell you that I am pregnant,' she announced. 'I have been pregnant now for many months.'

Mma Ramotswe clapped her hands with delight. 'I thought you might be, Mma. This is very good news.'

Mma Makutsi accepted the congratulations with due solemnity. 'We are both very pleased. Phuti is excited.'

'It is natural that he is excited,' said Mma Ramotswe. 'Men like these things just as much as women – mostly.' She paused. 'Well, not always, but very often.'

What Mma Makutsi said next rather surprised her. 'I don't want to talk about it, Mma. I hope you do not mind, but I do not wish to talk about something that has not yet happened – in case it might not happen.'

'I can understand that, Mma,' said Mma Ramotswe. 'But it's good to plan . . .'

Mma Makutsi shook her head. 'I do not want to discuss it.

Things can go wrong if you discuss things before it is time to discuss them.'

It was clear that there was to be no further conversation about pregnancy and no mention, therefore, of the issue of maternity leave.

Later that day, when Mma Ramotswe told Mr J. L. B. Matekoni about this exchange, he shook his head. 'You won't get her to change; you know what she's like.'

'But how can I make arrangements for cover while she is away?' asked Mma Ramotswe. 'I have no idea when she wants to go off, and for how long. She hasn't even told me when the baby is due, and I can't raise it with her.'

'You will have to wait,' said Mr J. L. B. Matekoni. 'It is very inconsiderate of her, but there we are. You cannot change people who will not be changed – and that is probably even more true when they're pregnant.'

Over the months that followed, Mma Makutsi's pregnancy became increasingly obvious, but her disinclination to discuss maternity leave remained.

'It's like having an elephant in the room and not mentioning it,' Mma Ramotswe said to Mr J. L. B. Matekoni.

'That is a very funny remark, Mma Ramotswe,' said Mr J. L. B. Matekoni, adding: 'In the circumstances.'

Chapter Two

Bones Never Lie

Mma Sheba Kutso was an unusually tall woman, which was why Mma Makutsi said, 'Here comes that giraffe lady, Mma Ramotswe.'

She said this as she was gazing out of the window in the office the next morning at the very time that Mma Kutso's car drew up and nosed into the shade under the acacia tree that was already half-occupied by Mma Ramotswe's tiny white van.

Mma Ramotswe looked in her assistant's direction. She was puzzled by the reference to a giraffe lady, but then Mma Makutsi was known to say strange, unexpected things – things that often seemed unconnected with anything else.

'Giraffe lady, Mma?' she asked. 'Who is this giraffe lady?'

'That woman,' answered Mma Makutsi. 'You know the one –

the tall one who calls herself a lawyer. She's parking right next to your van, Mma. Don't get too close . . . Ow!'

Mma Ramotswe sprang to her feet. 'Has she hit my van?'

'No,' said Mma Makutsi. 'Almost, but not quite. Now she is getting out – look at her. And . . . Ow! I think she has scratched the van with her door, Mma. Look, she's bending down to examine it.'

They watched as Mma Kutso, unaware that she was being observed, moistened a finger on her tongue and then dabbed at the paintwork of Mma Ramotswe's van. Mma Ramotswe raised an eyebrow but managed to appear not overly concerned.

'My van has had worse experiences than that,' she said. She paused before continuing. 'And Mma Sheba is a proper lawyer, you know, Mma Makutsi.'

Mma Makutsi shrugged. 'People should be more careful, especially lawyers.' She paused, and then muttered, 'So-called.'

Mma Ramotswe let the remark pass. She did not hold it against her visitor that she parked a bit too close to her van; it was never easy to judge these things exactly. Mma Makutsi was perhaps a bit too ready to comment adversely on the driving of others, when she herself was not the possessor of a driving licence and was only now getting round to having lessons from Patrick's Patient Driving School.

'Your lessons, Mma,' Mma Ramotswe asked. 'How is your own parking progressing?'

'It is very accurate,' said Mma Makutsi. 'We have done going forward into the parking place and now we are doing going backwards into same. Next it will be parallel parking.' She began to make her way to the door to admit Mma Sheba. 'I expect I shall achieve high marks in the test, when I take it.'

Ninety-seven per cent, thought Mma Ramotswe but did not say it, though she might have done so had Mma Sheba not entered the room.

The visitor greeted Mma Ramotswe courteously, asking after not only her own health but also the health of Mr J. L. B. Matekoni, of Motholeli and of Puso. She received a full answer to each of these enquiries: Mr J. L. B. Matekoni was in good shape, but could do to lose a small amount of weight; Motholeli had suffered from an in-growing toenail but this had been dealt with satisfactorily and she was far more comfortable now; and Puso was growing quickly, but still seemed to have a great deal of energy left to run about the place, ride his bicycle and climb trees.

'And I am very well too, Mma,' said Mma Makutsi loudly.

The lawyer turned round. Although the tone of Mma Makutsi's voice had been tetchy, she smiled civilly at their visitor.

'I'm pleased to hear that, Mma,' Mma Sheba said. 'You are certainly looking very well.'

Mma Ramotswe joined in. 'Mma Makutsi was married recently, Mma. You may have heard of it. It was a very good wedding.'

Mma Sheba nodded. 'I know the Radiphuti family – not very well, but a bit.' She smiled at Mma Makutsi again. 'You are a very lucky woman to have a husband like that. There were many ladies who could have been in your position.'

Mma Makutsi seemed taken aback by this remark, and it took her a few moments to react. When she spoke, her voice was strained. 'What are you saying, Mma?' she asked. 'I am not sure if I understand.'

Again Mma Ramotswe tried to defuse the situation. 'I don't think that Mma Sheba is saying that Phuti had lots of girlfriends before you. I'm sure he had none.'

Now both Mma Sheba and Mma Makutsi glared at Mma Ramotswe.

'I mean,' said Mma Ramotswe in a flustered tone, 'that he was not one of these men who spent a lot of time chasing girls – men like Charlie, for instance.'

'But why did you say he had none?' asked Mma Makutsi. 'There is a big difference between chasing lots of girls and having no girlfriends at all.'

'That is a very big difference,' contributed Mma Sheba. 'I certainly didn't say that he had no girlfriends at all. I do not know whether he had any . . . or none. I just do not know.'

'Then why did you say what you did say, Mma?' snapped Mma Makutsi.

Mma Sheba looked anxiously at Mma Ramotswe. 'But all that I meant was that he was a very good catch. And I meant, too, that there were many ladies who would have liked to catch him, had they even known him, which they didn't, I think.'

Mma Ramotswe threw a warning glance at Mma Makutsi. 'The important thing,' she said, 'is that we are all well. That is what counts.'

Mma Sheba, equally eager to prevent needless confrontation, quickly agreed with this sentiment.

'And now, Mma Makutsi,' said Mma Ramotswe, 'I'm sure that Mma Sheba would like a cup of tea.' She smiled at her visitor. 'Am I right, Mma?'

Mma Sheba nodded. 'That would be very good. It is never too late, or too early, for tea.'

'My view too,' agreed Mma Ramotswe. 'Now, what would you like? We have redbush tea or we have ordinary tea. Both are available.'

'Not everybody likes redbush,' said Mma Makutsi, hovering behind Mma Sheba's chair. 'I myself prefer what Mma Ramotswe calls ordinary tea, but which can be far from ordinary – if made correctly.'

'You choose,' said Mma Ramotswe. 'And you must not let others –' and here she looked directly at Mma Makutsi – 'interfere in your choice.'

'Information is not interference,' said Mma Makutsi. 'There is a difference, I think.'

'I think I'll try redbush,' said Mma Sheba. 'I have a friend who drinks it, and she swears by it.'

'As do I,' said Mma Ramotswe. 'It has no caffeine and therefore you can drink it even when you are about to go to sleep. And it is very good for the skin, I'm told.'

'Where's the proof?' muttered Mma Makutsi. But this question, barbed as it was, was ignored by Mma Ramotswe, who now looked expectantly at Mma Sheba.

'We have only met once before,' said Mma Sheba. 'Do you remember? It was at that lunch in the President Hotel some years ago – the Gaborone Professional Ladies' Lunch. Remember? We sat next to one another.'

Mma Ramotswe now recalled. 'Of course! I knew we had met somewhere, but I couldn't put my finger on it.'

Remembering the occasion, Mma Ramotswe felt a flush of ancient, rekindled embarrassment. The lunch had been an ordeal from start to finish. She had gone at the invitation of one of her clients, an accountant, who had thought it would be interesting for a group that consisted largely of lawyers, doctors and accountants to have a businesswoman from an entirely different field. This friend had been solicitous but had been unable to sit next to her guest at the table as the club's policy was to break up friends and mix people together. As a result, Mma Ramotswe had found herself seated next to Mma Sheba on one side, and a surgeon on the other. The surgeon was newly qualified but very conscious of her position. She had spoken to Mma Ramotswe politely at first, and then had asked her where she had done her training.

'But I have not had any training, Mma,' said Mma Ramotswe. She wondered whether reading Clovis Andersen's *The Principles of Private Detection* would count, but decided that it would not. Private detection was largely a matter of common sense, she had concluded.

The surgeon had shown surprise. 'No training?' she asked. 'So anybody can do what you do?'

Mma Ramotswe weighed her answer. 'Anybody? Probably not anybody, Mma. Some people might not be very good private detectives because they ... well, they might not understand people very well. You have to be able to understand people.'

The surgeon smiled. 'If that's all, then it must be very easy. Even my grandmother could be a private detective.'

Mma Ramotswe did not say anything and simply looked down at her place setting. A grandmother would make a very good detective, she thought: grandmothers had seen a lot of human nature and could use that knowledge well.

'Frankly,' said the surgeon, 'I'm not sure that private detection counts as a profession. No offence to you, Mma, but if something requires no training, then, well, I wonder whether it should be considered a profession at all.'

Mma Ramotswe kept her eyes fixed on her place setting before her. She soon became aware of a reaction from Mma Sheba beside her.

'Excuse me, Mma,' said Mma Sheba. 'I, for one, think that being a detective is a very important profession. I do not agree with you, but I suppose that you know no better, being so young and inexperienced in the world. Maybe you will think differently when you have the experience that our colleague –' she laid heavy emphasis on the word *colleague* – 'here has.'

That had ended the conversation, although Mma Sheba made a point of talking to Mma Ramotswe for the remainder of the lunch. The surgeon, smarting, had confined herself to talking to the woman on her other side. Mma Ramotswe had been grateful for the support, but her enjoyment of the lunch had been spoiled and she was relieved when it was over. Since then, she had not seen Mma Sheba.

'I have seen you,' said Mma Makutsi from the other side of the office. 'I have seen you going into your office in town. You are a lawyer.'

Mma Sheba half-turned to reply. 'You're very observant, Mma. But I suppose that is what comes with being a detective. You have to notice things in your job.'

'And in your job too, Mma,' said Mma Ramotswe. 'When you're reading through papers, you must always be looking for things that shouldn't be there.'

Mma Sheba laughed. 'Yes, you must. People will try to put things into contracts in the hope that the other side won't see them. We have to be on our toes.'

'So, Mma . . .' prompted Mma Ramotswe.

'Let me tell you a little about myself,' said Mma Sheba. 'Then you will feel that you know me better. And then . . .' She paused, with the air of one about to reveal an important secret. 'Then I shall tell you about why I have come to see you.'

'As you know, Mma,' said Mma Sheba, 'I am an attorney. My office – the one that your assistant—'

'Associate detective,' interrupted Mma Makutsi.

'That your associate detective mentioned. I have two partners in the firm, Mma. One of them is a woman, and one is a man. We all get on very well together and we have different areas of speciality. I am the one who does trusts and executories: I look after people's wills and estates after their death. We are quite busy these days, not because more people are becoming late but because there is more money in the country. The more money you have, then the more money there is in your estate after your death. I have one assistant, who is newly qualified, and I might even need to get another one before too long.'

'You are fortunate that your business is doing so well,' said Mma Ramotswe. 'Not everybody is in that position these days.'

'Indeed they are not,' said Mma Sheba. 'One of my partners handles insolvencies. He's very busy these days.' She shook her head sadly. 'People who have built up a good business over the years, who have worked hard all their lives, suddenly find that the economic climate is very different.'

'It is very sad for them,' said Mma Ramotswe.

Mma Makutsi had now made the tea and brought two mugs that she placed before Mma Ramotswe and Mma Sheba. 'These are both redbush,' she said. 'I shall be drinking ordinary tea myself.'

Mma Sheba thanked her, and Mma Ramotswe was pleased to see that some of Mma Makutsi's prickliness disappeared.

Mma Sheba continued with her tale. 'I drew up a will about four years ago,' she said. 'It was for a man who had been a client of my firm for some time – a farmer called Rra Molapo.'

'I know that family,' said Mma Ramotswe. 'Or rather, I know of them. Was his father not one of Seretse Khama's ministers?'

Mma Sheba nodded. 'Yes, he was in the government then. The Khamas and the Molapos were good friends, but I think the old man – that's the father of my client – became a bit bored with politics and so he bought a farm down on the other side of the Gaborone Dam. It was quite a good farm, and of course land was cheaper in those days. He was a skilled farmer, and the land was in good order when my client, that's Edgar Molapo, took over. The old man died and Rra Edgar took on the running of the farm. He did quite well: he won prizes for his Brahman bulls and I think they even used some of them for breeding on the other side of the border. He made a fair amount of money out of cattle.'

Mma Ramotswe thought of her own father, Obed Ramotswe,

whom she referred to as her 'late daddy'. Whenever anybody mentioned cattle, memories of him came back to her, and she was at his side again, at the cattle post, admiring the herd that he had built up through being able to judge them so well. She heard their lowing, and she smelled the sweet smell that always hung in the air above them – the smell of forage and dust, the smell of their hides when wet, the very smell of her country.

'There is nothing like a good herd of cattle,' she mused.

Mma Sheba agreed. 'No, there is nothing, Mma. And Rra Edgar was a happy man, I think. Except for one thing – he did not have any children of his own.'

Mma Ramotswe held Mma Sheba's gaze. And that is me too, she thought, although she had Motholeli and Puso, and she was grateful, and she loved them.

'So when he became ill and knew that his days were not going to be very long, he came to see me. His wife had died a few years back and the nearest relative was his sister. There had been three of them in the family – Rra Edgar, this sister, and a brother who had gone to Swaziland and had married a Swazi woman. He ran a hotel in the Ezulweni Valley and never came back to Botswana. He and Rra Edgar had fallen out with one another and did not speak. He was killed in a car crash over in Swaziland – you know what their roads are like – and then, of course, it was too late for any reconciliation. I think that Rra Edgar regretted this and he got his sister to arrange with his brother's widow, the Swazi woman, to send over his nephew, whom he had never met. He wanted this boy to come and stay on the farm during his school holidays, and that is what happened. Rra Edgar doted on him, as childless uncles can do. He picked up Setswana and became quite fluent in the language. Eventually he was just like a Motswana born and bred – you would never have known that he had been born in Swaziland.

'The sister stayed on the farm. Rra Edgar built her a small

house, and she settled in that. She had been married, but her husband had gone off with some bar girl from Francistown and that was it. They had no children, as the marriage had not lasted very long.'

Mma Makutsi had returned to her desk by now, but was listening avidly. Now she intervened.

'Men are always doing these things,' she said. 'Going off.'

'That is true,' said Mma Sheba.

They waited for Mma Makutsi to say something else, but she did not.

'About six months ago,' said Mma Sheba, 'Rra Edgar died. He dropped dead very suddenly and they found, when they opened him up, that his heart was not very good. They said that it was something of a miracle that he had lasted as long as he did – fifty-four years, Mma Ramotswe.'

'It is very early to become late,' said Mma Ramotswe. Obed Ramotswe had been only a year or two older, and she thought of all the years that her own father had missed. But then he had been a miner, and it was the dust that killed miners. It lined the lungs, so they said, and that lining turned, in due course, to rock.

'He had asked me to draw up a will,' Mma Sheba went on. 'I had done it and now I had to put the will into effect. There were one or two small legacies: one to the government school in his village, another to Camp Hill, and a small amount to his sister, who was living on the farm when he died. The main asset, though, was the farm.'

'That would have been worth a lot,' said Mma Ramotswe. 'And then there would have been the cattle. You must not forget the cattle.' It was her father's cattle that had made it possible to open the No. 1 Ladies' Detective Agency. Behind so many things in Botswana there lay cattle – it had always been like that.

'The cattle were very valuable,' said Mma Sheba. 'They went

with the farm. The will said: "the farm and all its stock and equipment".'

Mma Ramotswe thought she knew who got those. 'The nephew?'

Mma Sheba nodded. Behind her, seated at her desk, Mma Makutsi was silent.

'But . . .' Mma Sheba looked down at her hands.

'Yes, Mma?'

'But I'm not sure that the right person will get them.'

They waited.

'You haven't found the nephew?' asked Mma Ramotswe.

'I fear that is true, Mma,' said Mma Sheba. 'You see, what has happened is that a young man has stepped forward. He has come into my office and has claimed to be the nephew. He has shown me his birth certificate and his passport too. They both say he is Liso Molapo.'

Mma Ramotswe drew in her breath. 'But he isn't?'

Mma Sheba spread her hands in a gesture of uncertainty. 'How can I tell?'

Mma Makutsi could not contain herself. 'Surely the sister – Rra Edgar's sister – would know him? She's his aunt, after all. An aunt knows her nephew, I think.'

Mma Sheba turned round to address Mma Makutsi. 'Yes, an aunt should know her own nephew. And this aunt has said that this young man is who he is. The boy's father, of course, is late and I have been unable to track down the Swazi woman who is the mother of this boy. I have tried, but she seems to have left the country some years ago. The boy himself says that his mother went off when he was fourteen and that he had been looked after by a friend of his late father's. So there is no family for me to speak to – apart from his aunt, Rra Edgar's sister.'

Mma Ramotswe considered this. She sketched a brief family

tree out on a piece of paper in front of her: Rra Edgar, deceased brother, sister and nephew. It was not complicated. 'If she says he is who he claims to be and if he has documents to prove it, then what is the problem, Mma?'

Mma Sheba turned back. 'You want to know something, Mma Ramotswe? I have a nose for a lie. I've always had it. I think that this young man is lying. I think he is not who he claims to be.' She paused. 'I feel it in my bones, Mma.'

'Bones never lie,' said Mma Makutsi.

'No,' said Mma Sheba. 'Mine never have. Why would they start now?'

Mma Ramotswe noted what had been said about intuition and bones. She knew what Mma Sheba meant – she herself regularly used her intuition – but she was a detective and Mma Sheba was a lawyer. Lawyers were not meant to follow their noses, to rely on hunches and so on. Lawyers were meant to look at the evidence and weigh it carefully. That was how they were meant to work.

'Exactly what do you want me to do, Mma?' she asked.

The lawyer looked at her intently. 'I want you to prove that this young man is an imposter. That is what I want. I want you to find out just who he is.'

Again this struck Mma Ramotswe as a strange thing for a lawyer to say. Lawyers should not make up their mind in advance of a full understanding of the facts. It seemed that Mma Sheba had decided what she wanted the outcome to be. It was very strange, but just as there could be strange detectives, and strange mechanics for that matter, presumably there could be strange lawyers too.

'I shall do my best to investigate the situation, Mma,' she said. 'I shall try to establish the truth.'

'That is what we always do,' echoed Mma Makutsi. 'We establish the truth. That is our business, you see.'

Chapter Three

Snakes Are Very Shy

The house that Phuti Radiphuti and Grace Makutsi had built for themselves stood on a plot of land cleared from the bush at the edge of town. The land had been a haven for snakes and there were still a few who had survived its clearing. This came home to them when, two days after they had moved in, a cobra was discovered behind the washing basket in the bathroom, to be removed, hissing in anger, at the end of a long pole left behind by the builders. Grace would have preferred it had Phuti despatched the snake altogether with blows from the pole, but he did not believe in killing snakes.

'If we killed all the snakes in Botswana,' he pointed out, 'then we would be in serious trouble with rats. We would end up asking the snakes to come back.'

'I do not want all the snakes in the country killed,' said Mma

Makutsi. 'I want those in my garden, and now in my house, to be got rid of. That is all, Rra.'

'I am getting rid of him,' said Phuti.

This did not impress her. 'But he will come back. That snake is thinking: this man is putting me out, but I have my own ideas on that. I shall return when his back is turned and I shall find that nice cool place in the bathroom once more. And if he comes in again, I shall bite him to remind him that I am a cobra and we do not like being poked with sticks.'

'He will not come back,' said Phuti mildly. 'Snakes are very shy, Mma. They do not like to come into contact with people.'

'Then why do they move into our houses?' challenged Mma Makutsi, righteously. A cousin of hers up in Bobonong had been bitten by a puff adder, in the house itself, and had lost a leg as a result. She knew about these things.

Phuti had sighed and said something that she did not quite catch – something about conservation and respect for nature. But even if there were the occasional snake, neither of them felt anything but pride over their new house. For Mma Makutsi, in particular, it was an almost unimaginable leap from her modest quarters in Extension Two, where she had had what amounted to one and a half rooms, and water had to be fetched from an outside tap. Now she had a bathroom that she could only have dreamed of in the past – one with gleaming white tiles, and hot and cold running water, and a bath that would accommodate even Mma Ramotswe, or some other traditionally built person, with plenty of room left over. That was her greatest, most unimaginable luxury, and it would take more than the odd cobra to take the shine off that.

That day, after the visit of Mma Sheba to the No. 1 Ladies' Detective Agency, Mma Makutsi returned from work early. She explained to Mma Ramotswe that she was feeling tired, having been up late the previous night, and Mma Ramotswe had suggested that she go home to take a rest.

The house was quiet when she returned. Phuti sometimes worked from home in the afternoons, as he had found that he could do paperwork more efficiently without the disturbances that dogged him in the shop, but that afternoon he had meetings with suppliers and had said he would not be back until after six. The maid who had looked after him at his parents' home had been transferred to work in their new home, but it was a Thursday and that was her day off. So Mma Makutsi came home to a house in which the most noticeable sound was the creaking of the roof as it contracted with the dissipation of the day's heat. There were other sounds, though, and these were the sounds that can be heard in every house if one has the time to listen: the sighing of the wind under the door; the rattle of leaves against a pane of glass; the faint rhythm of a dripping tap. These may be sensed before they are heard, half-registered in the mind before they are recognised.

She decided to lie down. The doctor had told her that she might find herself feeling suddenly exhausted and she should not fight this. 'Remember,' he said, 'that your body tells you things.'

She went into their bedroom and kicked off her shoes. Then, lying down on the king-size bed that Phuti had specially ordered through his wholesaler, she closed her eyes and prepared to give in to her drowsiness. But sleep eluded her and she found herself listening to those small sounds, wondering which one of them might be a cobra. It was a hot day, and any cobra who knew anything about houses would realise that there would be plenty of cool places that offered sanctuary from the heat outside – places of darkness where a snake could lie and digest his meal and think about his next move. Places in bathrooms, places in cupboards, places under beds . . .

She opened her eyes. There was a movement on the ceiling above her – a movement that was almost undetectable because the creature that made it was so small. She saw what it was: a tiny gecko, attached to the ceiling by the curious sticky pads on its toes, had been stalking a fly and had pounced. She smiled. There was no reason to be frightened of creatures like that, which helped so much by keeping mosquitoes down.

Then she heard another sound. At first she wondered whether somebody had come into the house and was talking at the end of the corridor, but then, hearing it again, and louder now, she realised that it was in the room.

I'd be careful if I were you, boss.

She lay quite still. She had been wearing relatively new shoes and this pair had never addressed her before. But the voice was the same – and spoke with much the same accent as her other, older shoes.

'What was that?' she half-whispered.

I'd be careful, boss – that's all.

She sat up and rubbed her eyes. This was ridiculous. Shoes could not talk – as Mma Ramotswe would say, that is well known – and yet there was no doubt in her mind that she had heard something. She considered what they had said. *I'd be careful, boss.* What could it mean? In the past her shoes had restricted themselves to complaints or to Delphic utterances of no great importance – the sort of thing heard from subservient, disgruntled employees. This was the first time they had uttered a distinct warning.

She told herself that it was all in her mind. People imagined that they heard things, but it was just one bit of the brain convincing another bit of the brain that something had been said.

Don't say we didn't warn you, boss – that's all. But remember this: we can see things down here that you can't see up there.

Now Mma Makutsi was wide awake, and trying to make sense of what the shoes had said. What could they see that she could not? She shifted slightly so as to be able to look over the edge of the bed. Her shoes were there where she had slipped out of them, their toes pointed towards the bed. *We can see things down here that you can't see up there ...*

Mma Makutsi gasped. She was enough of a detective to work out that *if* – and it was an unlikely *if* – the shoes could see things that she could not, then, given the direction they were pointing in, whatever they were looking at would be under the bed. The thought brought a momentary surge of fear, but she made a conscious effort to control herself. You could make up all sorts of fears and then you would end up being too frightened to do anything. You had to be careful not to imagine things that were simply not there.

She took a deep breath and began to move her legs out over the edge of the bed.

Don't say we didn't tell you, boss!

She stopped, and looked down at the shoes. This was ridiculous. This was the sort of behaviour that ended in your being carted off to the special hospital in Lobatse. She completed the manoeuvre and stood up beside the bed. Then, decisively and deliberately, she slipped into her shoes. It crossed her mind that she should check them first to see that no scorpions had crept in – that had been known to happen – but now it was too late, and there was no sharp pain from a sting. No, it was all a matter of an overactive imagination, something to do with being pregnant perhaps.

But then she heard it. This time it was nothing to do with the creaking of the roof or the nudging of the wind. This time it was much clearer: the sound of motion, the sound of something sliding over something else. She edged away from the bed in the direction of the door. Then, very carefully, she bent down so that she could peer, from a safe distance, under the bed.

The snake was lying under the bed, stretched out, its upper body bent near the neck so that the head was pointed back in Mma Makutsi's direction and it looked directly at her. She saw its eyes, tiny points of reflected light; she saw the tongue move in a rapid flicker. It was watching her.

She did not scream, but moved very silently and deliberately. It had been drummed into her as a little girl in Bobonong that when confronted with danger one should not make sudden movements: they could trigger an attack from whatever it was that posed the danger. You must never run away from a lion, her mother had told her; the lion will think you are inviting him to chase you. He cannot help it.

Now, although there was a big difference between a lion and a snake, Mma Makutsi considered that the principle would be the same. Resisting every temptation to move as quickly as possible, she slowly rose and walked backwards out of the room, half-expecting the snake to dart out from under the bed and pursue her. But it did not, and she was able to close the door behind her and walk swiftly to the telephone in the kitchen.

Phuti Radiphuti, called out of his meeting with his suppliers, promised to come home immediately.

'But listen, Phuti,' Mma Makutsi said. 'It's no good just putting that snake out with a stick. You have to solve the problem permanently. That snake has to go.'

There was silence at the other end of the line.

'Phuti, are you still there?'

'Yes, I am here.'

'And so is the snake,' said Mma Makutsi.

'I'm thinking,' said Phuti.

Mma Makutsi sighed. 'Surely there is nothing to think about.

The snake must be killed; otherwise he will always be coming back into the house. Maybe he thinks it's his house already. Then all he will have to do is bite both of us and he will have it all to himself.'

'There is a dog,' said Phuti.

'It's not dogs; it's snakes.'

Phuti laughed weakly. 'There is a well-known dog. He belongs to the accountant here in the store. He's called Mealies.'

Mma Makutsi let her irritation show. 'I don't want to talk about dogs,' she said peevishly, 'whatever they're called. I want you to come home and hit that snake on the head. That is what you need to do.'

Phuti's voice was persuasive. 'This dog is a famous snake-catcher. I have seen him do it. The snake doesn't stand a chance.'

'Then it's a pity that he's not our dog.'

'I can borrow him. Other people have done that – they've borrowed Mealies and he's dealt with snakes. That is what we need to do.'

Mma Makutsi was doubtful, but agreed that Mealies could be tried – as long as he could arrive within the next half hour. 'I cannot wait in the house with a snake for longer than that, Phuti.'

'I'll fetch him,' said Phuti. 'He will be there.'

Phuti was as good as his word, arriving at the house only fifteen minutes later. With him was Mealies, an odd-looking dog with a thickset, muscular body and short, bowed legs that looked as if they had been taken from a much smaller dog and grafted on. Mma Makutsi met her husband as he emerged from his truck and watched with interest as he let the dog out of the back.

'He's a very peculiar-looking dog,' she remarked. 'Are you sure that he—'

He held up a hand to stop her. 'He's a famous snake-catcher, Mma. You'll see.'

He led the dog into the house while Mma Makutsi busied herself in the kitchen. She did not want to see what happened; she had seen a dog killing a snake in Bobonong and had not liked the sight. In spite of everything, she had felt sorry for the snake, which was a creature like the rest of us who just wanted to go on living. But her mind was made up on that cobra: you simply could not allow a highly venomous snake to take up residence in your house. It was a matter of survival, really.

She heard Phuti opening the bedroom door and then she heard the dog growling. This was followed by a furious barking and the sound of something being knocked over. Then silence.

'Phuti?' she called.

'He has done it,' Phuti called out from the bedroom. 'That snake is no more.'

She averted her eyes as Phuti carried the snake out by its tail. She caught a glimpse of a mangled head and she saw a small drop of snake blood, red and glistening, fall on the tiled floor. She shuddered.

'Take it outside, Phuti – I don't want to see it.'

Mealies, looking pleased with himself, the white fur around his jaws now stained red, swaggered into the kitchen on his short and bandy legs.

'You should reward him,' said Phuti. 'Give him some meat.'

Mma Makutsi looked down at the dog, who was gazing up at her expectantly. Crossing the kitchen to the fridge, she extracted a large piece of steak and cut off a small corner. This she tossed to the dog, who caught it in his jaws, swallowing it in a single gulp. Phuti now returned and washed his hands in the sink.

'I've left him outside,' he said. 'That will scare his wife away. They often come in twos.'

She looked away. She had wanted the snake killed – it was her doing – and now she had made a widow.

Phuti stood beside her. 'The important thing is that you are all right,' he said. 'It's not good to be frightened when ...' He reached over and placed a hand gently on her stomach.

She laid her own hand gently on top of his. 'I had a fright, but now I am feeling better. And he is feeling better too.' She glanced down at her stomach; she was sure it was a boy.

'How much longer?' he asked. 'I keep forgetting.'

She shrugged. 'Three weeks. Twenty-one days, in fact.'

He let out a low whistle. 'Have you talked to Mma Ramotswe about maternity leave yet?'

'I'll talk to her soon,' she said. 'I didn't want to bother people about our baby, Phuti. Just you. Just in case ...'

He understood. 'But now you can speak,' he said. 'Now the baby will be almost ready. Nothing can go wrong at this stage.'

She was worried by his saying things like that. There were plenty of things that could go wrong, even at this stage; men simply did not understand.

'I'll speak to her tomorrow,' she said.

'Tomorrow? Don't forget, then. It's not fair to keep her waiting.'

She smiled at him, her Phuti, the father of her unborn child, the man who had brought her to all this – this house, this state of comfort, this happiness.

After dinner, they spent an hour or so in the room they had pre-pared for the baby. Phuti had found the necessary furniture in the Double Comfort Furniture Store: a cot, a changing table and a chest of drawers. There was also an easy chair for Mma Makutsi to use when she came to comfort the baby at night, and a pair of curtains with a rabbit design. Now they set to sorting out a pile of baby clothes that Mma Makutsi had bought at a sale at Riverwalk and checking the contents of a drawer that she had stocked with baby oil, powder and a selection of other supplies.

Phuti was tired, and went to bed early. Mealies was to stay overnight, to be returned to his owner the following day, and he was bedded down on an old blanket on the kitchen floor. They had given him more steak, and a bowl of sorghum porridge mixed with gravy. This had been wolfed down with gusto, and the dog now looked even more barrel-like as he stretched out on the blanket.

Mma Makutsi was still getting used to her new kitchen and was happy to stand for long periods simply gazing at its pristine surfaces, at its capacious fridge and its numerous cupboards and shelves. She did this for a while after Phuti had gone to bed, and then, since it was a warm evening, she decided to go out into the yard with a final cup of tea before retiring.

Most of the garden was uncleared bush, but Phuti had made an attempt to cut the grass in the immediate curtilage of the house, giving it the appearance of a rough, half-cultivated field. This would be the beginnings of a lawn, she hoped, once they had the time to tend to it. She had already planted several small bushes that Mma Ramotswe and Mr J. L. B. Matekoni had given them as a housewarming present, and these were surrounded by neatly arranged rings of stones. She had never had a proper garden and was excited by the prospect of creating a small oasis of green in the surrounding brown. She would have a shelter, perhaps, under which chairs could be set out, allowing people to sit and drink tea in the fresh air. It was a thrilling prospect.

Sipping at her tea, she took a few steps away from the light spilling out of the kitchen door in order to accustom her eyes to the darkness. The sky above Botswana was a great expanse of stars – uncountable thousands of them – so dense in places as to give an impression that the heavens were decked with gossamer curtains of white. She looked for the reassuring presence of the Southern Cross, the only constellation she could name, and soon found it, hanging over the horizon above Lobatse.

She looked down. There was a shape in the grass not far from where she stood, and she gave a start. But she quickly remembered: Phuti Radiphuti had left the snake outside to deter its mate, and this was it, this thing that looked like an abandoned piece of hosepipe. She felt a momentary pang of sympathy. She had brought this life to an end, but she had to do it; she had to. There would be the baby coming soon and you simply could not have cobras in the house when you had a baby.

She moved forward to get a better view. The head was bent back, as one would expect; a dog will snap the snake's neck at first bite, knowing instinctively that there will be no second chance. She peered down at the snake and frowned. It was much smaller than she remembered. Had she thought it bigger when it was under the bed? Perhaps shock could have that effect? But no – this was definitely a smaller snake.

The realisation came quickly. The dog had caught a snake in their bedroom, but not the right one. That meant that Phuti was in the room with a cobra. She turned on her heels and began to run inside. She dropped her cup. She felt a pain, sudden, sharp and overwhelming, which stopped her in her tracks. She doubled up. She cried out.

Chapter Four

This Shall Be Botswana

The following morning Mma Ramotswe, as usual, spent the first fifteen minutes of her day in her garden inspecting her plants and taking advantage of the fresh morning air. It would be another hot day, she could tell: there was always something in the air at the onset of such a day. It was a matter of sound, she thought – one of those sounds you could hear but not quite hear, a tiny, distant thrumming that reminded you that at noon the heat would be like a physical blow falling from the sky. The rains would come soon, or so everybody hoped, and they would bring relief not only to people and cattle but also to the land itself. Yet there could still be seemingly interminable weeks of this heat before that happened.

Mr J. L. B. Matekoni usually drove Motholeli to school as it was easier to get her wheelchair into the back of his truck than into Mma Ramotswe's van. Puso could have gone with them, but he preferred to make his own way there, feeling that this was a badge of being the age he was. It was not a long walk and he picked up friends on the way. They did not rush, but spent time on the way tossing stones at paw-paw trees, finding interesting sticks with which to stage mock fights, and generally ensuring that they only arrived within seconds of the sounding of the bell that announced the start of the school day.

'Ask her about it,' mumbled Mr J. L. B. Matekoni, as he finished the last of his breakfast.

'Ask Mma Makutsi about what she wants to do?'

He wiped the crumbs from his lips and stood up. 'Yes. You can't let it go on for much longer. You have to know. What happens in the office if she suddenly goes off to look after a baby and nothing is arranged? What then?'

Mma Ramotswe thought for a moment. She could not imagine what it would be like if Mma Makutsi were no longer there in the office, sitting behind her desk, the lenses of her large round spectacles catching the light from the window, flashing the world back at itself. It was such a familiar sight that it made it hard to envisage what it would be like if that chair were empty and those comments – often helpful but sometimes not as constructive as they might be – were not being made. It would be a strange silence indeed.

The view from Bobonong, she mused; was that how the world looked to Mma Makutsi? It seemed an odd thing to say, and yet all of us had a view from somewhere; a view of the world from the perspective of who we were, of what had happened to us, of how we thought about things. Her view was the view from Mochudi, where she had been born and brought up by her late father, that great man, Obed Ramotswe. And his view had been the view from where? The view from Botswana, she decided: the view of the world that seemed essentially and naturally right, because it was a view that *understood* how things really were and how God must surely have intended them to be when He first made Botswana. She smiled to herself as she savoured the idea that God had looked at the world, seen a wide stretch of land and had said, *This shall be Botswana*. He had given it the Kalahari; He had given it the good land along the eastern border, and had added, for good measure, the Makadikadi Salt Pans. But then, just as He was about to give it wide and reliable rivers, He was distracted somehow and forgot to finish what He was doing, or found that He had already given all His rivers away and had only a few left for Botswana ... It was easily done when you were making a world, especially one as demanding as this, where there were so many people who thought they should have more rivers than they actually had, and who enviously eyed the land – and the rivers – of others.

'What then, Mma Ramotswe?'

She was brought back to where she was – not in the sky, looking down on Botswana, but in a very real and immediate part of Botswana, namely the kitchen of her house on Zebra Drive, where her husband was about to leave for work and where there were still many chores to do before she herself could leave for her office.

'When Mma Makutsi goes off on maternity leave,' she answered, 'then I shall have to get another assistant.'

Mr J. L. B. Matekoni looked unconvinced. 'Easier said than done, you know.'

He was right – she knew that. No doubt she would find somebody who fancied the idea of being her secretary. And this time, she resolved, the post would be very clearly and unambiguously described as a secretarial one, with no suggestion that it was a stepping stone to being an assistant detective or, as Mma Makutsi was at pains to insist, an associate detective, whatever that was. Yes, there would be many applicants for the job, but would any of them be as well qualified and efficient as Mma Makutsi?

It was difficult to see this happening, for the simple reason that there were presumably no secretaries with anything like Mma Makutsi's ninety-seven per cent in the final examinations of the Botswana Secretarial College. Mma Makutsi had reported that a young woman from Mahalapye had recently managed to get eighty-three per cent in the finals – a very creditable mark but still a whole fourteen per cent shy of her own.

'It was her shorthand that let her down,' Mma Makutsi had said, adding in a resigned tone: 'It always is, you know.'

Mma Ramotswe had replied, 'Yes, it always is,' as if she knew about these things. Perhaps she should have said, 'Yes, and I am let down too, as mine is very rusty,' but she did not.

Now, she too stood up from the breakfast table. If she had to get a new secretary, then that was what she would do. And even if she ended up with a secretary whose shorthand let her down – and that seemed to be something that it was simply impossible to avoid – she would make the best of it and the No. 1 Ladies' Detective Agency would continue in whatever way it could.

She would have to speak to Mma Makutsi that day. At least she did not have to broach the subject of pregnancy itself; at least Mma Makutsi had told her about that. It would be far more difficult for an employer if the employee had not said anything about being pregnant. That would not be easy, she thought, because if you went up to somebody and said, *Are you pregnant?* the question might be taken the wrong way. It might sound as if you had said, *Are you pregnant yet?* Or, *Are you pregnant yet again?* Both of these could be considered rude by some people, and would almost certainly be so viewed by Mma Makutsi, who was very sensitive to slight.

Another way of doing it would be to introduce the subject into the conversation by simply making a remark that suggested you knew. You could, for example, give somebody a cup of tea and then say something like, *Would you like a piece of cake as well – now that you're pregnant?* That would allow the other person to answer, *Well, cake is always welcome when one is eating for two.* Or she might say, *What makes you think I'm pregnant?* That could be awkward, because you could hardly say, *I thought you were pregnant because you're looking so large.* There were some people who became larger simply because of fattening foods, of cake or the like, or because they were traditionally built by nature rather than because of ... because of anything else. They might resent an inference that they were *too* large, and indeed there were those who might be trying to become pregnant and not yet succeeding; they might be upset if you reminded them of something they wanted but were not achieving. Or there might be people who could conclude that you thought that they *should* be pregnant, and they, in turn, might think, *What business is it of yours whether or not I'm pregnant?* There was no getting away from it: it was very difficult all round and even a discussion of maternity leave would have to be handled very carefully. There were undoubtedly many employees who were easy, with whom you could raise any issue without having to take care to be tactful, but Mma Makutsi, for all her many merits, was certainly not one of those.

She drove past the traffic circle at the university and then along the road towards the part of town known as the Village. Although she remembered it when it was a sleepy collection of meandering, tree-lined streets, it was less of a village now, since several large blocks of flats had been built on its periphery. Blocks of flats could change everything, thought Mma Ramotswe. They were designed for people, but people were not necessarily

41

designed for them. These flats at the edges of the Village, though, were made more human by the washing that was hung out to dry from their balconies; by the children who congregated in their doorways, or played with skipping ropes and dogs on their pathways; by the music that the residents listened to, melodies that drifted out of the open windows and throbbed with life. All of this made it harder for large new buildings to deaden the human spirit. It was like the bush: you could clear it and build something where once there had been nothing but trees and grass and termite mounds, but if you turned your back for a moment, Africa would begin to reclaim what had always been hers. The grass would encroach, its seeds carried by the wind; birds would drop the seeds of saplings that would then send tiny shoots up out of the ground; the termites would marshal their exploratory troops to begin rebuilding their own intricate cities of mud in the very places they had claimed once before. And sooner or later the bush would have covered all your efforts and it would be as it was before, the wound on nature completely healed.

By the time she reached the No. 1 Ladies' Detective Agency, Mr J. L. B. Matekoni had already arrived for work at his garage, Tlokweng Road Speedy Motors, with whom the agency shared premises. He was talking to a client who had brought in a car for repair – one of his regular clients, Mma Ramotswe noticed; one of that unfortunate category of people whose cars always seemed to be breaking down but who could not bring themselves to part with them and buy a new model. Mma Ramotswe understood that attitude only too well; she loved her van and had resisted every effort on the part of Mr J. L. B. Matekoni to trade it in for something newer. And when he had eventually succeeded, she had pined for her late van until it had been recovered, restored and given back into her ownership, where it was surely destined to be.

She nodded a greeting to the client, whom she knew slightly, before making her way into the office. Mma Makutsi was sometimes in before her. Good time-keeping, she had often pointed out, was one of the lessons learned in the Botswana Secretarial College – at least by those who were willing to learn, and that did not include people like Violet Sephotho, who learned nothing except, perhaps, how to distract men. This morning, though, it was Mma Ramotswe who opened up the office, pulling up the blind on the main window, filling the kettle, and brushing the ants off the top of the filing cabinet. The presence of the ants on the cabinet was a mystery; they were there every morning, a long line of pinheaded creatures, marching obediently across the painted metal wastes on some quite unfathomable mission. Mma Makutsi had suggested that the ants were there before the filing cabinet or the building itself; that this was some ancient ant highway that they still felt compelled to follow. She had been opposed to ant powder, as had Mma Ramotswe. These insects did not bite, nor did they have that curious unpleasant smell that the larger Matabele ants had – and they had none of the aggressive instincts of those warriors. Every child had been bitten at one time or another by a Matabele ant and, remembering the pain, learned to leave a wide berth when those determined black ants were on the march.

She filled the kettle and prepared her first cup of tea. It was, in fact, her third of the day, but she did not count the two that she had at home before she reached the office; those cups were merely preparatory and therefore exempt from tally. Her cup of tea in her hand, she stood by the window looking out at the acacia tree behind the office. She had not given much thought to yesterday's conversation with Mma Sheba, but now she wondered whether there was much that she could do. It seemed to her to be very odd that Mma Sheba should doubt the word of Rra Edgar's sister. She was, after all, the boy's aunt and if she said that Liso was the same boy who had been coming to stay on the farm every school holiday since he was very young, then that should be the end of the matter. Surely it would be easy enough to talk to the people who worked on the farm, or to the neighbours, and ask them whether Liso was the same boy. And if they said yes, which they no doubt would, then that would be the end of it. Why, she wondered, could Mma Sheba not have done that herself? And what interest, for that matter, would the aunt have in telling lies?

She was distracted from these considerations by the arrival of Phuti Radiphuti's car. He usually dropped off Mma Makutsi on his way to the Double Comfort Furniture Store, and that was what he would be doing now. Phuti was getting out of the car, yet she noticed immediately that he was not wearing his normal working outfit of neatly pressed black trousers, white shirt and tie. Instead, he was wearing a pair of denim jeans and an open-necked shirt. And where was Mma Makutsi, Mma Ramotswe wondered. Was she ill? She had rarely missed a day's work since she started; she came in even when she was beginning to go down with flu and had to be sent back to her bed. Something must be wrong or . . . She saw Phuti's expression. This was not a man about to deliver bad news, and at that moment she knew what he had come to say.

She opened the door as Phuti approached.

'*Dumela*, Rra. This is a surprise . . .'

'Mma Ramotswe, Mmmmmma . . .'

His mouth was open; he was stammering.

'It's all right, Rra, I am not in a hurry. I'm listening.'

'Itttt . . . it's . . .'

She reached out to take his hand. There was a momentary doubt that this was bad news rather than good, but his expression belied that. No, this man was a father. Any new father, whether or not he was given to stammering, might be expected to be nervous and to behave just like this.

She decided to take the initiative. 'Has she had it?'

He nodded, almost gratefully. 'Yes. Yes. She is now a father.' He shook his head and corrected himself. 'No, she is a mother and I am a father. It is a boy child. One boy.'

Mma Ramotswe smiled. It would have been much more difficult, she thought, for Mma Makutsi to have said nothing about twins. 'That is very good news, Rra! Very good. When did the baby arrive?'

'Seven days ago,' said Phuti. 'No, what am I saying? Seven hours ago. He is now seven hours old – my first-born.' He closed his eyes, as if uttering some sort of prayer. 'And it is three weeks earlier than we thought, Mma. Three weeks!'

She was still holding his hand, and she squeezed it. It was moist with heat and excitement. 'That is wonderful, Rra! Your first-born – a new Radiphuti.'

She saw that there were tears in his eyes.

'My father would have been very proud,' he said. 'But he is late now.'

Mma Ramotswe spoke gently. 'I think that there are some things that late people know,' she said. 'Wherever they are. This is the one bit of news that they get, I think.'

'Maybe,' said Phuti.

'And they will be very happy up in Bobonong,' went on Mma Ramotswe. 'It will be good news for all those Makutsi people up there.'

Phuti was now beginning to calm down. He gestured to a chair and asked whether he might sit.

Mma Ramotswe smiled. 'Of course, Rra. You will be very tired. Having a baby is very tiring – even for men, I think.'

Phuti extracted a handkerchief and mopped at his brow.

'That's true, Mma Ramotswe. Of course, it is the woman who has the hard work to do.'

Mma Ramotswe struggled not to laugh. 'I think that is probably true, Rra.' She paused. 'I am very happy for you, Rra – for both of you. This is very good. Well done.'

He acknowledged her tribute. 'Thank you, Mma. And do you know something? When I was at the hospital – at the Princess Marina – there were some men there who ...'

She looked at him expectantly. 'Doctors?' she prompted.

'No, not doctors. Ordinary men. Husbands. And they were going to be there in the room when the baby came. Right in the room.'

Mma Ramotswe shrugged. 'There are men who believe in that, Rra. They like to be with their wife when she has their baby. I can understand.'

Phuti Radiphuti frowned. 'It is not part of our culture,' he said gravely. 'Not in Botswana.'

'Traditionally,' said Mma Ramotswe. 'But things are changing, Rra. I think there are some men who want to be there when their child comes into the world.'

Phuti Radiphuti shook his head in wonderment. 'I take the traditional view, Mma. You know, there was a big row when I was there – not involving me, of course.'

Mma Ramotswe could not imagine Phuti being involved in any sort of row – big or otherwise. He was a mild man, and she had never heard him raise his voice. She had heard that this could be problematic at the Double Comfort Furniture Store, where he was sometimes required to deal with difficult staff. Awkward employees could be quick to sense when the person in authority over them was unprepared to be forceful.

'A row, Rra? In the hospital itself?'

Phuti nodded. 'Yes, there were three nurses on duty, you see.

There was a senior nurse, who was a lady like you, Mma . . . ' He made a gesture to indicate size, and then, realising what he was doing, he quickly dropped his hands.

'Traditionally built?' prompted Mma Ramotswe.

He looked sheepish. 'Yes, Mma. Traditionally built. And then there were two more junior nurses. And there was one of the fathers – or a man who was about to become a father – and he had asked one of the junior nurses whether he could go into the labour ward with his wife. He said that this is what she wanted, and he wanted it too. The nurse said that she thought this was a good thing to do. But then the older nurse started to shake her finger. She said to him that men had never been allowed anywhere near a woman who was having a baby and that he should be ashamed of himself for asking.'

Mma Ramotswe was not surprised. 'People have different views. Certainly she was right about the old Botswana views – that is the position. My late father would never have imagined that any man would ask such a thing. He was a child of his time – as we all are, Rra.'

Phuti Radiphuti went on to describe what had happened. The man had begun to shout, he said, and had asked whose baby it was anyway. 'The senior nurse shouted even more,' he said. 'She told him that the baby belonged to his wife and that he was just the father. He would be able to see the baby in due time, when his wife invited him to do so.'

'And how did he react to that?' asked Mma Ramotswe.

'He was not very happy,' replied Phuti. 'And then the other junior nurse, who had not said anything, started to support him too. That made it two nurses and one man against one senior nurse. There was a lot of shouting.' He paused. 'Then more shouting started – this time from one of the ladies who was having a baby. And that stopped the man.'

'He didn't like it?'

'No. He suddenly stopped shouting and he stood very still. I think he became frightened. Then he turned round and walked quickly away.'

Mma Ramotswe laughed. 'He'd changed his mind?'

'He decided that it was not a good idea after all,' said Phuti.

Mma Ramotswe looked out of the window. She was remembering. She tried not to think about it, but every so often it came back to her – the birth of her only child all those years ago. Her baby by Note Mokoti; her baby who had lived for such a short time before being taken away from her. Her child, her baby – the only baby that she would ever have. She closed her eyes, trying to fend off the memory of how she had held the tiny baby, uncertain whether life had gone yet, and how they had taken the bundle from her, restraining her in the raw depth of her grief, because they said that she could not hold the child's body for ever and would have to say goodbye. We all had to say goodbye, sooner or later, to those we loved – or they had to say goodbye to us. Those were the only two possibilities that this world allowed. But no matter how much we tried to face up to it, it never became easier.

She struggled to bring herself back. 'So you waited outside?'

He nodded. 'There is a place for fathers to go, but I think that most of us wanted to go outside. There were three other men there – the man who had changed his mind, and two others. One of them was a man who knew my cousin – a man who works in the Bank of Botswana. He has something to do with money.'

Again, Mma Ramotswe suppressed a smile. Phuti Radiphuti was just like Mma Makutsi, really: they both had a tendency to make odd, sometimes rather obvious, remarks. Married couples often reinforced one's another's quirks, she thought. Of course anybody who worked in the Bank of Botswana would have something to do with money. That, she thought, went with the job, although, to be fair to Phuti, there would be people there who were in charge of personnel, or the staff café, or some such thing, and they might be described as people who had nothing to do with money.

'And your son, Rra?' asked Mma Ramotswe. 'Have you seen him yet? Have you held him?'

Phuti's eyes glowed with pride as he answered. 'I saw him. He was in a special room for babies. There were a lot of cots and the babies were in those.'

'Very good,' said Mma Ramotswe. 'They look after babies very well there.'

'Many of the babies were crying,' Phuti continued. 'But my son was not one of them. He was behaving very well.'

Mma Ramotswe reached out to pat Phuti on the shoulder. 'He will be a very well-behaved boy, Rra. He is starting as he intends to carry on.'

Phuti seemed pleased with the compliment, but then he frowned. 'My aunt . . . '

'Ah.' Mma Ramotswe knew all about Phuti's aunt, whom she had met on more than one occasion. This was the aunt with the reputation for jealousy and interference, the owner of that unattractive brown car with its mean-spirited windows, the aunt who had tried to come between Phuti and Mma Makutsi.

'My aunt came round to the hospital. I don't know how she knew that Grace had been taken there, but she was there half an hour after we arrived. I think she has many spies throughout the town and one of them must have phoned her and told her.'

Mma Ramotswe summoned up as much sympathy as she could manage. 'I suppose she was very proud of you, Rra. I think it is always nice for an aunt when her nephew's wife has a baby. That can be a very big thing for an aunt.'

Phuti understood this. 'I am not saying that she should not have been there, but I do not agree with what she said. She said that Grace should go with her to her house and stay there for a month or two before they came back to my place. She said that is the traditional way and my father would have wanted it.'

Mma Ramotswe knew the custom to which the aunt was referring – and yes, that was the way it once was. The mother and baby would be secluded with female relatives until it was thought safe to let the baby out into the world. But things were changing and fewer and fewer people followed that custom these days. Babies might be kept inside for a matter of days, but it would be rare for them to be kept out of sight for months, as happened in the past.

'Simply tell her that this is not possible,' advised Mma Ramotswe. 'Tell her that you are not going to observe the old custom. Tell her that you and Grace are a modern couple and you are going to take the baby straight home – to *your* home – and that he will be taken out of the house whenever you want to do so.'

Phuti shifted uncomfortably in his seat. 'It is not always easy to tell my aunt things,' he said. 'She believes that she knows everything already. She does not think there is anybody who can tell her anything.'

'You didn't agree, did you?'

Phuti's discomfort appeared to grow. 'Not in those actual words. I did not say yes, but ... '

There were many different ways of saying yes and no, thought Mma Ramotswe.

'I see,' she said. 'So the baby is going to the aunt's place?'

'Only for a very short time,' said Phuti.

'And has Mma Makutsi agreed?' asked Mma Ramotswe.

'At first she did not say anything – I think that she felt too tired or too weak. But then she said that it would be all right if that was what I wanted.'

'You should have told her that it was not what you wanted,' said Mma Ramotswe.

'It is difficult to tell her something like that,' said Phuti.

She did not want to detract from his pleasure, and so she said nothing more on the subject. Instead, she asked about a name – had they decided?

'We discussed it,' said Phuti. 'We discussed it many times before the baby arrived.'

'It is not always easy to choose a child's name,' agreed Mma Ramotswe. 'I sometimes think that we have too many names in Botswana, with people inventing all these names all the time. In other places you do not have so much choice – you only have to pick from a very small list.'

'But that makes it better for us,' argued Phuti. 'If you have a name that nobody else has, then you feel more special. You know that there is only one of you.' He hesitated. 'There is no other Phuti Radiphuti in the whole world, I think.'

'Nor Precious Ramotswe,' ventured Mma Ramotswe, adding: 'As far as I know.'

'We are very fortunate,' said Phuti.

'And your son?' asked Mma Ramotswe.

Phuti Radiphuti looked down at the floor. 'We were wondering about Clovis,' he said hesitantly. 'Clovis Radiphuti.'

Mma Ramotswe was silent for a moment. Clovis Andersen was the author of *The Principles of Private Detection*, the book that had served her and Mma Makutsi so well for so many years. And then he had arrived unannounced in Botswana and introduced himself as a matter of professional courtesy. Their meeting with him had been one of the heights of her professional career – indeed, of her life.

Phuti was waiting for her reaction.

'I think it is a very good name,' said Mma Ramotswe. 'And we could tell Mr Andersen that the baby is named for him. That will make him very happy, I think.'

'I'm glad you like it,' said Phuti. 'We will only use it as his second name, of course. The first name will be a Motswana name. We haven't decided on that one yet. There are many family names that we need to consider before we finally decide.'

Mma Ramotswe agreed that a child's name should be chosen with some care, and only after carefully imagining how the child himself or herself might be expected to feel about it. There was a distressing habit in Botswana of calling people by names that might have amused the parents but would dog the child for the rest of his life. She remembered a boy at school in Mochudi whose name, when translated from Setswana, meant: *One who cries at the top of his lungs.* That might have seemed appropriate to the parents of a crying baby, but it would require a lot of explaining, and acceptance, on the part of the child in later life.

Phuti now moved on from names. 'Grace said that she had not discussed maternity leave with you yet,' he said. 'She was going to talk to you about it today, but then ... Well, I am talking on her behalf.'

Mma Ramotswe made light of this. 'Sometimes people don't want to talk about these things too early,' she said.

'Perhaps not,' said Phuti. 'But I think that it might have been better if she had discussed it with you a little earlier. She will need some maternity leave, you see.'

Mma Ramotswe said that she had assumed this would be the case. 'I shall be able to get somebody in,' she assured him. 'There are always people coming out of the Botswana Secretarial College. We get letters asking for a job almost every day. We have a big file of them.'

Phuti seemed relieved. 'Good,' he said. 'But you will only need that maternity leave person for a very short time. Grace does not want to sit about the house. She wants to get back to work.'

Mma Ramotswe was relieved. 'I'm very glad, Rra. It would be difficult to train somebody up to be an assist— an associate detective. How many months does she want?'

'Days, Mma. She said a few days.'

Mma Ramotswe let out a gasp of astonishment. 'That is not long at all, Rra.'

'It is the modern thing,' said Phuti. 'We shall have a girl to feed the baby. There is already somebody there.'

'A wet nurse?' asked Mma Ramotswe. She was surprised, and wondered why this would be necessary. Phuti meanwhile looked puzzled, and it occurred to Mma Ramotswe that he might not have understood what she meant.

'Wet nursing is where some other woman feeds the baby,' said Mma Ramotswe.

'That is what we are going to do,' he said. 'We already have a girl working in the kitchen. She will be feeding me too.'

Mma Ramotswe tried to keep a straight face. 'I think we are talking about different things, Rra. A wet nurse is a woman who feeds the baby with her own milk.'

Phuti frowned. 'From her fridge?'

Mma Ramotswe lost the battle against laughter. She chuckled, and then went on. 'No, from herself. Mother's milk, not cow's milk.'

Phuti shook his head. 'You mean one woman – a different woman – gives another woman's baby the milk that her own baby ...'

'That is exactly what I mean,' said Mma Ramotswe. 'It is unusual, but it happens. It may be a sister or a cousin who helps in this way if the woman herself cannot manage to feed the baby. It is a kindness, you see.' She paused. 'There is usually a reason.'

He looked at her with interest, and she thought, This is a man who needs to go to those classes they have for new fathers.

'What is the reason?' he asked.

'It may be uncomfortable for the mother,' said Mma Ramotswe. 'That is a good reason. But I believe that there are some places where the mother just doesn't have time to feed the baby. Maybe she is too important.'

'But feeding a baby is very important,' said Phuti.

Mma Ramotswe was inclined to agree. You passed on more than mere sustenance in feeding a baby – you passed on love, and tenderness, and a bit of Botswana too, she thought. A bit of what it was to come from this place and be born into this nation.

'So the young woman in the kitchen—'

He interrupted her. 'No, she will not be doing that – certainly not. She will make the baby's food and give it to him if Grace is busy at the office.' He paused. 'Grace also thought that it would be all right to bring the baby to the office. Not every day, of course, but from time to time.'

Mma Ramotswe was on the point of saying that she would be delighted to have the baby in the office, but then she thought, Will I? She was very fond of babies, and sometimes when she went to see Mma Potokwani at the orphan farm she would spend hours playing with the babies they had there. But offices were different. One had to work in an office, and babies sometimes did not realise that – indeed, they *never* realised it. And what would happen if an important client were to arrive at the office for a meeting and the baby should choose that moment to protest about any one of the numerous things that babies tended to protest about? What then? Or if the baby needed changing and, in the middle of a meeting at which a prospective client needed to be impressed, Mma Makutsi started to change him in full sight of the client? Of course, she could take him through to the garage, but somehow Mma Ramotswe hardly dared to imagine a baby being changed in a garage alongside a lot of cars that were having their oil changed.

Her answer was cautious. 'Well, I'm sure that it will be nice to see him – from time to time. But I don't think we really have suitable facilities for him to come too often. Poor baby! What baby wants to sit about in an office? No babies I know would like that.'

Phuti appeared to weigh her response. 'Our baby will probably sleep a lot of the time. I don't think he will make a noise.'

Mma Ramotswe looked at Phuti incredulously. 'I'm sorry, Rra, but I'm not sure I'd agree with you there. Babies are very noisy things. That is well known.' She paused, before adding, 'At least to some.'

'Oh, I know a lot about babies,' said Phuti.

'That is very good, Rra. That is definitely a good thing.'

Phuti smiled. 'I asked them at the hospital if babies came with instruction books – you know, like fridges do, or cookers, or any electrical appliance. You get those instruction books, sometimes with pictures, telling you what to do.'

'That would be very funny,' said Mma Ramotswe. 'But on a serious note, Rra, you can get books. There are many books on babies.'

He seemed surprised. 'Whole books, Mma?'

She nodded. She had recently read about a new one in one of the magazines. It was a book that told you how to raise very intelligent babies. You had to read to the baby all the time and show it how to add and so on. It would not be very much fun being one of those babies, thought Mma Ramotswe. Babies – ordinary babies – liked to look at the sky, or watch chickens, or suck on blankets. They did not want to add.

'I think it is mostly common sense,' said Mma Ramotswe. 'Give babies lots of love and keep them warm and don't let flies settle on their noses. Those are all matters of common sense, and if you do things like that, the baby will be happy.'

Phuti nodded. 'I agree with you, Mma. Everybody can raise a baby.' He hesitated. 'Of course, it is best to learn a few special things, and I have been told all those by Grace. She has given me lists of things I should know about, and she has made up a few small tests for me. It has been very helpful in making me an expert.'

Once again, Mma Ramotswe reached out to take his hand. She pressed it in congratulation and empathy. 'Your baby will make you very happy, Phuti. That is something that babies are very good at.'

He nodded. 'I am already happy. I have Grace, and a furniture store, and now a baby. Three big things in my life.'

'Well, there you are,' said Mma Ramotswe. 'It is a very good idea to make a list like that – to remind yourself of what you have.'

'And you, Mma,' said Phuti quietly. 'You have many things in your life too. You have ...' He nodded in the direction of the garage. 'You have a very fine husband. You have your own business. You have that white van of yours.'

'Yes,' said Mma Ramotswe. 'I am lucky. But I have the two children I look after – Motholeli and Puso. They are the most important things I have, I think.'

'Yes, they are very important.'

'And I have a very good assistant.'

Phuti beamed with pleasure. 'Yes, her too.'

'And the assistant's husband and the assistant's baby. All of these are good things in my life.' She paused. 'And this country, of course. I have this country too.'

She gazed out of the window, towards the acacia tree. The birds that had been nesting in its branches – the two Cape doves – were not there, but they would return at some point in the day. For a moment she imagined what, if birds could think about these things, they might think they had, and what their list would be. It would be a simple list, but the few things on it would be good: the shelter of an acacia tree, sky, air, Africa.

Chapter Five

The Modern Husband Course

Of course, she had to buy a present for Mma Makutsi's baby, which she would take with her when she went to see him for the first time. Following his early morning visit to her office, Phuti rang her up later the same day and told her that his wife would be coming out of hospital after two or three days and Mma Ramotswe was welcome to visit any time after the weekend. Grace and the baby were not going to the aunt's house after all; he had spoken to his aunt about that and had stood his ground, as Mma Ramotswe suggested he should.

'Grace is looking forward to seeing you,' said Phuti.

'I would not like to bother her too soon,' Mma Ramotswe said. 'Perhaps I should wait until she has been at home for three or four days. Then I should come.'

'No, Mma Ramotswe, that is not what Grace wants. She said

to me in the hospital that she was looking forward to showing you her baby as soon as she came home. She said that it would be good for the baby to meet people like you right at the beginning.'

'I doubt if the baby will take much notice of me,' said Mma Ramotswe. 'Babies are busy enough sleeping and ... doing the other things that babies do. They don't really notice us very much.'

Phuti disagreed. 'Babies are like blotting paper. They soak up everything they see. They start learning Setswana more or less from the first day, or so I'm told.'

Mma Ramotswe doubted that, but did not wish to disillusion him. New fathers were famous for attributing all sorts of abilities to their first-born, and it was harmless enough. Indeed, it was a good thing; a parent who did not believe in a child was not much of a parent. Most parents – mothers, in particular – believed the best of their children, come what may. A boy, or even a man, would always be forgiven by his mother, even if he did something unspeakable. She remembered Note Mokoti's mother who had thought her son incapable of wrong, even in the face of all the evidence to the contrary. She had heard her say, 'My son is a very good man – one of the best men in the country. He is so kind.'

So kind! She closed her eyes. She would not allow herself to remember how Note had treated her, and many others too, she suspected. She had forgiven him, yes, but she still did not like to remember. And perhaps a deliberate act of forgetting went along with forgiveness. You forgave, and then you said to yourself: *Now I shall forget*. Because if you did not forget, then your forgiveness would be tested, perhaps many times and in ways that you could not resist, and you might go back to anger, and to hating.

Then Phuti said something that worried her.

'There is plenty of help for her in the house, Mma. There is that girl who works in the kitchen – she is a very good cook. And she keeps things clean too. And then there is my aunt.'

'Your aunt?' Mma Ramotswe said sharply.

Phuti sighed. 'She is coming to the house for six weeks,' he said. 'Grace's mother is late now, and she says that there must be a senior female relative to help with the baby and all the things that need to be done. She says that it is her duty to come, since we will not let the baby go to her place. In fact . . . '

She waited for him to continue but he was having difficulty with the words. Mma Makutsi had told her that it was always like that – when Phuti was upset or nervous about something, the words would not come, or would come out in pieces, or sometimes in the wrong order.

'Has she already come to the house?' she asked.

'Y . . . yes. She is there now.'

Mma Ramotswe was not sure what to say. Phuti's aunt was a difficult woman, by any standards, and could try even the patience of Dr Moffat, the most patient of men, who would listen to people talking about their problems and their sorrows for any length of time and never urge them to hurry up, because our problems and our sorrows may be a story that is very long in the telling, and he understood that. And Professor Tlou had been the same – that wise man who knew more about the history of Botswana than anybody else, but who had always been prepared to listen to people telling their own story, even if he had heard similar things from many others before. He was late now, but he had not been forgotten and it was as if his wisdom and kindness were still there; which they were, in a way, because people still remembered and that made them a little bit wiser and kinder themselves.

The aunt was not in that company. She was, Mma Ramotswe feared, someone who would probably never improve very much, even if there were times that she appeared to be a little less difficult. But it was always worth trying; there were few people who were so unpleasant that you could not get through to them with courtesy or praise. That was often what such people really wanted – to be praised, to be loved – and that was what could change them.

'I am sure that she will be a great help,' she said. 'It is important for a new mother to have support, and aunts are just the right people for that.' But not that aunt, she thought. She did not say so, of course, though she sensed that Phuti himself felt it but was prevented by loyalty, of which he had a good measure, and decency, of which he had even more, from expressing doubt as to the helpfulness of his difficult relative.

Mma Ramotswe thought that Mma Makutsi had probably agreed to the arrangement in a moment of weakness, or possibly even in a state of drowsiness. You were never at your best in hospital, and after having given birth you might agree to all sorts of things. Mma Makutsi was saddled with the aunt for now, but perhaps would be capable of dealing with her when she became a bit stronger. Those six weeks that the aunt proposed to stay might, with a bit of skilful negotiation, become six days. That would be bearable, Mma Ramotswe thought.

On the day on which Mma Makutsi was due to return home, Mma Ramotswe closed the office early. It had been a slow day, with not a single client appointment, no mail to speak of, and few continuing investigations. It had, in fact, been a rather quiet period at the No. 1 Ladies' Detective Agency, which was not unusual, Mma Ramotswe had noted, in the weeks before the onset of the rains. It was always hot then, and it seemed as if people felt too lethargic to be aware of their problems, or, if they were aware, to be bothered to do anything about them. Once the rains came, it would be different. That was a time when life seemed to start all over again, and this meant that people who had something to worry about – some matter of doubt or uncertainty that required the services of Mma Ramotswe – would think about doing something about their problem. And she, of course, was just the person for that. As the motto of the agency proclaimed: *Satisfaction Guaranteed.*

She wrote out a note to leave on the door, in case a client should turn up. *Closed*, she wrote, *but open again tomorrow morning as normal. Please return with your problem then.* Having dashed off the note, she looked at it more closely. She was not sure whether it was enough to say that a business was closed. Somebody who had made a special trip to consult her might be forgiven for being annoyed at not receiving an explanation; might conclude, perhaps, that this was a business that could close for no reason at all – on a whim. There were businesses like that, she knew; their owners thought nothing of bringing down the shutters because they fancied an afternoon of shopping, or because they felt a little bit tired and wanted to go home to rest, or simply because they were fed up with working. So she felt that she should give some explanation, and perhaps also change the word *problem* to *matter.* She had found that people rather liked their problems being described as *matters*, a term that, she had observed, was much used by lawyers. It was more tactful, she thought.

She reached for a fresh piece of paper and wrote, in large, easy-to-read letters: *We are closed today on account of the joyful arrival of the first-born son of Mma Makutsi (Associate Detective). We shall re-open for business matters tomorrow morning, same as usual. Signed, Precious Ramotswe, Owner, No. 1 Ladies' Detective Agency.*

It was a good sign, one that would reassure even the most troubled of clients – and all the clients of detective agencies *were* troubled, no matter how much they might try to conceal it. If anybody could help them to become less troubled, then undoubtedly it was the signatory of that sign.

She parked her van near the coffee shop at the edge of Riverwalk and made her way past the cluster of traders' stalls. These stalls were a fruitful source of presents, but not, she decided, ones for a new baby. There were leather belts, and jewellery, and animals made out of polished soapstone, but her real destination was a shop near the large supermarket. This was Mother and Baby, a small shop sandwiched between a men's clothing store – Kalahari Fashions – and an electronics store – Loud Sounds. She had noticed the store before, having been attracted by the colourful displays mounted in its window, but had never gone inside. It belonged, she had heard, to a woman whose husband was the proprietor of an unsuccessful – but determined – football team unkindly referred to by nearly everybody as the Gaborone All-time Losers. Mma Ramotswe had met this man on one or two occasions as he brought his car to Mr J. L. B. Matekoni for servicing. For the proprietor of a lost cause, he always seemed very cheerful, and she had heard that his wife had a similar approach to life.

She did not look in the window but went straight inside, where one or two other customers were examining a selection of lace bonnets of the sort that people liked to put on babies' heads. Some of these were attractive enough, in Mma Ramotswe's view, but others were unduly fussy and only succeeded in making the baby look absurd.

The woman who owned the shop was busy with the bonnets, but smiled in Mma Ramotswe's direction and gave her a look that seemed to say, *These people are being very slow to make up their minds, but I shall be with you before long.* It was quite a lengthy message for a single look to convey, but it did so clearly enough.

You could not buy a boy baby a bonnet like that, thought Mma Ramotswe. A cap, perhaps – one of those woollen caps that could be pulled down over the baby's ears in cold weather. That would be a good present, though inappropriate in this heat. So one might get the baby one of the stuffed toys that were arranged along a section of shelving towards the back of the store. There was every imaginable creature: lions, chickens, even a stuffed anteater. She moved towards the shelf and reached for a lion. It was rather large for a stuffed toy – almost the size of a real lion cub – and it occurred to Mma Ramotswe that a baby might get something of a fright if given such an object.

She replaced the lion and picked up in its stead a long green crocodile, complete with teeth represented by short tabs of white felt. What would a baby make of a crocodile? And was it a good idea to give a baby such a creature to love when real crocodiles were so completely unlovable? Should you not tell very small children to keep well away from crocodiles, rather than give them the message that crocodiles were suitable companions in the nursery?

She looked at the crocodile. As it stared back at her with its carefully stitched brown eyes, she remembered that a long time ago, at the very beginning of her career as a private detective, she had been obliged to deal with a crocodile that had eaten somebody during a baptism ceremony in a river. It had been such an ill-advised thing to do – to immerse the new believers in a river known for its crocodiles. What did people expect? That the crocodiles would stay away out of respect? She shook her head. People forgot about obvious dangers and then were reminded sharply that Africa could be a dangerous place, for all the sunlight and the music. Yet everywhere was dangerous. The Tlokweng Road was dangerous if you tried to cross it in the face of a careering minibus or a truck. All roads were like that, wherever you went in the world, and if there were crocodiles in rivers in Botswana, then there were sharks in the sea off Durban, and Australia had even more poisonous snakes than Africa. She had read, too, that there were pirates in the Indian Ocean, and so it went on. You had to be aware of all the dangers, but you should not worry about them too much or you would end up sitting in your room afraid to go outside in case something bad happened.

'Mma Ramotswe?'

It was the owner of the store, who had now finished with her other customers.

Mma Ramotswe struggled to remember the name of the woman.

'Mma . . .' she began.

'I am Mmakosi. Your husband looks after my husband's car, I think. He has seen you there, going into your office next to the garage.'

Mma Ramotswe put down the stuffed crocodile and returned the owner's greeting. She noticed that she used the naming practice that a woman might use in Botswana: Mmakosi, meaning that she was the mother of Kosi, who would be her first-born.

'I have come about a present,' said Mma Ramotswe. 'It is a present for a new baby.'

Mmakosi nodded and smiled. 'It's Mma Makutsi?'

Mma Ramotswe was taken aback. Gaborone was a large town, but there were many occasions on which it behaved like a village – and a small village too. This was an example of exactly that: not only did Mmakosi know who she was, but she was also aware of the birth of the young Radiphuti.

Mmakosi noticed her customer's surprise. 'Do not be too astonished, Mma. We hear these things. It is useful information for a shop like this.'

Mma Ramotswe recovered her composure. 'I should take lessons from you, Mma. I am a detective but so, it seems, are you.'

'Informants, Mma – that's the secret. Make sure that you have informants in the right places.'

'Such as maternity wards?'

Mmakosi's eyes sparkled. 'But you must always remember never to reveal your sources,' she said. 'I'm sure that you know all about that in your profession.'

'I understand that,' said Mma Ramotswe. 'And if ever you need a new job, Mma, perhaps you could call me on the telephone . . .'

They both laughed. Then Mmakosi said, 'I hear it's a boy.'

'That is so, Mma. That's good news for Phuti Radiphuti – he is the husband – but I always feel it must secretly be a bit disappointing for the mother. You can't dress boy babies up in the same way as you can dress up girls.'

'That's changing, Mma. It used to be the case, but these days there are clothes that suit both sorts of baby.'

'They're putting lace on boys?'

'Not quite,' said Mmakosi. 'But that may come. Men are wearing more feminine clothes these days, haven't you noticed?'

Mma Ramotswe was not sure whether she had noticed this or not. What were Charlie and Fanwell wearing these days? They were young men of fashion, but all she ever saw them in was mechanic's overalls. For an absurd moment she saw the two of them in greasy overalls with lace cuffs and necks. And Mr J. L. B. Matekoni also in overalls with a delicate lace trim along the edge, perhaps with only a trace of grease here and there . . .

'You're smiling, Mma?'

The ridiculous image faded. 'I was thinking. My husband's a mechanic, as you know, and his clothes are . . . Well, they are the sort of thing that men wear. They don't like fussy clothes, as a general rule.'

'Of course, Mma,' said Mmakosi. 'I understand that very well.

My own husband is like that. His head is full of football, and there is no room for clothes.' She paused. 'Mind you, Mma, there is a course, you know. They have a course for men called the Modern Husband course. Have you heard of it?'

'I have not, Mma. It sounds interesting.'

'It is very good. I hear they teach men how to cook, or at least to think about cooking.'

Mma Ramotswe's attention was immediately engaged. 'That sounds very useful.'

'And then they have lectures on clothes and how to look smart. Then – and this is very important – there is part of the course called "How to make your wife feel special". They teach them about buying presents for ladies and how to remember your wife's birthday.'

Mma Ramotswe laughed. 'Men could write the date on a piece of paper and put it on the wall. Or they could have a book that had dates like that – birthdays, wedding anniversaries, and so on.'

'They could do all of that,' agreed Mmakosi. 'But do they, Mma? Would men remember their wedding anniversary if we didn't tell them? I do not think they would.'

It was true, thought Mma Ramotswe. There were many things that men did not do, or only did because there were women there to remind them to do it. Some men, she believed, were almost entirely dependent on their wives and had to be reminded, perhaps, to breathe ... 'Remember to breathe,' the wife might say as the husband left the house in the morning. 'In, out. In, out. That's it.'

'This course, Mma? Where is it?'

'I read about it in the newspaper, Mma. I forget where they said it would be. They were hoping to hold it again because it had been a great success the first time round.'

'I shall look out for it,' said Mma Ramotswe. 'But now, Mma, there is the more pressing question of what to get for this new baby of Mma Makutsi's.'

'Come this way,' said Mmakosi.

Mma Ramotswe left Mmakosi's shop with a parcel that was far too small to contain a soft toy – a stuffed lion, or elephant, or even a stuffed anteater. It was a neat rectangular package in which, wrapped in coloured tissue paper, nestled a pair of child's shoes, size zero. These were made of soft leather, dyed red, with bright blue laces, and had been chosen by Mmakosi herself, who had convinced Mma Ramotswe that they were an ideal present for the young Radiphuti.

'That assistant of yours – your Mma Makutsi – is a lady who likes shoes, I believe,' said Mmakosi. 'And if the mother likes shoes, then you can be pretty sure that the baby is going to like shoes too.'

Mma Ramotswe was astonished that Mmakosi should have known this detail of Mma Makutsi's life, and expressed her surprise.

'But I have seen her,' exclaimed Mmakosi. 'I have seen her going into the Pick and Pay. You can tell that she is a woman who appreciates shoes. You just have to look at her feet.'

'I suppose so,' said Mma Ramotswe. 'She has some nice pairs of shoes now that she is married to Phuti Radiphuti. But even when she was single – and did not have much money – she was careful with her shoes.'

'She is very wise,' said Mmakosi. 'If you look after your shoes ...' She left the unfinished aphorism hanging in the air, imparting to it a slight air of warning. And what, wondered Mma Ramotswe, would be the consequences of *not* looking after your shoes?

'Then your shoes will last a long time,' Mmakosi concluded.

Mma Ramotswe savoured this piece of wisdom. 'That is certainly true, Mma,' she said at last. 'As long as the shoes are well made in the beginning. That is the important thing.'

Mmakosi was in complete agreement. 'You get what you pay for,' she said. 'You don't get what you deserve.'

This, Mma Ramotswe felt, was dubious. Mmakosi's observations about shoes might be true enough, but she was not sure that this proposition about life in general was entirely supportable. 'That may be so sometimes, Mma,' she pointed out. 'But there are many cases, I think, in which people get exactly what they deserve. And that may not be what they think they should get.'

She was thinking of Violet Sephotho as she said this. Violet, who seemed to have dedicated herself to being Mma Makutsi's nemesis – on the grounds of jealousy going way back to their days in the Botswana Secretarial College – had got her just deserts in that her ploys had consistently failed. She had been dramatically exposed when she worked for a short time as an assistant at the Double Comfort Shop, her short-lived political career had been nipped in the bud, and her attempts to secure a wealthy husband had similarly met with no success. She had brought all of this on herself, and so she had, in a sense, got what she deserved. But even so, Mma Ramotswe reminded herself, she had a soul like everybody else and one should not crow over the defeat even of those who richly deserve to be defeated. That was dangerous because then you yourself might get what you deserve for revelling in the misfortunes of another. It was safer, perhaps, not to think of Violet at all . . .

They had returned to the subject of shoes. 'Children's feet grow so quickly,' said Mmakosi. 'So I always say to people: get shoes that are always slightly too big for your child. Then turn your head for a week or two and – whoosh – the child's toes will have filled the extra space. That is what I say, Mma Ramotswe.'

Mma Ramotswe examined the tiny red shoes – boots, really – that had been selected for Mma Makutsi's son. 'These are size zero, Mma,' she said. 'Perhaps we should go for size one. Then he will grow into them.'

Mmakosi shook her head. 'No, Mma. These shoes are not like ordinary shoes. If you feel the toes, you will notice that the leather is very supple. These shoes can expand very easily to allow for growth. And they are not shoes for walking in, you know. These shoes are called crawling shoes. They are for when the child begins to crawl.'

'But he's only a few days old,' said Mma Ramotswe. 'He's going nowhere.'

'But he will,' said Mmakosi. 'He will start to crawl before too long, and these shoes will be there, ready for him. They are a very sensible present.'

Mma Ramotswe was drawn to the shoes. It tickled her to think that she was giving shoes to Mma Makutsi, who had always taken a rather condescending attitude towards Mma Ramotswe's own shoes, which were designed for comfort rather than for fashion. They were always the same: flat and brown, and fairly wide too, to cater to traditionally built feet. But they had never let her down and, unlike Mma Makutsi's shoes, had never been sarcastic.

'You know something, Mma?' Mma Ramotswe said to Mmakosi. 'Mma Makutsi's shoes are very unusual. They ...' She stopped herself. She had been about to mention that Mma Makutsi's shoes appeared to speak, but she realised that this would sound very odd to the shopkeeper.

'Yes, Mma?' prompted Mmakosi.

'They are a very unusual colour. And so I think she will like these red shoes.'

The purchase made, Mma Ramotswe went out into the covered

square. The managers of the shopping centre had thoughtfully provided concrete benches for the comfort of tired shoppers, and for those who might not have been tired out by shopping but were tired at the thought of shopping. A few of these people now sat about on these benches, plastic bags of purchases resting at their feet, in some cases watching passers-by, in others looking vaguely into the distance, and in yet others half dozing in the drowsy warmth of the afternoon. A small group of four or five teenagers had congregated around one bench and were chatting about the things which teenagers liked to chat about and which adults, for all their efforts, singularly failed to understand. There was laughter and raised voices from this group, sufficient to attract a scowl of disapproval from a middle-aged man on a nearby bench. But Mma Ramotswe did not disapprove. Laughter, even teenage laughter, was something of which she would never disapprove, unless, of course, it was cruel laughter, which was always so easy to recognise from its higher pitch and sharper edge.

Mma Ramotswe decided to sit down. She was not particularly tired – it was simply one of those occasions when she felt like sitting down. There was no reason why one should always be on the move. That was half the trouble with the world, she thought: not enough people took the time to sit down for a few minutes and look up at the sky or at whatever it was that was before you – a herd of cattle, perhaps, or a stretch of bush dotted with acacia trees, or the sinking of the evening sun into the Kalahari. You did not have to sit for long; even a few minutes was enough to remind you that if you spent your life rushing about, then the years would slip through your fingers without your really noticing it until suddenly they were gone and you were old and before long it would be that moment that comes to everybody – the time to leave Botswana for ever.

A morbid notion, and Mma Ramotswe was not given to such

things, so as she lowered herself on to the bench, the gift parcel on her lap, she turned her mind to something else altogether: the Sheba case. Although she had not started her actual investigation, she had been thinking about it, and thinking about a problem – even in a rather dreamy way – was often a good way of allowing the mind to come up with possibilities. What puzzled her about this case was that if anybody was lying, it would be the aunt: she was the one on whose word the whole matter rested. If Mma Sheba was right and Liso was not the real Liso, then there had to be a reason for the aunt to go along with that deception. Would she have an interest in stopping the real Liso from inheriting the farm? Would it be because he might evict her from her house? That was possible. Or did she want this other young man to inherit it because she could control him in some way? Perhaps she wanted to buy the farm at a knockdown price and had a secret agreement with him to sell it to her if she lied about his identity in order to enable him to inherit. Unlikely, she thought. Very unlikely.

Her chain of thought was diverted when she looked up and saw two workmen struggling with several large plywood boards. The boards had been covering the window of a shop undergoing renovations, and now the renewed shop beneath was being revealed. She tried to envisage what had been there before. It had been, she seemed to recall, a shop that sold gardening equipment: spades and trowels, specialist rakes and gloves. These were things that people liked to own, and would find quite useful, but not things that they would bother to buy. If you wanted a trowel, you hunted through the piles of old possessions that naturally accumulated in sheds and garages and as likely as not you found one, soil-encrusted and ancient, but a trowel nonetheless; you did not think of buying such a thing.

She shook her head as she thought of the shop-owner's

disappointment at becoming yet another commercial failure. People had said that the same fate awaited her when she started the No. 1 Ladies' Detective Agency. They had laughed and said that nobody would want the services of a detective agency in a society in which there were few secrets, and where, moreover, everybody prided themselves on how easily they could find out anything they wished to know. That is what they had said behind her back and in some cases even to her face. Yet here she was, years later, with a firm that had defied these Jeremiah-like predictions and was a well established, prosperous concern. Well, if not actually prosperous, then at least not a business that lost too much money.

One of the workmen paused to mop his brow with a handkerchief. Yes, thought Mma Ramotswe, it is very hot, even here in the shade. Yet people had to work, even in this heat; they had to take boards off the front of shops, they had to cook meals in kitchens, they had to lie under cars and struggle to undo the nuts on oil sumps, they had to ... Her attention was caught by the workman's renewed struggles with the board. He had prised it off successfully and was shifting it to one side, revealing the lettering painted on the glass behind.

Mma Ramotswe stared at the name: *The Minor Adjustment Beauty Salon*. It took a moment or two, but then it came to her: she knew about this business. She had met Mma Soleti, its owner, who had previously operated her beauty salon from such unpromising small premises – no more than a shack, really – and who now was moving into this much smarter accommodation. This was indeed a business success.

She got to her feet and approached the workman.

'*Dumela*, Rra,' she said. 'You are doing a very good job.'

The man, breathless from his exertions, mopped his brow again. 'It is too hot to be working, Mma.'

'Yes,' she said. 'The only thing to do in weather like this is to sit in some cool place somewhere. But ... ' She paused as she peered into the shop's interior. 'But business has to go on, Rra, and, as it happens, I know this lady. I know Mma Soleti.'

The man scrutinised her for a moment. 'You have been a client, Mma?'

Mma Ramotswe smiled. 'Not really, Rra. I am not a lady who spends a lot of time on fashion and such things. And you, Rra? Have you ... ' She left the question unfinished.

He laughed. 'Men do not go to these places.'

'Perhaps they should, Rra. Perhaps men should go and have the wrinkles taken out of their faces.'

For a moment the workman looked anxious, and his hand went involuntarily to his face.

'I am not being serious,' Mma Ramotswe reassured him. 'Women do not notice the wrinkles on men's faces. Women are mostly interested in what is in a man's heart. Is he a kind man? That is the question, Rra. And there are many kind men who have many wrinkles.'

The workman nodded. 'This woman, this Mma Soleti, is coming here soon to open up her shop. That is why we are getting it ready.'

'Soon soon?' asked Mma Ramotswe.

'Yes. She should have been here already, but maybe there is traffic and she is delayed.'

Mma Ramotswe nodded. The traffic was getting worse – particularly at lunchtime and in the late afternoon – and one could no longer say with certainty when one would arrive. There were too many cars, and it would be a good idea to round up all the cars and throw away half of them, to make things better for the surviving vehicles. Such a solution, though, was hardly practicable and of course there was Mr J. L. B. Matekoni to think of. Cars were his livelihood and by extension hers too, in a way, until the No. 1 Ladies' Detective Agency became much more profitable – which it would not, unless people started to have rather more problems than they currently did, and who would wish more problems on other people?

She became aware of somebody approaching, and she turned round.

'Mma Ramotswe!'

Mma Soleti, carrying a bulging canvas bag in each hand, was struggling towards her. Instinctively Mma Ramotswe reached out to help her, but this only caused the other woman to lose her grip on one of the bags. A cascade of plastic bottles – shampoos, creams, lotions – scattered about their ankles.

Apologising profusely, Mma Ramotswe scooped up the bottles and jars and stuffed them back into the bag.

'This is the last load,' said Mma Soleti, fumbling for her keys with her free hand. 'Once we have these on the shelf, I shall be ready for business.' She looked at Mma Ramotswe as if she were planning something. 'In fact, Mma, would you like to be my official first customer?'

It took Mma Ramotswe a little while to answer. She realised that she did not have very much money on her – the purchase of the baby shoes had been more expensive than she had expected, and the remaining one hundred and fifty *pula* she had in her purse had been earmarked for the purchase of groceries. It would hardly do for her to reveal to Mr J. L. B. Matekoni that there was nothing to put on the table because she had spent the house-keeping money on beauty treatments. Tolerant though he was, no man could fail to be disappointed by such information; some would even be angry, but those particular men would do well to ask themselves how much of the household budget went on beer. If men bought beer, thought Mma Ramotswe, then women should be entitled to spend money on beauty treatments. At least beauty treatments made you look better, while beer generally made you look worse. She had to admit, though, that both were capable of making you feel more cheerful – in moderation, of course.

Mma Ramotswe clapped her hands in gratitude. 'That is very kind, Mma, but I'm afraid that I'm having to watch my *pula* these days and I don't have much money on me. Some other day perhaps.'

Mma Soleti shook her head vigorously. 'Oh no, Mma. I was not going to charge my first customer. The treatment would be entirely free. On the house. Nothing to pay.'

Mma Ramotswe was grateful, but still felt unable to accept. 'That is very kind, Mma, but it is not a good way to run a business. If you did not charge for your treatments, then you would be out of business pretty quickly.'

Mma Soleti was having none of this. 'But of course I'm going to charge for the treatments. All I'm saying is that I won't charge you, Mma Ramotswe, as you will be the first customer in my new premises. That is all I'm saying.'

Mma Ramotswe looked at her watch. The supermarket would be quite busy, she thought, and she would need time to cook Mr J. L. B. Matekoni's dinner. She also had to call on Mma Makutsi to deliver the present. 'Time is the problem for me,' she said. 'There are so many things to do.'

'It would not take long, Mma,' said Mma Soleti, peering at Mma Ramotswe's face. 'I think the main thing would be doing something about those slightly enlarged pores at the side of your nose. And there's a bit of dry skin near your ears, if I'm not mistaken. It's this weather, Mma. The sun dries a lady's skin very quickly and when we have as much sun as we're getting on days like this, then moisturiser is the only solution.'

'Fifteen minutes?' asked Mma Ramotswe.

'Twenty,' countered Mma Soleti.

'Then I accept. Thank you, Mma.'

Mma Ramotswe was impressed by the interior of the Minor Adjustment Beauty Salon.

'This is very luxurious, Mma,' she said as she lay down on Mma Soleti's treatment couch. 'Your last place was . . . very nice, but it was a . . . '

'Shack,' said Mma Soleti. 'You have to start somewhere, Mma, and that is where I started. Now we have this new salon complete with hot and cold running water and a fan to keep the customers cool. It is very different.'

'It must have cost a lot,' said Mma Ramotswe. Through her mind was going the question that always went through people's minds but they never liked to ask: Where did the money come from?

Mma Soleti would understand that question – everybody in Botswana was familiar with it. In rural Botswana, everybody, no matter how long they had lived in a town, helped one another, would not let another go hungry and were polite in their dealings with their fellow villagers; yet there was one major failing shared by all – a human enough trait, of course, but a failing nonetheless – envy. People could be envious of the material success of others, and almost everybody knew of some case where something spiteful had been done purely out of envy. So if somebody suddenly had a lot to spend, it was envy that fired up curiosity as to where the money had come from.

'You will be wondering where I got the money,' said Mma Soleti. This was no accusation – her tone was matter-of-fact.

'I must admit the thought crossed my mind, Mma,' said Mma Ramotswe.

Mma Soleti twisted the lid off a jar of cold cream. 'I had some money saved,' she said. 'A good amount, in fact, but not nearly enough to pay the rental deposit on this shop. Nor to pay the builder. No, I was able to borrow money, Mma – and at a very competitive rate of interest.'

'That is good because you must have needed a lot,' said Mma Ramotswe. 'Even this couch ... ' She ran her hand over the surface. It looked expensive and it *felt* expensive too.

'Two thousand *pula*,' interjected Mma Soleti. 'It came all the way from Johannesburg. It is the latest thing. Except it's second-hand, of course.'

'Many old things are very good,' said Mma Ramotswe diplomatically. 'Things are rather like people in that respect, Mma ... '

Mma Soleti waited for Mma Ramotswe to finish, but her voice died away. Perhaps, thought the beautician, that is all she wanted to say; perhaps there was no conclusion to the observation.

From her supine position on the couch, Mma Ramotswe looked up at the ceiling. Two flies were engaged in a display of complicated footwork – an upside-down argument over upside-down territory. Or a dance of love perhaps. From the flies' perspective, she thought, the ground was the sky, the thing you looked at when you craned your neck and looked up. And what were we to them? Great elephants lumbering around, strangely attached to that sky; our exposed flesh, moist with sweat in this heat, wide expanses of swamp for courageous flies to explore; our hair the jungle; our nostrils great caves emitting gales of heated air, places into which only a foolhardy insect would venture.

At length Mma Soleti spoke. 'I think you're right, Mma Ramotswe. Many people improve as they grow older. They become less foolish. They behave more thoughtfully towards others. There is a long list of these things.'

Mma Ramotswe smiled. 'I suppose that is what I meant. Mr J. L. B. Matekoni thinks that about cars, you know. He says that an old car has a big soul. Those were the words he used – the exact words.'

Mma Soleti had now arranged three jars of cream on a tray beside the couch. 'Close your eyes,' she said. 'This will feel nice and cool.'

Mma Ramotswe did as she was bidden. The cream, applied by Mma Soleti's gentle fingers, felt pleasant, and it smelled good too. She wrinkled her nose slightly in an effort to identify the scent.

'That cream is made of aloes,' said Mma Soleti. 'But they have added lemon to it. That is what you're smelling, Mma.' She paused, spreading the cream in generous quantities across Mma Ramotswe's brow. 'Lemon juice is a very good skin cleanser, Mma,' she continued. 'It is good for oily skin and when you mix it with aloe then it heals very well too. You can drink lemon juice with honey in the mornings – that will clean your skin from within.'

Mma Ramotswe frowned. 'I drink tea in the mornings, Mma. I drink redbush tea.'

'That is very good for the skin too,' said Mma Soleti. 'You can put cold redbush tea on your skin if you have a rash. Then you can drink what's left over so that you are cleansed inside and outside.'

Mma Ramotswe relaxed. She liked the idea of being cleansed inside and outside. And then she thought of Mma Makutsi and her difficult complexion. She had never broached the matter with her assistant, but she knew that skin problems had troubled Mma Makutsi for some time, although more recently her complexion seemed to have settled down. She was not the easiest person with whom to raise delicate issues, but Mma Ramotswe wondered whether she might suggest that her associate put lemon juice in her tea rather than milk. Perhaps it would be possible to do that tactfully, for instance by saying that she had heard that people who were concerned about their skin spoke highly of lemon juice. Not that she would be implying that Mma Makutsi was a person who needed to worry about her skin; she would not say anything like that.

Of course, having a husband always took the sting out of your minor imperfections. Now that Mma Makutsi was married to Phuti Radiphuti she would no longer have to be concerned about attracting men and could stop worrying about skin issues and having to wear very large round glasses and so on. Mind you, no woman, Mma Ramotswe thought, should give up entirely and not concern herself with looking good for her husband. The best solution lay somewhere in the middle, as it always did: you could relax a bit but you should always remember that it gave your husband pleasure to gaze at a beautiful wife over the breakfast table. And beauty, she reminded herself, was both an inside and an outside quality. You could be very glamorous and beautiful on the outside, but if inside you were filled with human faults – jealousy, spite and the like – then no amount of exterior beauty would make up for that. Perhaps there was some sort of lemon juice for inside beauty . . . And even as she thought of it, she realised what it was: love and kindness. Love was the lemon juice that cleansed and kindness was the aloe that healed.

Neither woman spoke for the rest of the treatment. Mma Ramotswe found herself feeling drowsy and at one point came close to sleep. It was very comforting sensing the potions on one's skin and breathing their perfume. It was highly relaxing to feel Mma Soleti's fingertips coaxing tension out of the skin. And so, when the creams were rubbed off and some final unguent applied, Mma Ramotswe found herself feeling vaguely disappointed, as when the final drops of a much looked-forward-to cup of tea are drained.

'There we are,' said Mma Soleti. 'You can open your eyes now, Mma. The treatment is over.'

Mma Ramotswe sat up. Her face felt as if it was glowing, as if she were basking in the first rays of an early morning sun. She raised a hand to touch her cheek. 'It feels very smooth, Mma.'

'That is because the creams have done their work and now it *is* smooth,' said Mma Soleti, a note of pride in her voice. 'Just like a baby's skin.' She paused. 'Mma Ramotswe, I'm glad that you have enjoyed being my first customer in this new salon. First *free* customer. Free, remember.'

Mma Ramotswe noticed the emphasis on the word *free*. Some things that are free are not free, she thought. She was wary.

'You were very kind, Mma. Thank you.'

Mma Soleti had her back turned to her as she was replacing the jars on the shelf. 'Mma Ramotswe,' she said, 'there is something that is worrying me.'

Mma Ramotswe realised that her instinct had been right: this free beauty treatment came at the cost of a favour. Well, that was how the world worked, and she knew that she should not be surprised. Life was a matter of exchanges; you did things for people and they did things for you. And it had to be that way because you started life with the assistance of the one who brought you into the world – the midwife – and you ended it with the assistance of those who laid you in the ground. Between those two extremes, you often needed the help of others; you needed their company, you needed their love, and they, in turn, needed those things from you.

She did not show her feelings. She was there to help, after all – that was what being a private detective was about, even if whatever problem Mma Soleti had looked as if it would not involve any remuneration. It would not be the first *pro bono* case she had undertaken; there had been many of those and there would no doubt be many more. One client had even suggested that *she* – Mma Ramotswe – should pay *her* to investigate her case. That was unusual by any standards, but the fact that it had occurred went to show that one should not be surprised by anything that people suggested – or did, for that matter.

'Tell me what is worrying you, Mma,' said Mma Ramotswe. 'Sometimes, you know, the things that worry us are not so bad when you tell another person about them.'

Mma Soleti turned to face her. She looked at the shop's glass front door. 'Can we speak in the office at the back, Mma?'

Before Mma Ramotswe had the chance to reply, Mma Soleti took her by the arm and started to lead her into a room at the back of the salon. This was furnished with a desk, some chairs and a telephone. An unopened cardboard packing case labelled *Beauty Products: Urgent* stood on the floor near the desk. Mma Ramotswe could not conceal a smile. She wondered how anybody could consider beauty products to be urgent. Medicines yes, but not aloe extract and lemon juice. Of course, everybody considered their own orders of supplies urgent. Mma Makutsi often became concerned if her stationery orders took longer than a week to arrive. 'How do they think we are going to be able to write to people, Mma?' she complained. 'Perhaps on scraps of old newspaper? Perhaps on the back of envelopes?'

Mma Soleti invited her to sit on one of the chairs and then settled herself on the other one. 'I have received a parcel,' she said. 'Through the post.'

Mma Ramotswe looked down at the case of beauty products.

Mma Soleti shook her head. 'Not that, Mma. This was a very small parcel – about the size of a packet of cigarettes.'

Mma Ramotswe waited for her to continue. Mma Soleti had

lowered her voice, although there was nobody who could possibly hear them. People did that, Mma Ramotswe had observed – and it was usually a sign that they were frightened.

'I opened it,' went on Mma Soleti.

Mma Ramotswe nodded her encouragement. 'And, Mma?'

'I wish I hadn't.'

Mma Ramotswe reached out to soothe her. Mma Soleti was shivering. This was unfeigned fear.

'It is very difficult not to open a parcel, Mma Soleti.'

'I know that. But in this case I wish that something had happened to this parcel before it arrived at my house.'

'May I ask why, Mma?'

'Because it contained something very bad, Mma.'

Mma Ramotswe was silent. She had an idea what Mma Soleti was going to say.

'It was a feather,' whispered Mma Soleti.

Mma Ramotswe had not been expecting this. She had expected a bone, or a powder of some sort. Those were the usual devices of witchcraft, and no matter how logical or modern one was in one's outlook, such things were capable of bringing terror. People had died simply because they received such things. There was no scientific reason for them to do so, but the heart and the head were not the same thing in the darkness of the night.

'Was there anything with the feather?' she asked. 'Any *muti*?' She used the word commonly used for such things. *Muti* was at the heart of curses and spells – at least for those who believed in such things, which she did not. But she knew very well that it took only a handful of gullible people to give a witchdoctor his lucrative practice.

Mma Soleti shook her head. 'I did not know what the feather meant, and so I took it to a person I know who is a big expert in birds. He took one look at it and told me. It was a feather from a ground hornbill.'

Mma Ramotswe let out a sigh. 'So, they have sent you a sign from that bird.'

Mma Soleti nodded miserably. 'I threw it away immediately. I washed my hands, more than once – three or four times, I think – but I had already touched it. I already had had it in my pocket.'

Mma Ramotswe tried to make light of the incident. 'But, Mma, listen to me: I know people say that this poor bird is bad luck, that it will bring all sorts of bad things—'

'Including death,' interjected Mma Soleti. 'If that bird comes to your house then ...'

Mma Ramotswe wagged a finger. 'Hush, Mma! That is complete nonsense. It is untrue. How can an innocent bird bring death? That is nonsense.'

'It is not innocent,' said Mma Soleti. 'It is a wicked bird.'

'A bird cannot be wicked. It cannot.' She paused. 'Birds don't think, Mma. Look at their heads – they are very small. All that a bird can think about is food and things like that. They do not think about harming people.'

Mma Soleti was not convinced. 'Even if a bird can do nothing, a person can. And there is some person somewhere who wants to frighten me, who would like me to be late.'

Mma Ramotswe became firmer. 'No, Mma, you cannot say that. You cannot say that there is anybody who wishes you to become late. There is some person – some very foolish and childish person – who wants to frighten you, yes. But what power has that person got if you refuse to be frightened? A rock rabbit, a tiny little *dassie*, can laugh at a leopard. Even he will not be frightened if he does not let himself feel that way.'

'Until the leopard eats him,' said Mma Soleti.

'I think my example was not very good,' said Mma Ramotswe.

'But look at ...' She racked her brains for a more suitable example. Surely there were instances of small and plucky people standing up to larger bullies and facing them down, but now that she needed them she could not bring any to mind. Meerkats were plucky, no doubt about that, but when they saw the shadow of a hawk they ran for cover.

'So what do I do, Mma Ramotswe?'

'Ignore it,' she answered. 'If you ignore stupid people, they lose interest. That is very well known, Mma.'

'Is it, Mma?'

Mma Ramotswe was adamant. 'Definitely, Mma. It is definitely well known throughout Botswana and, I'm sure, elsewhere.'

Then her example came to her: Sir Seretse Khama, the first President of Botswana. People had tried to frighten him when he declared his intention of marrying Ruth, the woman from a very different background whom he loved. Everybody had leaned on him, scolded and cajoled him, including the tribal elders of the Bamangwato people, for whom he was royalty; the British and the South Africans had done the same. But he had refused to be cowed and had triumphed in the end, creating modern Botswana, with all that it stood for in terms of decency and courage.

'Think of Seretse Khama,' she said, rising to her feet. 'What would he say to you, Mma?'

Mma Soleti looked nonplussed.

'I'll tell you, Mma,' supplied Mma Ramotswe. 'He would say: Do not be afraid of people who lurk in the shadows. Stand up for what you believe in. The people in the shadows are no match for people who are not afraid of light. That is what he would say, Mma. I am sure of it.'

She watched the other woman and thought: Yes, she is becoming stronger. But then she thought – strictly to herself and without saying anything about it – what sort of enemies has this Mma Soleti acquired, and how?

Mma Soleti was watching her, a look of disappointment on her face. Noticing this, Mma Ramotswe understood that she would have to say something.

'You may be wondering what to do, Mma,' she said.

'I was. Yes.'

Mma Ramotswe nodded her head. 'At the moment, nothing,' she said. 'There are some situations where it is best to wait and watch.'

'Is this one of those?' asked Mma Soleti.

'Yes,' answered Mma Ramotswe. 'This is one of those cases where doing nothing is doing something, if you see what I mean, Mma.'

Mma Soleti hesitated, but then she said, 'If that's what you say, Mma.'

'It is,' said Mma Ramotswe.

Chapter Six

That is My Baby, Mma

L ater that day Mma Ramotswe received word from Phuti
  Radiphuti that Mma Makutsi had returned home from hospital, and was back on her feet and looking forward to a visit in the
afternoon. She sent a message back saying that she was very happy
to hear all this and that she would be at the Radiphuti house
shortly after four. She said that she would not stay long, as she
knew how tired people could be after childbirth, and that it would
not be necessary even to make so much as a cup of tea for her.

The hours before four dragged. Without Mma Makutsi,
the office was a disturbingly quiet place, and although Mma
Ramotswe had a number of reports to write, she found that she
could not settle to the task. Shortly before three, she rose from
her desk, put aside a barely begun report, and made her way into
the garage workshop next door.

Mr J. L. B. Matekoni, her husband and by all accounts the finest mechanic in Botswana, was busy attempting to instruct his two assistants, Charlie and Fanwell, on an obscure point of engine tuning. They had broken off from their technical discussion and turned to an issue that Mma Ramotswe believed was causing a degree of friction – how they should be referred to at work. They had both been taken on as Mr J. L. B. Matekoni's apprentices, but Fanwell had now qualified and so had to be addressed as an assistant mechanic. Charlie had failed his examinations, several times, and seemed doomed to perpetual apprentice-status, but did not like to be described as such.

'I know as much as Fanwell,' he protested, 'and you do not call him an apprentice. So why should I be called that?'

Mr J. L. B. Matekoni tried to explain that there were formalities in life that had to be completed, and examinations were just such formalities. 'Take Mma Makutsi, for instance,' he said. 'She did not get her job just like that – she had to write exams and get her ninety-seven per cent, or whatever it was.'

Charlie sniggered. 'Ninety-seven per cent of nothing is nothing, boss. Or it used to be.'

'You may laugh, Charlie,' warned Mr J. L. B. Matekoni, 'but ninety-seven per cent is ninety-seven per cent more than you ever got. You got no marks at all for the last exam – they sent me the result. Nought per cent. Nothing. *Nix.*'

Charlie shrugged. 'What counts is this: can you fix a car? Exams are nothing beside that. Would you want Miss Ninety-seven Per Cent to fix your car? No? Neither would I, boss.'

'She has a baby now,' remarked Fanwell. 'She will not have the time to fix any cars.'

'Yes,' said Charlie. 'A baby! A ninety-seven per cent baby! And that baby will be sitting there with big round glasses like his mother's. A secretary-baby!'

Mr J. L. B. Matekoni glanced at Mma Ramotswe, who was following this conversation from the sidelines. 'You were a baby once, Charlie. Don't you forget that.'

'Ha!' said Fanwell. 'An apprentice-baby! Trying to fix a little toy car ...'

Mma Ramotswe decided to go back into her office. There was a curious thing about male conversation that she had noticed – men often ended up poking fun at one another. Women did this only rarely, but men seemed to love insulting one another. It was very strange. Mr J. L. B. Matekoni followed her into the office, wiping his hands on the ubiquitous lint that he kept for the purpose.

'I'm sorry about that,' he said. 'Those boys ...'

'They are young men,' said Mma Ramotswe. 'They'll grow up one of these days.'

'I hope so,' said Mr J. L. B. Matekoni. He looked at her enquiringly. 'Did you want to discuss anything with me back there?'

'No,' said Mma Ramotswe. 'I was killing time. I'm going to see Mma Makutsi at four.' She paused, fiddling for a moment with a manila file that was sitting on her desk. 'May I ask you something, Rra?'

Mr J. L. B. Matekoni stuffed the lint into his pocket. 'You may ask me anything, Mma – anything at all. You know that.' He thought it unlikely that there was anything that he knew that she did not – unless, of course, it was about cars. But on all other subjects, he deferred to his wife.

'What would you do if somebody sent you a ground hornbill feather?'

For a moment Mr J. L. B. Matekoni did not answer. Then, when he did, his voice was strained. 'Those birds are very bad luck.'

Mma Ramotswe waited for him to say something more.

'If I were sent a feather like that, I would know that there was somebody who wanted me dead.' He looked at her severely. 'I would say that it was very serious, Mma. I would say that sending somebody a feather like that would not be a joke at all.'

'Who does that sort of thing these days? It's so ... so old-fashioned.'

Mr J. L. B. Matekoni snorted. 'That thing never goes away, Mma. There will always be somebody prepared to pay those people to put a curse on his enemy.'

'Don't the police do anything about it?'

Mr J. L. B. Matekoni scratched his head. 'If they hear about it; but nobody wants to report it to them. It is always the same. Fear works.'

Mma Ramotswe agreed, but her fundamental question remained unanswered. What sort of person would do such a thing?

'Let me put it this way, Rra,' she said. 'If you received a feather or something like that, whom would you suspect?'

He answered quickly. 'My enemies.'

'But you have none, Rra.'

He looked puzzled. 'Perhaps not. But if I did, then they would be the suspects.' He paused. 'Or a rival, I suppose. Anybody can have rivals.'

They were silent for a while, and Mma Ramotswe stared out of the window at the acacia tree. A small bird – not one of the doves who made their home there, but something altogether more modest – was arguing with another bird about the possession of a few inches of branch. The prize was nothing much, and there were plenty of unoccupied branches nearby, but for the birds it was worth fighting for. She watched the birds in their tiny rage, and was joined by Mr J. L. B. Matekoni, who stood at her shoulder.

'Ridiculous birds,' he said. 'They are always squabbling with one another.'

'Like people,' muttered Mma Ramotswe. 'We are always fighting too – over the same things that animals fight over. Land. A place to live or work.'

'Maybe.'

'Yes, we are. And the people who are in a place first think that this means that everybody else can be shooed away. Like that bird over there. He was there first, he says. The other bird is the intruder.'

He was thoughtful. They both knew what was being discussed. 'But don't people have the right to protect their place? This Botswana of ours – everybody would want to come and live here. All those people from countries where things don't work, or where they are in a big mess – they would want to come here. And we couldn't manage that, Mma Ramotswe . . .'

She understood the point he was making. You could not open your doors to everybody because you would go under if you did. So you had to harden your heart; you had to be selfish, which she did not like. But you cannot turn another away, she thought; you cannot.

'It is very hard,' she said. 'But I suppose you're right. We cannot take on all the problems of Africa. Nobody can.' That was true, she realised, though she wished that it were otherwise.

She looked again at the birds. Mma Soleti was the bird that had come to the tree more recently. The other bird, the defender, was the bird that was already there.

She drove to the Radiphuti house in her tiny white van. Because the new house that Phuti Radiphuti had commissioned from the This Way Up Building Company was on the very edge of town, in an area yet to be adopted by the council, the road was rough and bumpy, and the van threw up a cloud of fine dust that seemed quite out of proportion to the vehicle's size. It would be impossible for anybody to approach the house by stealth, thought Mma Ramotswe, as long as they drove and as long as they came by day.

She saw that Phuti's car was parked beside the house, which did not surprise her as he had told her that he was taking a few days off while Mma Makutsi and the new baby settled. It would be good to see him; she had grown to like Phuti Radiphuti immensely, and she looked forward to witnessing his joy in his new son. There was another car, though, that Mma Ramotswe recognised, and this was a less welcome sight. It was a low-slung, rather old brown car – the colour of cattle dung, she could not help but observe – and had small, mean-spirited windows. It was a car, she thought, for a person who did not want to be looked at by the world, and wanted, in turn, to gaze out at the world only through narrow and defensive slits. It occurred to her that it might even have previously been a military vehicle, and that the purpose of the small windows was to stop people shooting at the occupants within.

The car belonged to Phuti's contrary aunt, and for a brief moment she imagined the aunt driving off to the shops under the fire of her enemies, of whom there surely were many. She smiled at the picture.

She began to park the van next to the unpleasant brown car, but then she thought better of it. She was by no means as ready as Mr J. L. B. Matekoni was to attribute emotions to cars, but she did not like the thought of her van being so close to the brown car. It was ridiculous, she knew that, but she would feel more comfortable if she found another parking place. Very slowly, she drove round the side of the house. There was no real driveway there, but there also seemed to be no garden – yet.

She stopped the van and got out, remembering to take with her the small parcel of baby shoes. As she approached the house, she had a feeling that she was being watched. *Trust your feelings,* Clovis Andersen had written in *The Principles of Private Detection. If the back of your neck tells you that you're being watched, listen to it!*

The back of Mma Ramotswe's neck now told her that there was somebody looking at her. She turned and glanced at the windows that were slightly above her. She thought she saw a movement, but she could not be sure. She continued on her way to the front of the house.

As Mma Ramotswe feared, it was the aunt, rather than Phuti, who opened the door to her.

'Yes?' said the aunt. 'Who are you, Mma?'

Mma Ramotswe was certain that the aunt must remember who she was. 'We have met before, Mma. Perhaps you have forgotten. I am Mma Ramotswe.'

The aunt feigned sudden enlightenment. 'Oh, that woman. The one from that garage.'

'From the No. 1 Ladies' Detective Agency,' corrected Mma Ramotswe. 'It is next to a garage, but it is not a garage itself.'

The aunt ignored this. 'I'm sorry that there is nobody in,' she said abruptly. 'Come back some other time.'

Mma Ramotswe caught her breath. She had never been able to understand how some people could lie like this when it was so obvious that their lies would be exposed. 'But, Mma, Mr Radiphuti's car is here.'

The aunt hesitated. 'Is it? Well, he must have come home, but I think he must be asleep. We cannot wake him. Sorry about that – you must go now.'

'No,' said Mma Ramotswe. 'I have been asked to come here by Mma Makutsi herself. She will want to see me.'

She began to push past the aunt, who resisted for a few moments, but, in military terms, it was light armour against heavy, and heavy armour won, as it always does. A final push was all that was required, and Mma Ramotswe was in the living room. From deep within the house she could hear Phuti's voice, and she made her way towards that.

Phuti was in the kitchen, as was Mma Makutsi, wearing a loose pink housecoat. They were both seated when she entered. Phuti rose to his feet, while Mma Makutsi remained in her chair. Mma Ramotswe gave a small cry of joy and crossed the room to embrace her assistant.

'This is good news, Mma,' she said. 'This is very good news.'

Mma Makutsi adjusted her glasses. She was beaming with pleasure.

'I am very happy too,' she said. 'It is a boy, Mma, as I think Phuti told you.'

Mma Ramotswe turned to smile at Phuti Radiphuti. 'He did. He is a very proud father. Where is the baby?' asked Mma Ramotswe. 'I have brought him a present.'

Mma Makutsi nodded in the direction of the corridor that led off the kitchen. 'He is sound asleep. He has just been fed, and now he is sleeping.' She paused. 'Would you like to see him, Mma?'

A voice came from behind them. The aunt had entered the room and was standing in the doorway. 'It is not good for babies to be seen by too many people,' she said, shaking her head in disapproval. 'You should know that.'

Mma Ramotswe turned to face the aunt. 'I'm not going to touch him, Mma. Only look.'

The aunt shook her head again. 'There are traditions,' she said. 'You people may have forgotten them, but I haven't.'

Phuti Radiphuti had been silent, but now he spoke. 'We all know about those, Auntie. But these days—'

'These days makes no difference,' the aunt spat out. 'These days, these days. That is all that people say when they don't want to follow tradition. And then . . . ' She made a gesture to suggest the collapse of everything.

'I am the mother,' said Mma Makutsi. 'I am the one who must decide.'

'Yes,' said Phuti Radiphuti. 'Grace is the . . . ' He was silenced by a look from the aunt.

The aunt addressed herself to her nephew. 'It is not men's business, Phuti. This is women's business and men should not put their noses into it.'

Mma Ramotswe looked anxiously at Mma Makutsi. She did not think it a good thing for somebody who had just given birth to be subjected to strain.

'I think that I can see the baby a little bit later,' she said. 'This is not the time. Now is the time for me to talk to Mma Makutsi.' She looked first at Phuti Radiphuti and then at the aunt. 'And I think we should talk in private. These are business matters, you see.'

Phuti Radiphuti crossed the room to stand by his aunt. 'You're quite right, Mma Ramotswe,' he said. 'Auntie and I will go and sit on the veranda – it's cooler there.'

'Well!' said Mma Ramotswe. And then, because she could not think of anything else that would adequately express her feelings, she said again, 'Well!'

Mma Makutsi rolled her eyes. 'She is the senior aunt, as you know. I have no family down here – all my people are up in Bobonong.'

Mma Ramotswe sighed. She understood the system and the perfectly legitimate claims that Phuti's aunt had as the senior female relative. 'I know, Mma,' she said. 'But it can't be easy for you. Is she taking the traditional view?'

Mma Makutsi explained that Phuti Radiphuti's aunt was *extremely* traditional. 'She said that the baby should be kept inside for three months, Mma. She also wanted to rub ash into his skin – you'll remember how they used to do that in the villages. But I said that nobody was going to put anything on my baby except Vaseline.'

Mma Ramotswe smiled. 'There is nothing better for a baby than to be covered in that jelly,' she said. 'It helps to . . . ' She faltered. She was not sure what purpose was served by polishing babies with petroleum jelly, but there must have been some reason, or it would not have been done. Some people said that it was an old custom and should be given up, but she thought it harmless, even if it was difficult to think of any scientific reason to do it.

'It helps the mother,' said Mma Makutsi. 'If the mother sees that the baby is nice and shiny, then that makes the mother feel better, and if the mother feels better, then she looks after the baby better. There is a lot of evidence for that, I think.'

Mma Ramotswe wondered whether Mma Makutsi was going to disclose that she had learned this information at the Botswana Secretarial College, but she did not. 'I am sure you are right, Mma,' she said.

Mma Makutsi glanced towards the doorway through which Phuti Radiphuti and the aunt had disappeared. Then she looked at Mma Ramotswe.

'Would you like to see him?' she whispered.

Mma Ramotswe suppressed a giggle of glee. 'Yes, I would love to, Mma. She needn't know.'

Quietly, like stealthy conspirators, they crept out of the kitchen and into the small bedroom that was acting as nursery. There was a large green cot in one corner of this room, a changing table and a tall chest full of baby supplies: powder and creams and neat piles of woollen clothing. There was also that wonderful, evocative smell of a small human creature – a smell of softness, a smell of milk, a smell of life just beginning.

'There he is,' said Mma Makutsi. 'See him, Mma Ramotswe? See my baby?'

Mma Ramotswe leaned forward over the little figure in the cot. She reached out and very gently touched one of the tiny hands – carefully, as one might touch a butterfly or a delicate flower. The baby did not stir, not beyond the tiny movements of a sleeping infant – the almost imperceptible rise and fall of the soft blanket under which he slept, and the occasional twitch. She thought: for all he knows, he might still be in the womb, except here, in his new life, there was light and colour and the warm embrace of Africa.

She straightened up and looked at Mma Makutsi, who was still gazing raptly at the minor miracle before them. She noticed that her assistant's large round glasses had misted up. She reached and put an arm about Mma Makutsi's shoulders. It was a long road they had travelled together over the last few years; a long road that led from that very first day when the newly minted secretary had talked herself into the job, with Bobonong behind her but poverty still snapping at her heels. A road that then led to the meeting with Phuti Radiphuti and now to this – to motherhood and all the happiness it brought.

Mma Makutsi took off her glasses and dabbed at the lenses with a handkerchief. 'My heart is full,' she said.

'That is why we are crying,' said Mma Ramotswe.

Mma Makutsi replaced her glasses, but still there were tears in her eyes. 'That is my baby, Mma,' she whispered. 'That is my own baby.'

It is your own baby, thought Mma Ramotswe. It is yours, as these other things you have are yours. And none of this came to you at the start of your life, because then you had nothing, or next to nothing, and you have earned all of it, Mma, every single bit of all this by your hard work and your sacrifice and by being kind to Phuti Radiphuti and loving him for what he is rather than because he has many of the things of this world. This is all yours, Mma Makutsi – your ninety-seven per cent share of everything.

They left the baby, returning to the kitchen where, for a few minutes, they sat together in complete silence, each with the thoughts that such a moment will always bring. There was no need for words, for there are times when words can only hint at what the heart would wish to say.

Chapter Seven

In the Chair of a Very Great Man

It felt very strange to be carrying out an investigation without Mma Makutsi's advice and assistance. Mma Ramotswe had become so accustomed to discussing issues with her assistant that now, on her own, it seemed to her as if a standard office procedure had suddenly changed. With Mma Makutsi at her desk on the other side of the room, she could toss ideas into the air in the certainty that they would be examined, debated and then either confirmed or rejected. Now she had only herself with whom to conduct those meandering dialogues by means of which she was used to sorting out the tangled issues that people brought to the No. 1 Ladies' Detective Agency. And these issues were sometimes hopelessly tangled – and then it was only through some extraordinary serendipitous insight that the situation became clearer. Often that insight was triggered by something that Mma Makutsi said, by some question that she asked. Not now, though, and, rather to her surprise, Mma Ramotswe felt vulnerable as a result. There was Mr J. L. B. Matekoni to run ideas past, but helpful though he was he did not have feminine insight – for which she could hardly blame him. Feminine insight did not always go with mechanical ability – it *could*, of course, especially now that men and women were being encouraged to do the same things, but as a general rule it did not. One had to be realistic about that.

Mma Ramotswe was relieved that Mma Makutsi's absence was not going to be a long one, but she could hardly shelve all cases until such time as her assistant returned. So the day after she had paid that first visit to the Radiphuti house to inspect the new baby, she decided that it was time to tackle the matter that Mma Sheba had recently entrusted to her. She had done nothing so far, and Mma Sheba had said something about phoning up to hear about progress in a week or so. She could not put it off any longer.

Seated at her desk in the office, a cup of freshly brewed red-bush tea within reach, she took a blank piece of paper and wrote a summary of what she knew. It was always useful – and some-times sobering – to write down what you knew. Occasionally the paper remained blank, which was instructive, if somewhat unsettling.

It was not blank that morning. *Rra Edgar*, she wrote. *Had farm. Had brother. Brother went to Swaziland and had son, Liso Molapo. Sister, aunt of boy in Swaziland, stayed in Botswana, on farm. Rra Edgar dies. Farm goes to Liso. Liso comes back and claims legacy. Mma Sheba thinks he is not Liso. His papers say he is. Aunt on farm confirms his identity.*

Those were the facts of the case as she recalled them. But that was only the beginning. Now came the questions.

How do we know that the boy is Liso? Papers: he has a passport that says that he is Liso Molapo. He has a birth certificate that says same. The aunt says that he is Liso Molapo. If he is not, then somebody is lying. The passport? The birth certificate? The aunt?

She put down her pen and looked at what she had written so far. It seemed to her that the important questions had been asked, and now it was simply a matter of finding answers. That, however, was the difficult part; questions were easy enough to pose, but the answers to these questions were not always ready at hand. There was, however, one very obvious answer, and it was the one that she thought she should consider before she looked at any other possibilities. This was that Liso Molapo was indeed Liso Molapo, and that Mma Sheba's doubts were unfounded, and even ill-intentioned. Did Clovis Andersen say something about that? She rose to her feet and took the well-thumbed copy of *The Principles of Private Detection* from the shelf above the filing cabinet.

It did not take her long to find the relevant passage, and she read it out loud just as she would have done had Mma Makutsi been there. *Remember,* wrote Clovis Andersen, *that of all the possibilities you may address, the truth may lie in the simplest explanation. So if you are looking for something that is stolen, always remember that it may not be stolen at all, but mislaid. Similarly, if you are investigating a homicide, it is always possible that the victim died a natural death. Do not exclude this possibility even where the death seems very suspicious. I knew a man who stabbed himself to death. Everybody thought that he had been murdered, and they found plenty of suspects – he was one heck of an unpopular guy – but then they discovered a note in which he said that he was going to do this in order to make things look bad for his principal enemy. He even used his enemy's knife to do it!*

Mma Ramotswe let out a little cry, half of surprise, half of disapproval. She had forgotten about that example but now it came back to her. It must be very unusual to stab oneself; people shot or poisoned themselves, but self-inflicted stabbing was an altogether different matter. She reminded herself that there was nothing like that in this case. Yet Clovis Andersen's words brought home to her that it was entirely possible that Liso Molapo was quite genuine. Indeed, the more she thought about it, the more she felt that this was the likely outcome and that ... She stopped herself. Was it possible that Mma Sheba stood to benefit in some way if the legacy of the farm to the boy were to fail? What if he were really Liso but was shown, falsely perhaps, to be an imposter? Who would get the farm then?

She explored the possibility for a few minutes. She was well disposed towards Mma Sheba because she had been kind to her at the lunch all those years ago. But lawyers could be calculating people and perhaps she should be cautious about accepting her story at face value. Again, Clovis Andersen said something about being politely sceptical and not trusting everything that a person told you, even if you liked the person. Friends can be good liars, he said. Yes, that was true; presumably liars had friends, as everybody had. But did liars lie to their friends, or did they tell them the truth while they went about lying to other people? She stared up at the ceiling but saw no answer there. She would have to think about that again – perhaps when Mma Makutsi returned to work. She could say: 'Mma, I have been thinking about liars and whether they can have true friends.' And Mma Makutsi would say, 'Don't ask a liar that question, Mma,' and they would both burst out laughing, as they often did.

She closed *The Principles of Private Detection* and returned it to the shelf. She had now decided what she needed to do, which was to go to the farm, introduce herself, and form her own assessment of the situation. She had wondered about how she could explain her interest in the matter without revealing her client's suspicions.

This was going to be difficult as she did not like using deception. Of course, she could claim to be lost. Nobody in Botswana would turn away somebody who had lost her way, or they would not do so in the Botswana in which she had been born and brought up; whether that was still the case in the Botswana of today, she was not so sure. But she thought, on balance, that however much things might have changed on the surface, people were still good at heart and had not forgotten everything that the country had tried to teach them. No, people will not turn another away. Not yet at least, not until the old Botswana ways – the code that had been followed by her father, the late Obed Ramotswe, and had served him so well all his life – no longer accounted for anything at all, which was not the case, she felt, thank heavens.

'Don't worry, Daddy,' she said under her breath. 'Botswana has not changed – not in the things that really matter.'

There was silence. She would have loved him to reply. She would have loved to hear his voice again saying, *Precious, my Precious, I know, I know.* And behind that voice she would perhaps hear the lowing of those cattle that he always said lived in heaven and were there to greet us when it was time for us to go. But she heard none of this, and so, with a sigh at the inevitability of duty, she closed the office and set off down the Lobatse Road towards the farm that was the cause of the trouble.

Further reflection on the way led her to rule out any deception. She would not pretend to be lost, but would tell the truth – that she was working for the lawyers and had come to check that everything was in order. That was quite true, even if it was one of those truths that left something unsaid. But you did not have to say everything all the time, especially if you were a detective and you were interested in trapping those who might be less attached to the truth than you were.

*

The Lobatse Road was straight as an arrow here – an undulating strip of black tar that shimmered in the noon heat. Mma Sheba had told her where to turn, and the landmark appeared on cue. Now she was on a rough farm track that meandered off into scrub bush. Behind the level of the trees, squat hills that had seemed blue from a distance now took on the grey-green hue of acacia. The track had been scraped into the red earth carelessly, without regard to the land it crossed, and was interrupted here and there by obstacles it had not bothered to avoid – an outcrop of rock, a cluster of termite mounds, the beginnings of a *donga* – one of those deep eroded ditches that criss-crossed the land. The tiny white van had been through worse, and its suspension was in such a state that little by way of potholes or humps could discourage it further. Even so, Mma Ramotswe drove with caution; a broken axle or a shattered oil sump would no doubt bring renewed suggestions from Mr J. L. B. Matekoni that the time had arrived to get a new van. It would also mean a long walk back to the Lobatse Road in the full heat of day, hard enough for anyone but particularly demanding for those of traditional build.

It took the best part of half an hour to reach the farm gate. Once through this, the track improved somewhat, and showed signs of recent use. She noticed the tyre-tracks in the dusty ground and reflected on how a good Kalahari tracker could have told her precisely when the last vehicle had passed by and whether it had been lightly or heavily laden. For those trackers with the necessary knowledge, an antelope or a truck were much the same, both leaving on the earth information about themselves that could be as clearly read as if it were writing on a page.

A farmhouse came into view – a low-slung building with a red tin roof and a long, shady veranda. Behind the house were several outbuildings, including an open-sided garage and a high water-tank made of corrugated iron. A metal windmill of the sort that was common on farms stood beside the tank, its vane sticking out behind it like a pointing finger, its blades turning slowly. The trees themselves were still, but the windmill, being taller, had picked up an invisible breeze, enabling it to pump water into the tank. She stopped the van and got out to stretch her legs. She had not been to this farm before, but the scene seemed both familiar and peaceful. This, she thought, was how you should live, if you possibly could: with your cattle around you, with the land beneath you, with this air about you.

She sniffed at the air. It was pure and dry, and it carried the scent of cattle and dust, and of acacia too – a smell you could never describe, but you took in nonetheless. She listened. There were cicadas somewhere, that shrill note that seemed to fill the sky, and, barely audible, the familiar clanking of the windmill pump. It was a miracle that there was water in such a place, but it was there, deep below; water that came from a long way away but was cool and fresh and pure.

She got back into the van and completed her journey. As she pulled up in front of the house, a door opened and a woman stepped out on to the veranda to peer at the unexpected visitor. Inside the van, Mma Ramotswe composed herself. She felt as she often did before she started an investigation: there was a familiar fluttering of the heart, a feeling of risk, an awareness that she had to be on the lookout for any information that might be presented to her by the body language of the other. It is the first few minutes of any encounter, said Clovis Andersen, that can be most revealing; it is what people do before they have the chance to work out what they *should* be doing.

The woman came down the couple of steps that led from the veranda. She greeted her visitor courteously, but Mma Ramotswe could sense the curiosity that lay behind the greeting.

'I work for Mma Sheba,' said Mma Ramotswe. 'I have come to see that everything is all right.'

The woman visibly relaxed. 'You are very welcome, Mma. I am Mma Molapo – I am the sister of my brother, who is late.'

Mma Ramotswe lowered her gaze respectfully. 'I am sorry about that, Mma. I am very sorry.'

Mma Molapo accepted the sympathy gracefully. 'It was too early, Mma, but when it is the will of the Lord, then we must accept it.'

'That is true, Mma,' said Mma Ramotswe.

There was a brief pause before Mma Molapo invited her in. 'Would you like some water, Mma?' she asked. 'Or perhaps some tea?'

'If there is tea,' said Mma Ramotswe, 'then I will be very happy.'

'There is tea.'

'Then I am very happy.'

Mma Molapo led her into the house, into a rather dark and empty corridor, and then, from there, into a sitting room. The room was furnished with several green armchairs, angular and box-like in their construction, with wooden facings on the arms that provided a place for chrome ashtrays. The dark green fabric of the chairs had been stained here and there by ancient cups of tea that had toppled and spilled. The shabbiness of the furniture was compounded by the appearance in one or two places of cigarette burns. On the walls, several pictures hung from a picture-rail below the ceiling. There was a picture of a Brahman bull with its great white hump; another picture of a Dakota aircraft on the runway of the old Gaborone airfield; and a framed photograph of Sir Seretse Khama meeting a much younger Prince Charles.

Mma Molapo noticed Mma Ramotswe's interest in the picture of Seretse Khama. 'Do you like that picture, Mma?' she asked.

Mma Ramotswe nodded, and moved closer to examine it.

Mma Molapo, who had been polite but perhaps a bit reserved, became animated. 'If you look at Prince Charles you can see that he knows that this is a great man whose hand he is shaking.'

Mma Ramotswe continued to stare at the picture. She had a plate with a picture of the Queen on it, and a biscuit tin with Prince Charles on the top. 'My father met Seretse,' she said. 'When he came to Mochudi, he met him.'

Mma Molapo absorbed this. 'You know who my father was, Mma?'

'I do, Mma. He was a good friend of Seretse's.'

Mma Molapo smiled. 'I met him too. Many times. He came to this house once and sat in that chair over there, Mma – that very chair.'

Mma Ramotswe looked at the shabby green armchair that suddenly seemed so important.

'Why don't you sit in it, Mma?' said Mma Molapo. 'I'll fetch tea.'

Mma Ramotswe lowered herself into the armchair. It felt much as any other armchair, if perhaps a little bit harder, but she was aware of the historical significance of the moment. She was sitting in an armchair that had once supported the greatest man in Botswana's history, a man who had set an example to all of Africa, and to the world, in much the same way as Mr Mandela had done. And here was she, an ordinary woman from Mochudi, of no particular distinction – at least in her mind, even if she was the first lady private detective in Botswana – seated in the great man's chair.

Mma Molapo returned with two cups of tea. 'Is everything going all right with the execution?' she asked.

Mma Ramotswe was puzzled. 'Execution, Mma? Who is being executed? I do not know of anybody who is going to be executed.'

'The will,' said Mma Molapo. 'Lawyers make a big fuss over the execution of the will.'

Mma Ramotswe laughed. 'That is executry, I think, Mma. They call it executry.'

Mma Molapo waved a hand airily. 'I often get words mixed up. I'm hopeless that way, Mma.'

Mma Ramotswe found herself warming to the other woman. She knew that it was too early to reach any conclusion, but she found it difficult to think of this well-mannered and modest woman being a liar.

'Mma Sheba is taking a long time,' said Mma Molapo as she sipped her tea. 'Are there any difficulties, Mma? Is that why she sent you?'

Mma Ramotswe detected a note of anxiety in Mma Molapo's voice, but thought that anybody would be anxious when discussing the timescale against which lawyers conducted their business. 'I don't think there is any particular problem,' she said. 'These things are slow. They have to check and double-check everything. She sent me to find out that everything was all right at this end.' That, she thought, is true; I have not told any lies.

Mma Molapo sighed. 'I know about lawyers. They are like tortoises. Some people say that they are the tortoise's cousins. And I also know that I shouldn't be impatient; it's just that my nephew would like to get everything sorted out. You know how young men are.'

Mma Ramotswe saw her opportunity. 'Is your nephew here? Could I meet him, do you think?'

'Certainly you can, Mma. He is outside, working in the shed. I shall go and fetch him.'

Mma Molapo left the room and Mma Ramotswe sat in the Seretse Khama armchair, deep in thought. After a minute or two, she got up and crossed the room to the window, and looked out.

Her eye was first caught by the windmill; the breeze had stopped and the blades were still, etched sharply against the blue of the sky. But then she saw, standing in front of the shed, Mma Molapo and a tall young man wearing a bright red T-shirt and one of the narrow-brimmed round hats that were all the fashion with young men. Mma Ramotswe did not like those hats, which she thought made the wearers look like children; but that, she reflected, might be the idea behind them. Some young men did not want to grow up and seemed to cling to the things of boyhood. But then she thought: perhaps they have good reason to do that. Perhaps what they saw in the world of adults was conflict and competition that scared them. And anyway, hats were nothing much – young people had always worn hats that older people considered ridiculous. It had always been so, probably since hats were first invented.

She watched the two figures, making sure that she was standing well enough back from the window so as not to be seen. Mma Molapo appeared to be lecturing her nephew about something. He made a defensive gesture and then nodded his head, as if agreeing to the terms of some bargain. She watched them. Something was happening, but she had no idea what it was.

They began to walk towards the house, and Mma Ramotswe went back to her chair. A few minutes later the door opened and Mma Molapo came into the room, followed by the tall young man. Mma Ramotswe noticed that the red T-shirt had been replaced by a smart white open-necked shirt; of the ridiculous round hat there was nothing to be seen.

Mma Molapo effected the introduction, and Liso stepped forward to offer his hand politely. He spoke in Setswana to begin with before switching to English, and Mma Ramotswe noticed that his Setswana was perfectly enunciated. If he had been brought up in another country, it certainly did not show in his accent.

'So, Liso,' Mma Ramotswe began. 'You are going to be a farmer soon.'

Liso was modest. 'I will have to learn how to do it, Mma.'

'You've never lived on a farm?'

He hesitated, but only slightly. 'I used to come here when my uncle was alive.'

'He stayed with us,' said Mma Molapo. 'Every school holiday, he stayed with us.'

'But back in ... where was it? Swaziland? On that side you stayed ...'

'In a hotel,' supplied Mma Molapo. 'His father, my other brother, who is late too, was the manager of a hotel in the Ezulweni Valley. Do you know Swaziland, Mma?'

Mma Ramotswe shook her head. 'I would like to go some day, but I only really know Botswana, I'm afraid.'

It seemed that Mma Molapo was pleased to hear this answer. 'It is a much smaller country, Mma, and much greener too.'

'I have heard that they have forests,' said Mma Ramotswe. She directed the comment to Liso, but again it was intercepted by Mma Molapo.

'There are many forests,' said Mma Molapo.

'And rivers,' said Mma Ramotswe. She turned to Liso. 'Liso, there are some good rivers in Swaziland, aren't there? Always full of water. Do you like that one, the river that ...'

She was interrupted by Mma Molapo. 'The Umbeluzi,' she said. 'That is the one you like, isn't it, Liso?'

The young man nodded. He had been looking at Mma Molapo, but now he turned to Mma Ramotswe and beamed at her. 'There are crocodiles in the Umbeluzi, Mma. I used to walk beside it when I was a little boy and my father used to say, "You be careful of old croc! Old croc would like you for his dinner!"'

'I do not like crocodiles much,' said Mma Ramotswe.

'Nobody likes crocodiles,' said Mma Molapo.

This brought a chuckle from Mma Ramotswe. 'Except their mothers, perhaps.'

This remark seemed to have a strange effect. Liso looked at Mma Molapo, who pursed her lips together discouragingly. Mma Ramotswe was puzzled. Why, she wondered, should a remark about nobody liking crocodiles produce this reaction?

Mma Molapo changed the subject. 'When Liso is the owner of this farm,' she said, 'he is going to get the fences fixed. I'm afraid that my late brother allowed them to deteriorate and now they are in a very bad state in some places.'

Liso greeted this comment enthusiastically. 'I can do a lot of it myself,' he said. 'I have helped to mend the fences here before.'

Mma Ramotswe was watching him. 'When was that, Liso?' she asked.

He frowned. 'Last time.'

'Last year?'

Mma Molapo looked at her watch. 'My goodness,' she said hurriedly. 'It gets late so quickly.'

Mma Ramotswe decided to ignore the intervention. 'You helped your uncle last year?'

Liso looked away briefly, but then turned to smile at Mma Ramotswe. 'Yes, Mma.'

'But your uncle was very ill then, wasn't he? Was he strong enough to work?'

Mma Molapo rose to her feet. 'My poor brother was ill but he was able to walk until the very last day of his life. Now, Mma Ramotswe, I must go and do some work. You must excuse me.'

Mma Ramotswe replied quickly, 'That is quite all right, Mma. You do your work and Liso can show me the outbuildings. We have to make sure that everything is correct on the inventory, you see. You can do that, can't you, Liso?'

Had Liso not answered, Mma Molapo would probably have vetoed the suggestion. Certainly she began to say something, but the young man had already accepted. 'I can do that, Mma. Yes, I can do that.'

It was clear that Mma Molapo was reluctant to allow the two of them to go outside together, but she had insisted that she had work to do and she could hardly go back on that. 'Very well, Mma,' she said. 'He can show you. But he must not take too long. He has some work to do too, I think.'

Mma Ramotswe rose from the Seretse Khama armchair and started to make her way towards the door, followed by Liso. Once outside, she pointed to one of the sheds and asked the young man what it contained. 'There are some ploughs in there,' he said. 'And there is a tractor. It is quite new, I think. It is a good one.'

They walked across to the shed to inspect the ploughs and the tractor. 'Where were you at school in Swaziland?' asked Mma Ramotswe.

He did not hesitate. 'Manzini. I was at school there, Mma.'

She absorbed the information. She did not know very much about Swaziland, but she knew that the two major towns were Mbabane and Manzini.

'Wouldn't it have been easier to go to Mbabane?' she asked.

He said nothing.

'Don't you think so?' she pressed.

'Why, Mma?'

'Well, it's closer than Manzini. Your father ran a hotel, didn't he? Wasn't that in the Ezulweni Valley?'

'It was,' he said. 'Manzini was further away but it has a very good school. There is one down by the hospital there – you know the place? It was run by the Fathers. They are Catholic. I came top of the class for two years, Mma.'

Of course she did not know the school, but she nodded.

He opened the door of the barn. The air inside was stale and hot, and it smelled of a mixture of spilled oil – a scent she knew very well from Tlokweng Road Speedy Motors – and straw. She saw the straw – bales of it at the back, stacked almost to the ceiling like giant building bricks. She wanted to sneeze.

'That's the tractor,' he said proudly. 'I have started it to make sure that the battery doesn't go flat, but I have not driven it yet. Driving a tractor is different, you know, Mma, from driving a car.'

'You can drive, Liso?'

'Yes, I can drive, Mma. I do not have a car yet, but I can drive.'

'You passed your test in Swaziland?'

He nodded. 'Last year.'

She stored the information away. Mma Sheba had not told her the age of the real Liso. If this Liso, whether or not he was the real one, had passed his test in Swaziland last year, he must be at least eighteen, assuming that the minimum driving age there was the same as it was in Botswana.

They left the barn, and he led her to a shed a short distance away. 'This is where they keep the dip for the cattle, Mma,' he said. 'It has a very strong smell – you will not like it.'

She smiled. 'I know that smell well,' she said. 'I used to count the cattle going through the dip when I was a little girl. It is a bit like tar, but different. I will never forget that smell, Liso.'

He grinned back at her. 'I spilled some on my shirt once when I was helping my uncle. I had to throw the shirt away.'

He spoke so naturally that she knew the story was true. But then one could spill cattle dip on one's shirt in any circumstances, and he might well have a memory of such an incident that had happened elsewhere.

'I can show you the septic tank, if you like,' Liso now offered. 'It is over there, Mma.'

She declined the offer. 'I mustn't hold you up, Liso,' she said. 'I have things to do in Gaborone and your aunt says you have some work to do too. I have seen that everything is in good order. I will tell the lawyers.'

He smiled at her. 'That is kind, Mma. And could you ask them to hurry up? I do not want to waste too much time.'

'I'll do that, Liso. But you have plenty of time, don't you think? You are still seventeen, and that is not old.'

'Eighteen,' he corrected.

'Of course – eighteen. But when you're eighteen you still have most of your life ahead of you. You will be staying on this farm for a long, long time.'

She searched his expression as she pronounced the sentence of years on the farm. She was not sure what sign she was looking for, but it had something to do with an awareness on his part that he knew that he was not going to be there for the rest of his life, a sign that he had other plans. But he showed no emotion, and appeared to accept what she said with equanimity.

As she walked back towards her van, she saw a movement at the window. She was not surprised; Mma Molapo would have been watching them. There was an innocent explanation for that. If you lived out in the bush as they did, and somebody came to see you, you would be watching. There was not much else to do out here, and a stranger was intriguing, whatever her business.

'Thank you for showing me round,' said Mma Ramotswe, offering Liso her hand to shake. He took it, and used the proper formalities, placing his right hand on the forearm of his left: a sign of respect. Top marks again, she thought . . . for what? For acting?

She started the van. The young man was standing there respectfully, waiting for her to leave. She caught his eye, and it seemed to her that there was between them a momentary exchange of fellow feeling. She felt ashamed. You should trust people, she thought, and not seek to trip them up or unmask them. Unless, of course, you were a private detective, and were paid by others to do just that. As she turned the tiny white van down the farm track, she found herself thinking something that had not occurred to her during all the years she had been running the No. 1 Ladies' Detective Agency. And that thought was this: *Should I be doing something else? Should I return to a world where there was no call to be suspicious?* She wondered about that. That was how she wanted the world to be, and that, in a way, was what her work was intended to bring about. She sighed, and decided to focus on something quite different. Fruitcake came to her mind unbidden – a large fruitcake rich in sultanas and candied peel; the sort of cake that would torment and tantalise those on a diet. But Mma Ramotswe was neither dieting nor planning to do so, and she welcomed the vision wholeheartedly. She had not had fruitcake for a long time, and the idea of a generous slice – or possibly even two slices – seemed very attractive. It meant, of course, a slight detour on her journey back. There were two ladies in Botswana who made good fruitcake, and Mma Potokwani was one of them.

Chapter Eight

He Was the Light of Our Lives

There were two places called Mokolodi. There was the small game reserve to the south of Gaborone, barely a mile off the Lobatse Road, and there was the farm with its large stone house, the original Mokolodi, where Mma Ramotswe's friend Gwithie lived. They had all been one large farm in the past, until the land was given to the children of Botswana for a nature reserve. Mma Ramotswe knew the reserve well, and had some years previously helped them with an issue of superstitious staff being frightened by the presence of a ground hornbill. That bird! Now here was Mma Soleti being driven into a state of fear by a single feather. It was ridiculous, completely ridiculous, that otherwise sensible people should believe in things like that. Except that they did. People believed all sorts of things and were not easily persuaded that what they feared was really harmless.

And the things they believed by day were often different from the things they believed at night. The shadows you saw on the ground at midday were just that: shadows caused by some very ordinary object that blocked out the sun. The shadows you saw by night, by contrast, could be the shapes of things with no name: things that moved silently and changed their form; things that could touch the skin with icy coldness; things that could draw the breath out of your body and leave you gasping for air. It was all very well saying that such things did not exist, but to the people who saw them and felt them they were as real as the ground beneath their feet.

The gates of Mokolodi were topped, as it happened, with an ornamental hornbill worked in iron. This was the ordinary hornbill, though – the cousin of the bird that spent much of its time grounded – and it did not have the same power to frighten. Perhaps, she thought, if you wanted gates to do the job of discouraging unwanted visitors, you might put the ground hornbill there.

She passed through the gates and drove up to the main house. Here she parked in the shadow of the house itself – a cool well of shade that would keep the cab of the van from feeling like an inferno when she returned to it. As she got out, her friend appeared from the side of the house, a gardening trowel in one hand and a basket of plant cuttings in another.

Gwithie put down the basket and walked over to the van to welcome Mma Ramotswe.

'Mmapuso,' said Mma Ramotswe as she got out of the car. '*Dumela*, Mmapuso.' She used the name by which the other woman was generally known – Mmapuso, the mother of Puso. She too had a Puso, the same name as one of Mma Ramotswe's foster children. Mmapuso had lost hers some time ago now, but the name remained.

The two old friends embraced and then Mma Ramotswe took Gwithie's hand and pressed it, not once but several times. No words were exchanged, but the gesture of sympathy was understood. They had both lost the one thing in this life that is hardest to lose.

They went into the garden at the side of the house, crossing an expanse of grass that was dominated by a large jacaranda tree whose umbrella branches stretched out to provide an enticing circle of shade. In spite of the late dry season, the beds around the edge of the grass still had colour, surviving on the tiny amounts of water doled out to them by a drip-feed system of irrigation. The husbandry of water was well understood here: the using of every precious drop, the giving of water to those plants that needed it while the waxy desert plants like cacti were left to wait until the rain eventually brought them relief.

They made their way to the shade and sat down on chairs arranged around a low wooden table. On a tray by one of the chairs was a teapot with two cups.

'In case of visitors,' said Gwithie, pointing to the extra cup.

'Very wise,' said Mma Ramotswe. 'Tea and cake is always . . .' She had not intended to mention cake, but somehow it came out and she felt embarrassed.

'Oh,' said Gwithie. 'Cake. Yes, well, I must do some more baking. I had one last week but we had the grandchildren in the house and cake doesn't seem to last very long when children are in the house.'

'Of course.' Mma Ramotswe laughed, but she was disappointed. She could always bake herself a fruitcake – she had copied out Mma Potokwani's recipe by hand into her own recipe book and she made a perfectly good version herself – but somehow the eating of one's own cake was different from the eating of another's.

'Next time you come to see me,' said Gwithie, 'I promise you we shall have cake. Several slices, in fact.'

As her friend poured the tea, Mma Ramotswe looked out over the garden. Beyond the trees at its edge, the ground rose up to make a ridge, and beyond that were the hills looking down over the game reserve. There was no other building in sight. It was a small corner of undisturbed bush – Botswana in its untouched state. This was the land that Obed Ramotswe had known: the grey-green acacia scrub that ran for hundreds of miles along the country's border to the east and, to the west, into the great Kalahari. This was the land over which the great dome of African sky presided; the sky that would, they all hoped, soon fill with towering, rain-filled thunderclouds from somewhere far away – the annual gift of the wetter and more temperate lands beyond their borders.

'Rain,' remarked Mma Ramotswe. She did not need to say anything more.

Gwithie shrugged. 'Next week? I have somebody who helps me in the kitchen who has an uncanny habit of knowing when the rains will start. She's been right year after year. It's extraordinary.'

'And she says next week?'

Gwithie nodded. 'Towards the end of next week, and she says the rains will be good.'

'I am very happy to hear that,' said Mma Ramotswe. 'My own garden is looking very sad now. It is very thirsty. And my husband's vegetables ...' She sighed. Mr J. L. B. Matekoni grew beans, but the plants had shrivelled under the onslaught of the sun and she found it hard to imagine that they would recover once the rains arrived. But plants did survive the harshness of even prolonged drought; they somehow kept themselves alive. The soil could be dry and dusty, parched and apparently lifeless, and yet under it there would be seeds and roots ready to spring into life within hours of the first rainfall.

'Things will grow, in spite of everything.' Gwithie paused. 'Were you on your way somewhere?'

'I was passing by,' said Mma Ramotswe. 'I had to go to the Molapo Farm. You must know the place – it's on the other side of the Lobatse Road, not far really.'

'I know it,' said Gwithie. 'We used to see a bit of Edgar Molapo. We don't know his sister at all well. She keeps to herself, and always has done.'

'I met her for the first time this morning.'

Gwithie was looking at her with interest. 'You were there professionally?'

Mma Ramotswe was careful. Even with friends, she knew the importance of confidentiality. Her clients told her things that she should not reveal and she always observed that trust, difficult though it was at times.

'Nothing serious,' she said non-committally.

Gwithie did not press her. 'They say that the farm is going to Edgar's nephew from Swaziland.'

'So they say,' said Mma Ramotswe. 'Do you know him – the boy?'

Gwithie shook her head. 'He used to come over to Botswana a lot when he was younger. We never saw him then.'

'He speaks very good Setswana,' said Mma Ramotswe. 'He must have spent a lot of time in this country.'

'Yes,' said Gwithie. 'I met him the other day. But we spoke in English.'

Mma Ramotswe was interested. 'He came here? With the aunt?'

'Yes,' said Gwithie. 'They were interested in buying cattle from a man who's been working on one of the buildings here. Some complicated transaction, so Edgar's sister came over to do it. She brought the boy – well, I suppose he's a young man now – with her. He was interested in some fruit trees I've been trying to grow and I showed him. Nice young man.'

'He is,' said Mma Ramotswe. 'He has good manners.'

Gwithie seemed to remember something. 'It was a bit odd, though. He said something that made him very flustered.'

Mma Ramotswe leaned forward. 'Yes?'

'He referred to his aunt as his mother. He said, "I must show this to my mother." I then asked him where his mother was, and he turned round to point at the aunt who was talking to somebody at the other end of the fruit garden. And then he stopped and he seemed dismayed by the slip. He said something like, "I mean my aunt. I mean my aunt." I made nothing of it, but it struck me as odd.'

Mma Ramotswe was silent.

'A slip of the tongue, no doubt,' said Gwithie.

Mma Ramotswe put down her teacup. 'No doubt,' she said, while thinking: Of course, of course. Quite suddenly, seated under the tree with her friend, with the air so still and hot, with a fly buzzing about the lip of the milk jug on the tea-tray, with all Botswana yearning for rain, it became clear to her. It had not occurred to her before because there was no reason for her to suspect that there was any other relationship between Mma Molapo and the young man who claimed to be Liso. She had been acting on the assumption that he was either her nephew or he was not, and the second of these options had not included the possibility that he was even more closely related to her – that he was a son. But now it seemed so obvious. If Mma Molapo had a son, then she would undoubtedly prefer him to succeed rather than her nephew. So if the nephew proved to be hard to locate, or had vanished altogether, then all she would have to do would be to substitute her son. And if he succeeded, then she could stay exactly where she was; whereas a nephew may well have views of his own as to whether his aunt continued to live on the property. The problem, though, would be that it would not work. There must be many people who had seen the boy over the years – neighbours and people who worked on the farm – and they would know if suddenly a different young man came along and claimed to be the person they had seen over the years. So a substitution was impossible, and that meant that Liso could not be Mma Molapo's son.

Gwithie said a few words that Mma Ramotswe, sunk in thought, did not catch. Now she repeated them.

'I'm sorry, Mmapuso,' said Mma Ramotswe. 'I was thinking of . . . something I hadn't been thinking about . . . before, that is.'

'I asked whether you would like to come for a walk with me,' said Gwithie. 'A brief walk.'

Mma Ramotswe knew where they would be going.

'Of course,' she said. 'I would like to go with you, Mma. Of course I would.'

They made their way through thick acacia bush, following a rough twin-tracked road. The earth was red here, and there was little vegetation to hide it, with only the acacia trees providing a note of green. The track curved and then dipped down towards the lake that, though diminished by the dry season, was still home to a small family of hippos and flocks of water birds.

Neither spoke much on this walk, although Gwithie stopped at one point and drew Mma Ramotswe's attention to a plant by the side of the track.

'Look at this,' she said. 'I have a soft spot for this plant. It has quite a few Setswana names but the one I use is *kgaba*. Do you know it?'

Mma Ramotswe tried to remember. Her father had shown her plants when he had walked through the bush with her, and he had taught her the Setswana names, but she had had difficulty in remembering them. The old words, people said, were slipping away, remembered only by a handful of elderly people. The world as described in Setswana was becoming smaller and smaller with each year that passed. Gwithie, she knew, was working on a book of wild flowers and had gone out of her way to learn the old names before they were lost.

She peered at the plant. Like everything else it was struggling, and a thin layer of red dust had coated its leaves. But she thought she knew its blade-shaped leaves, and she nodded.

Gwithie reached down to touch the plant gently, as a doctor might touch a patient. 'People use this for a variety of complaints,' she said. 'Like almost everything in the bush, it has its uses. This is good for arthritis and rheumatism, apparently. And you can also eat it as a sort of spinach.' She straightened up, smiling as she spoke. 'It can also be used to treat children who fail to look after their parents,' she continued. 'And to bind together the members of football teams.'

Mma Ramotswe laughed. 'It must be a very busy plant,' she said.

They continued on their walk. Now the track drew near the edge of the lake and she knew that this was the spot. Mma Ramotswe had been there on that sad day, and she remembered.

They stood before the rock, a natural boulder that had been used by rhinos as a rubbing stone. She saw the smooth parts of the stone where, for generations and for centuries, the animals had rubbed their hide. These were their landmarks, the monuments of animals that had once been plentiful; now, in many places, only the stones remained. As she stood there, she recalled a fragment of a story that her father had told her a long time ago, just a line of it: *Our brothers, the rhinos, who are gone now.*

A small brass plaque with the name *Puso Kirby* was attached towards the base of the rubbing stone. Underneath were the words: *Light of Our Lives.*

Mma Ramotswe took her friend's hand. 'Yes, Mma,' she said. 'This is his place.'

Gwithie was looking out over the waters of the lake. 'You know, Mma,' she said, 'on the day that we lost him we heard a leopard nearby. We very rarely hear those creatures – they are so shy and secretive – but we heard a leopard. There is no mistaking them. And it was here when we buried him.'

Mma Ramotswe said nothing, but she pressed her friend's hand in sympathy.

'And then,' Gwithie continued, 'there was an extraordinary thing. I don't expect people to believe it, but it happened. When the children came, much later, to see their father's grave, as we were walking down here, we saw the leopard. He was following us, but we felt no fear – not for one moment.'

Mma Ramotswe looked at her. 'Do you think it was him? His spirit?'

Gwithie lowered her eyes, and her head moved slightly. Her voice was quiet. 'Why should I not think that?'

'There is no reason why you should not think that,' said Mma Ramotswe. 'It is a lovely thing to believe. He loved wild animals. They were his work, weren't they? He loved the bush. He loved the rocks that leopards love. So that is where your son must be, Mma. He must be. We are always in the place we love, Mma. We never leave it.'

They moved away, with Mma Ramotswe still holding Gwithie's hand until they turned the corner, and the stone, with its heart-felt inscription, was no longer in sight. *The light of our lives.* Yes, thought Mma Ramotswe. That is what we should be to one another: light that shines whatever the darkness of loss. Always.

It did not seem right to return to the Molapo case until much later, when she had left her friend and was travelling back on the final stretch of road towards Gaborone. Then she allowed herself to wonder how she would be able to prove what might be the truth. One slip of the tongue by a young man could hardly be considered evidence sufficient to unmask an imposter. And then a further thought came: what if it were simply a mistake on his part? Liso Molapo – the real Liso Molapo – had not seen his mother for a long time and might easily call his aunt by that name because he viewed her as a substitute for the mother he no longer had. That was entirely plausible and, if true, it meant that she was no further along the road to sorting out this affair.

By the time she reached Zebra Drive it was four o'clock, and doubt had replaced the certainty of earlier. An hour later, she no longer knew what to think. She took a pumpkin out of the store cupboard and began to prepare it by splitting it with the heaviest of her kitchen knives. Pumpkin was something uncomplicated, something completely certain, and cooking a pumpkin, she felt, was a good thing to do when you did not know quite where you were.

Chapter Nine

All Men Can Benefit

There had been periods – sometimes rather long ones – in Mma Ramotswe's life, as in the lives of most of us, when nothing very much had happened. There had, for instance, been the period shortly after the foundation of the No. 1 Ladies' Detective Agency when there had been a marked paucity of clients – there had been none, in fact – and she and Mma Makutsi had spent long days trying to find tasks to do without giving the appearance of having no real work. It had been easier, perhaps, for Mma Makutsi, as she had been able first to invent and then to refine an elaborate filing system that, she claimed, catered for all possible eventualities. Thus there was an entry in this system entitled *MEN*, which at one level below was subdivided into *FAITHFUL MEN* and *UNFAITHFUL MEN*. Matters relating to men could also be filed under such disparate headings as: *DISHONEST MEN*, *GENERAL MEN* and *UNKNOWN MEN*. Then there were files for *CLIENTS WHO HAVE NOT PAID THEIR BILL* – rather a larger file than Mma Ramotswe would have liked – and for *CLIENTS WHO MIGHT NOT PAY THEIR BILL*. The judgement on whether or not a client was likely to pay the bill was one made entirely by Mma Makutsi – on criteria that Mma Ramotswe had tried unsuccessfully to get her to clarify.

'It is not only done on the way they look,' said Mma Makutsi, in answer to Mma Ramotswe's enquiry.

'I'm glad to hear that, Mma,' Mma Ramotswe said.

But then Mma Makutsi went on firmly, 'Although that is a very important factor. You see, dishonest people look dishonest, Mma. There is never any question about that.'

'Well,' said Mma Ramotswe, 'I'm not at all—'

'I never have any difficulty,' Mma Makutsi cut in. 'There are many ways of telling, Mma. There is the way their eyes look, for instance – if they are too close together.'

Mma Ramotswe frowned. 'I don't think so, Mma. There are many—' She was not allowed to finish.

'Oh, make no mistake about it, Mma. If the eyes are close together, that person is going to be trouble. I've always said that, Mma. And the same goes for those whose eyes are too far apart – the same thing there. They will be up to no good.'

Mma Makutsi stared intently at Mma Ramotswe, the light flashing off her large round spectacles. It was as if she were challenging her employer to contradict a fundamental scientific truth. Mma Ramotswe said nothing at first; she was at this time discovering that Mma Makutsi in full flight was not to be interrupted lightly. But when no further assertions came, she very gently ventured a question as to where Mma Makutsi had learned to discern character in this way.

'Life experience,' said Mma Makutsi. 'There are some things you cannot learn from books. You cannot be taught instinct.'

Mma Ramotswe absorbed this. 'But surely you must be careful, Mma. People cannot help the way they look. A person who is good inside may look bad outside. I am sure there are many cases of that.'

Mma Makutsi's glasses flashed a danger signal. 'Really, Mma? Name one, please. Name one person who looks bad outside but who is good inside.' She paused, before adding, 'I am waiting.'

Mma Ramotswe looked up at the ceiling. She was sure that there were such people, but she found it difficult to bring anybody to mind. 'Violet Sephotho?' she suggested. 'What about her? She looks all right on the outside but is definitely bad on the inside.'

Mma Makutsi let out a hoot of laughter. 'Violet Sephotho, Mma? You say that she looks good on the outside? She does not, Mma! She does not! That woman looks on the outside exactly as she is on the inside. And that, I must say, is bad, very bad.'

Mma Ramotswe was kind. Surely even Violet Sephotho, for all her manifest faults, had her better moments. 'I'm not sure that she looks bad absolutely one hundred per cent of the time, Mma,' she said. She had almost said ninety-seven per cent of the time, but managed to stop herself. 'I have seen her smiling sometimes.'

This was as a red rag to Mma Makutsi. 'Smiling, Mma? A smile is the most dangerous disguise of all. Many people smile to disguise what they are thinking inside.'

There had been no further debate on the issue, and Mma Ramotswe had learned to steer clear of certain topics – such as that one – that could be guaranteed to elicit an extreme response from her somewhat prickly assistant. Mma Makutsi had many merits, she came to realise, and these easily outweighed her occasional faults. And now, with Mma Makutsi on maternity leave and the office seeming strangely quiet as a result, there was something else that she came to realise: she missed her assistant in a way and to a degree that she had never anticipated. She missed her occasional outbursts; she missed her comments on what was in the newspapers; she even missed the way in which she would intervene in the conversation Mma Ramotswe was having with clients, dropping in observations from her position to the rear and making them stop and turn their heads to reply to somebody over their shoulder – not an easy thing to do. All of that she missed, just as she missed Mma Makutsi's knack of putting her teacup down on the desk in a manner that so completely revealed her thinking on the subject under discussion. There was nobody else she knew who could put a cup down on a desk to quite the same effect. It was, she decided, one of the many respects in which Mma Makutsi was – and here she could think of only one word to express it – *irreplaceable*. There simply could never be another Mma Makutsi. There could never be another woman from Bobonong, of all places, with flashing round glasses and ninety-seven per cent in the final examinations of the Botswana Secretarial College. There could never be another person who was even remotely capable of standing up to somebody like Mma Potokwani, or putting Charlie in his place when, with all the confidence and ignorance of the young male, he made some outrageous comment. If Mma Makutsi decided not to return from maternity leave then Mma Ramotswe thought that the No. 1 Ladies' Detective Agency would never be the same again, and might not be worth continuing with.

She looked about her. She had worked as a detective for some years now, and in that time she had done her best for her clients. She liked to think that she had made a difference to the lives of at least some people and helped them to deal with problems that had become too burdensome for them to handle on their own. Now, however, surveying the shabby little office, she wondered whether she really had achieved very much. It was a rare moment of gloom, and it was at this point that she realised she was doing something that she very seldom did. She supported many people in their tears – for tears could so easily come to those who were recounting their troubles – but there were few occasions on which she herself cried. If you are there to staunch the tears of the world, then it does not cross your mind that you yourself may weep. But now she did, not copiously but discreetly and inconsequentially, and barely noticeably – except to Mr J. L. B. Matekoni, who chose that moment to come into the room, wiping the grease off his hands, ready with a remark about what he had just discovered under the latest unfortunate car.

For a moment he stood quite still. Then, letting the lint fall from his hands, he swiftly crossed the room and put his arm about his wife's shoulder, lowering his head so that they were cheek to cheek and she could feel the stubble on his chin and the warmth of his breath.

'My Precious, my Precious.'

She reached up and took his hand. There was still a smear on it – some vital fluid of the injured car to which he had been attending – but she paid no attention to that.

'I'm sorry,' she said. 'There is really no reason for me to cry. I am being silly.'

'You are not silly, Mma. You are never silly. What is it?'

With her free hand she took the handkerchief from where it was tucked into the front of her dress. She blew her nose, and with some determination too. After all, the blowing of a nose can be the punctuation that brings such moments to an end.

'I am much better now,' she said. 'I have been sitting and thinking when I should be working. And without Mma Makutsi to talk to, well, you know how hard it can be to sit with the problems of other people.'

He knew, or thought he knew. Yes, he knew how she felt. 'Just like cars,' he said. 'You sit and look at a car and you think of all its problems, and it can get you down.'

'Yes, I'm sure it can.' She smiled at him. 'I'll be all right, Mr J. L. B. Matekoni. Mma Makutsi will come back and everything will be the same again.'

He removed his hand from her shoulder and stood up. 'I will make you tea,' he said.

She looked at him with fondness. For some reason, Mr J. L. B. Matekoni did not make very good tea. It was something to do with the quantities of tea he put in the pot, or with not allowing the water to boil properly, or with the way he poured it. For whatever reason, his tea was never quite of the standard achieved by her or by Mma Makutsi. So she thanked him and said that it would be good for her to do something instead of sitting at her desk and moping, and then she made the tea for herself and for her husband, and for Charlie and Fanwell too, and Mr J. L. B. Matekoni took his cup back into the garage where he sipped at it thoughtfully while he decided what to do.

Later that afternoon, on the pretext of taking a recently repaired car for a test drive, Mr J. L. B. Matekoni went out along the Tlokweng Road in the direction of the orphan farm. There was a good reason for taking that particular car on that particular road – he had fitted new shock absorbers and he wanted to check that they were properly bedded in – but his real motive was to see Mma Potokwani. Mr J. L. B. Matekoni held the matron in high regard, in spite of her habit of finding something for him to fix whenever she saw him, and he wanted to talk to her about what had happened earlier that day.

She was in her office when he arrived and happened to be looking out of the window.

'So, Mr J. L. B. Matekoni,' she called out to him as he got out of the car. 'So you're coming to see me.'

He waved to her and made his way into the small building from which Mma Potokwani, as matron and general manager, ran the lives of the children under her care. She welcomed him warmly and enquired after the health of Mma Ramotswe and Mma Makutsi.

'Mma Makutsi is doing fine,' he said. 'She has a baby now.'

'So I've heard,' said Mma Potokwani. 'That is very good for her and for Mr Radiphuti. They will be very happy.'

'They are, although Mma Ramotswe tells me that Phuti's aunt has moved in. I think that is difficult for her.'

Mma Potokwani made a face. 'That is a very sour woman, that aunt. I think she eats too many lemons.' She paused. 'And Mma Ramotswe, Rra? What about her?'

He suspected that she had sensed that something was wrong.

His reply was hesitant. 'I think that in general she is all right, but . . . '

She waited for him to go on. He looked down at his hands. It was sometimes difficult for him, as a mechanic, to find the words that seemed to come easily to women.

'Something is wrong, Rra,' she prompted.

He drew in his breath. 'Mma Potokwani, may I talk to you in private?'

She looked surprised. 'Of course, Rra. There's nobody else here. And remember I am a matron, and a matron hears all sorts of secrets. I could tell you, Rra! Only this morning there was . . . ' She stopped herself in time. 'So you can talk, Rra.'

He looked awkward, and she made a further suggestion. 'Why don't we go for a walk, Mr J. L. B. Matekoni?' she said. 'It is easy to talk when you are walking.'

She did not wait for an answer, but rose and guided him out of her office. It was warm outside, but the afternoon sun was less oppressive than it had been earlier in the day and they were not uncomfortable. Mma Potokwani suggested that they follow a path that skirted round the edge of the grounds. This would enable them to see the children playing on the small sports field – now not much more than a square of parched and frazzled grass – and also to inspect the new vegetable patch that had been planted near the borehole.

Mma Potokwani did not walk fast. This was not because of any physical impediment, but because of her tendency to stop and examine what she came across; the ancient habit, he thought, of a matron who was used to inspecting and prodding things – and people – for whom she was responsible. So they stopped and looked at a gate that might need rehanging – if anybody could find the time to do it. And as she said this, she looked meaningfully at Mr J. L. B. Matekoni, who nodded meekly and made the offer she was expecting.

'I should be able to do that some time,' he said. 'I can bring Charlie or Fanwell and they will give me a hand.'

'That is very kind,' said Mma Potokwani. 'I was not going to ask you, Rra, of course.'

'Of course.'

'But since you offer, what about next week some time?'

He nodded.

'But tell me, Rra,' Mma Potokwani said. 'What is the trouble? It is not a marriage thing, is it?'

He shook his head vigorously. 'No, never that.'

'I didn't think it would be. I know that you and Mma Ramotswe are very happy.'

'We are,' he said. 'But she is happy and unhappy, if you see what I mean.'

Mma Potokwani frowned. 'I'm not sure that I do, Rra.'

'I found her crying.'

She appeared to absorb this for a few moments. Then she asked why this was.

'I don't know,' he said. 'She said it was to do with sitting there and thinking about problems. She said that was why she was crying. But she normally never cries – not even when she has a whole lot of problems to think about.'

Mma Potokwani's pace became even slower. 'Do you remember what happened to you, Rra?' she asked. Normally Mma Potokwani spoke in stentorian tones – the result of having to make herself heard over the voices of hordes of children; now her voice was softer, gentler.

Mr J. L. B. Matekoni was not sure what she was referring to. 'Many things have happened to me,' he said. 'In fact, Mma, things happen to me every day.'

'No, no, Mr J. L. B. Matekoni. I am not thinking of ordinary things. I am thinking of when you were ill. Some years ago – remember?'

He stopped in his tracks. 'Oh . . . '

Mma Potokwani was looking at him intently. 'People get depressed, Rra – it is very common. One of the housemothers here had that happen to her just a few months ago. She sat and sat and thought about problems. One of the children came to me and said that the mother cried too much and sometimes could not manage to heat up their dinner. I knew what the trouble was.'

'And this lady – how is she now?'

'Good as new,' said Mma Potokwani. 'I took her to the doctor and they knew what was wrong. It was the same thing that happened to you.'

'That was thanks to Dr Moffat,' said Mr J. L. B. Matekoni.

'Yes,' said Mma Potokwani. 'He is very kind.'

'But I do not think she's depressed,' said Mr J. L. B. Matekoni. 'She is eating as much as ever. She is keeping the house very well. She has no trouble with her sleeping. Dr Moffat told me that if you're depressed you usually do none of those things.'

'Are you sure?' asked Mma Potokwani.

'I am very sure, Mma. She is still laughing. When I was depressed I did not do any laughing.'

They resumed their walk. They were now near the patch of grass and dust where a group of children were playing football. They were all wearing the khaki shorts and shirts of the classroom, but were barefoot. Two teams of six, running and wriggling with all the energy that young boys can muster, battled over a somewhat deflated old leather ball, urging each other on exuberantly and raising a cloud of dust that darted about the pitch like a tiny, localised tornado.

Mr J. L. B. Matekoni called out encouragement, and Mma Potokwani gave a good-natured wave of her hand.

'Boys,' said Mr J. L. B. Matekoni. 'Their batteries never seem to run down, do they, Mma?'

'No,' said the matron. 'They're on the go all day. Non-stop. I think that ...' She broke off and turned to look at Mr J. L. B. Matekoni. 'Batteries, Rra.'

He made a gesture towards the boys. 'Yes, look at them ...'

'No,' she said, shaking her head. 'Not the boys'. Mma Ramotswe's batteries.'

He took a little while to reply. Then he said, 'Her batteries are run down? Is that what you're saying, Mma?'

'You see, Rra, women have to do so much. They have to run a house. They have to look after children. They have outside jobs to go to as well. Nearly every woman has three or four jobs altogether if you add everything up.'

He understood that. 'We men often just have one.'

'That is so, Rra. You men work hard, but it is often only at one job.' She paused. 'Not that I'm criticising men, you understand, Rra. It's just that sometimes it all gets too much for women and it would help a great deal if their husbands could be a little bit more modern.'

'More modern, Mma?'

She tried to explain. 'Modern husbands support their wives more. They help around the house. They pay more attention to their wives. They try to look a bit smarter for their wives, too. That helps, you know. If men go around looking very run-down and scruffy, then that is not nice for their wives. A modern husband takes that into account.'

'Oh.'

'And there's another thing,' said Mma Potokwani, warming to her theme. 'A modern husband is more sensitive. He knows how his wife is feeling.'

'I see.'

'Not that I am looking at you when I say any of this, Rra.'

'No. That is good.'

'Except it might be an idea – just an idea, Rra – if you were to think about these things and see how you might become a bit more modern.'

He looked down at the ground. He would not claim to be modern and had never considered whether he might be at fault in that regard. But he had come for Mma Potokwani's advice, and he knew from his own experience of advising people about their cars that advice, once sought, should be followed if at all possible.

'I have been reading in the newspaper about a course,' said Mma Potokwani. 'It might help if you could go on that.'

'I have heard of that course,' he said, guardedly. Mma Ramotswe had told him about it after the woman in the baby supplies shop had mentioned it to her.

'Do you think you might try it?' asked Mma Potokwani. 'If you took that, it could help Mma Ramotswe a lot. She would be very much cheered up by having a modern husband.'

He made up his mind. 'You're right, Mma Potokwani. I shall find out about this modern husbands course and go on it. It will make a big difference, I think.'

Mma Potokwani was pleased. 'If you were able to take my husband too,' she said with a sigh, 'that would be very good. But I'm afraid there are some men who are too old-fashioned to benefit from courses like that.'

Mr J. L. B. Matekoni thought this was true. He enquired where the course was held, and Mma Potokwani explained that she believed it was held in the evening in one of the buildings at the university. 'I'm sure they will find you a place, Rra,' she said. 'I have heard that they turn nobody away, not even the most unpromising men. All men can benefit, Rra.'

He went over those words in his mind. *All men can benefit.* It would make a wonderful slogan for anything – even for a beer advertisement. But he stopped this train of thought, as he suspected that modern husbands did not allow themselves to think such things, at least not in public.

Chapter Ten

Not a Lady With Many Enemies

If Mma Ramotswe had felt at all defeated – and she had, after all, found herself in tears at her desk – then that feeling was a temporary one. It was not in her nature to be morose or to engage in self-pity; she saw these things in others and was always sympathetic to those who felt that the world was in some respect too much for them, but was herself rarely in anything but an equable state of mind. So while the sight of her in a momentary low state was enough to trigger alarm in Mr J. L. B. Matekoni, Mma Ramotswe was, within a matter of minutes, back to normal. Yes, she was missing Mma Makutsi, and yes, it was not easy to run a detective agency by yourself and with nobody to bounce ideas off, but these setbacks were minor irritations compared with the lot of so many other people; and anyway, they were not destined to last. Mma Makutsi had said that she did not intend to take a long maternity leave, and even in the time that she was away Mma Ramotswe could still consult her on any matter on which she needed advice. And she would do that, she decided, over the next day or so: she would visit Mma Makutsi and see what she made of the troublesome case of the young man who claimed to be Liso Molapo and who might or might not be lying.

That thought gave her pause. The young man might be lying – that was certainly possible – but there was another aspect of the situation that had not occurred to her. If Liso was telling the truth, then did that necessarily mean that he was the real Liso Molapo? Or could it be that he was not lying, but still was not the person he said he was? That could be the case if he *believed* himself to be Liso Molapo, having been told that this was who he was, but all the while he was actually somebody else altogether? The possibility was enough to make her head ache, but now it had come to her, she had to think it through.

This, she told herself, was how it might work: eighteen years ago, Edgar Molapo's brother – the one who lived in Swaziland – has a son, and he and his wife call this boy Liso. Then, in a terrible accident of the sort that is always happening on those mountainous Swazi roads, Liso loses his life. The father, in his misery, takes under his wing the child of one of the women working in his hotel. This woman has more children than she can manage – four or five, perhaps – and the grieving parents informally adopt one of these children and call him by the name they had given to their own son. Liso is replaced by a new Liso, who at the same time is Liso but is not Liso. Edgar, of course, thinks that the child is his nephew, and treats him accordingly. But he is not ... or is he? If Edgar thought of him as Liso Molapo, his nephew, then when he made provision for him in his will, he was thinking of that actual child. And if that were so, then why should the young man who was treated as Liso Molapo not benefit from something that was meant for him – as a person, rather than as a name?

It was a possibility, she felt, but only a remote one, and it did not really bring her any closer to a solution. The problem with being a private detective was that people expected you to provide them with a clear-cut answer to their query. Sometimes that could be done, and Mma Ramotswe was able to provide a full account of exactly what happened, but there were many occasions on which that simply was not possible and a more tentative answer was all that could be given – or no answer at all. Some matters remained obstinately unresolved because that was what life was like. Not all the uncertainties we faced were capable of being resolved – there were many strings left untied; there were many events that happened and could not be explained; there were many injustices that remained injustices because we could not find out who had perpetrated them, or who could rectify them. As a child she had believed that wrongs would always be righted, that somehow the world would not let the innocent suffer, but now she realised that this was not true. Old oppressors were replaced by new ones, from another distant place or from right next door. Old lies were replaced by new ones, backed up by old threats. There had been so much suffering in Africa, and nobody had done a great deal to stop it. In some places the suffering continued: through wars fought by child soldiers, crying behind their guns; through famine and disease, quick to take root in the shanty towns that perched on the edge of plenty. People waited for intervention, for rescue, but it never came – or only rarely, and then too late. Contemplating this vast human suffering, you might be tempted to shrug your shoulders, but you could not. You had to try, thought Mma Ramotswe – you had to try to sort things out for others and point them in the direction of the truth that they were so anxious to find.

Now that she had resolved to talk to Mma Makutsi about the Molapos, the decision seemed to relieve her of the anxiety that had been building up around the case. And there were other everyday things to occupy her time and her mind, including the shopping. Men might believe that food appeared miraculously in the kitchen, but women, Mma Ramotswe included, knew better than that. They could hardly forget that there was a lot of trudging around shops to be done, and the choosing of this item rather than that one, which sometimes involved squeezing things to determine ripeness, or sniffing them to gauge freshness. This, she had noticed, was not something that men tended to do; they did not squeeze things in shops.

She decided that she would do some shopping and at the same time collect the mail, a task usually performed by Mma Makutsi. Letters were placed by the post office in serried banks of private boxes, each opened by the owners with small keys entrusted to them by the postal authorities. She could check her box, and the box rented by Tlokweng Road Speedy Motors, before going on to the nearby shops. Then, if she felt in the mood – and that morning she thought she did – she could have a cup of coffee at the Equatorial and watch what was happening around the market stalls – which was always something interesting if one enjoyed people-watching, which she did.

Her walk from the post boxes to the supermarket took her directly past the premises of the Minor Adjustment Beauty Salon. As she approached, she saw that Mma Soleti was standing in the doorway, looking out at the concourse. Mma Ramotswe hesitated. She had not come up with any further advice for Mma Soleti and she felt vaguely guilty that she had not been able to offer her more comfort when she had received her threat. But what could she do? It probably really was best to ignore things like that, as the issuer of such a threat wanted a reaction and might lose interest if the victim did nothing. Yet if you were on the receiving end of hatred, inaction might seem a rather weak response. People wanted others to do something; to express their outrage, and not merely to say, as Mma Ramotswe had said, that they should let it be.

She took a deep breath and steeled herself. It would be easy to stick to the other side of the concourse and thus avoid Mma Soleti, but she could not do that. She would do her duty, which was to speak to her and find out whether anything else had happened. If another threat had been sent, then it might provide some clue as to the motives of the sender; or, of course, it might not, and in that case her advice would have to be the same.

The beautician had seen her and beckoned to her from her doorway. Mma Ramotswe waved back and began to make her way over towards the salon. Greetings were exchanged before Mma Soleti said, 'You should come inside, Mma – it is too hot to stand outside.'

Mma Ramotswe looked up at the sky. 'The rains will be here any day, Mma. We shall not have to wait long now.'

'It is still too hot,' said Mma Soleti. 'And besides, there is something I need to talk to you about, Mma.'

Mma Ramotswe followed her into the salon. All the devices of Mma Soleti's trade – the creams and oils, the astringents and the unguents – were laid out neatly on trays, and at the foot of the treatment couch a pristine white towel had been folded and placed ready for use. But there was no sign of any customers.

Mma Ramotswe knew, from experience, how tact was required when one commented on the slow pace of another's business. And so she chose her words carefully. 'It's good to have time to get everything ready, isn't it, Mma?' she said. And then added, 'I'm sure you'll be busy later on.'

Mma Soleti gestured for her guest to sit down. 'There have been no clients for three days, Mma. Three days! I have been here every morning at eight to open up. I have stayed until one minute past five each day, and there have been no clients – not one, Mma.'

Mma Ramotswe made a sympathetic clicking sound. She remembered such days in the first months of the No. 1 Ladies' Detective Agency's existence. She remembered the leaping of the heart when it looked as if somebody might enter the door, a potential client, and then the awful sense of let-down when the passer-by proved to be just that – a passer-by.

'And it's not because they don't need beauty treatments,' continued Mma Soleti, before adding, with some solemnity, 'I believe that the need has never been greater.'

Mma Ramotswe puzzled as to the meaning of this last remark. Were people looking worse than before? Had there been some sudden and terrible deterioration in the general standard of looks – a widespread communal sagging of chins and stomachs? Was it something to do with the temperatures being endured in this late part of the hot season – an endemic drying out of skin and a melting of muscle into pools of flab?

Mma Soleti made a frustrated gesture towards her stacks of supplies. 'What's the use of all this expensive stuff, Mma, if there is nobody to apply it to?'

'That is a great pity, Mma,' said Mma Ramotswe. 'This beautiful salon and no clients ... It is a great shame.' She paused. 'Do you think people are holding on to their money? Is it to do with that?'

Mma Soleti was shaking her head vigorously. 'No, it has nothing to do with money. It is because of the rumours that are being spread.'

'Rumours about your salon, Mma?'

'Yes. People are saying some very wicked things about my salon. Would you go to a beauty salon that everybody said bad things about?'

Mma Ramotswe said that no business could survive a whispering campaign. At the back of her mind was a precise example, but what was it? It took a moment or two, but then she remembered. 'That restaurant,' she said. 'The one that everybody used to say was so good. The one that had that very traditionally built chef.'

Mma Soleti looked confused. 'What has this got to do with restaurants, Mma?'

'I was thinking of another business that had this problem, Mma. It was a restaurant out on the road to Molepolole. Somebody said that they were serving dogs as beef. They said they were going out at night and catching people's dogs. The next day the dogs would be on the menu, but not as dogs, of course. Now they were cattle.'

Mma Soleti's eyes widened. 'That is a very wicked thing to do,' she said. 'I'm glad that I never went to that place.'

Mma Ramotswe found it hard not to laugh. 'Hold on, Mma,' she said. 'You've fallen into the same trap as everybody else. You believed a rumour.'

'But you said—'

'No, Mma, I said that those poor people whose business collapsed were the victims of a made-up story.'

Mma Soleti wrinkled her nose. 'I would not like to eat dog,' she said.

'Some people like it,' observed Mma Ramotswe. 'I would not like to eat dog either, but then you know, some people do.'

'I'm sorry to hear that,' said Mma Soleti. 'Dogs are meant to be our friends, and you shouldn't eat your friends.'

'As a general rule, you should not,' said Mma Ramotswe. She sensed that the conversation was drifting – just as it sometimes

144

did when she was in discussion with Mma Makutsi, who might suddenly start talking about what happened in Bobonong or at the Botswana Secretarial College, or something of that sort, while all the time you were hoping to talk about the matter in hand.

'What have they been saying about your salon, Mma?'

The question brought pain. 'It is very unkind,' said Mma Soleti. 'And it's untrue too. They say that I put the wrong cream on somebody and her face came off – actually peeled right off. That is what they have all been saying.' She waited for the enormity of the defamation to sink in before she continued. 'Your face can't peel off, Mma. It isn't possible. People who know about faces will know that.'

Instinctively, Mma Ramotswe raised a hand to her cheek as if to reassure herself that it was still there. There would be a lot to peel off in her case, not that there was any danger of that ever happening – if Mma Soleti were to be believed.

'I heard the story from the woman who sells vegetables over on the other side of the road,' Mma Soleti went on to explain. 'She said that she heard it from two different people. They both said, "Don't ever go to that place – there is a woman now who has no face left because of her." That is what she said, Mma. She said that she was only telling me about it because she thought I should know what people were saying.'

Mma Ramotswe shook her head in disbelief. 'People can be very foolish,' she said. 'They believe everything they hear; they don't ask themselves whether it can be true.'

'And then I have a daughter, Mma, as you might know,' continued Mma Soleti. 'She came home from school crying. She said that there were girls whispering the same story to each other, looking at her and sniggering. The children said that somebody had found this woman's face in a bucket. She was very upset.'

'This is very bad, Mma,' said Mma Ramotswe. 'But I don't think you should leap to any conclusions.'

'I have not leapt to any conclusions,' retorted Mma Soleti. 'All that I am saying is that it is the same person – it is the same person who sent me the feather. That is the person who has started this wicked rumour about my salon.' She looked at Mma Ramotswe defiantly. 'There can be no doubt about that, Mma.'

'That is a conclusion, Mma,' ventured Mma Ramotswe, thinking of what Clovis Andersen said in the very first chapter of *The Principles of Private Detection*. He wrote: *You wouldn't leap on to the first bus or train that came along without knowing its destination, would you? Find out the evidence first, examine the possibilities, and then see if you have grounds to draw a conclusion.* It was sound advice – like all the advice that Clovis Andersen offered in his book. What a nice man he was, too, thought Mma Ramotswe nostalgically. And to think that she and Mma Makutsi had actually *met* him, had sat with him drinking tea – a man who had written a *book* had sat talking to them and had been so courteous in his manner. That was what Americans were really like, she reflected. Not some of the Americans you saw on the cinema screens who were always shouting at people and chasing one another in cars – not those Americans, but the Americans like Clovis Andersen who listened politely and spoke without shouting.

Sensing that her version of events was doubted, Mma Soleti issued a challenge. 'Well, who else could it be, Mma?'

Mma Ramotswe suggested that the rumour might not have been started deliberately. 'These stories can start in all sorts of ways,' she said. 'Somebody may think they've heard something, or may hear half a story and then decide it ends in such and such a way. They may not know that they're spreading a rumour; they may think it is true, Mma.'

Mma Soleti gave a snort. It was only too clear to her. 'It is the same person, Mma. It is that person who sent me the feather. I am very sure of it.'

Mma Ramotswe had to admit that it was a possibility, but when pressed to come up with a suggestion as to how to identify the author of Mma Soleti's misfortunes, she could only think of a list of enemies. It was not a very novel idea, she had to admit, but it could throw up something useful.

Mma Soleti received the suggestion thoughtfully. 'I am not a lady with many enemies, Mma,' she said. 'But I shall try to think.'

'It is not always easy to know our enemies,' said Mma Ramotswe. 'I think that is because enemies are often enemies for no real reason, and so we do not think they exist.'

'But all the time they are there?'

'Perhaps,' said Mma Ramotswe.

Mma Soleti had already reached for a pad of paper. 'I had an enemy at school,' she said. 'It was when we were very young – maybe seven or eight. There was a girl who hated me for some reason. She used to creep up behind me and pinch me. I was very upset by it.'

'That is quite understandable,' said Mma Ramotswe. 'Has she continued to be your enemy?'

Mma Soleti shook her head. 'I haven't seen her for many years. But she might still be—'

Mma Ramotswe cut her short. 'No, Mma. We are not looking for an enemy from back then. Usually people forget the enemies they had as children. Sometimes they become good friends.'

Mma Soleti had thought of somebody. 'There is a neighbour,' she said. 'She says that my children stole her paw-paws. That is not true, but I can see that she still thinks it.'

Mma Ramotswe was doubtful. 'Those little arguments between neighbours are usually not enough to make somebody do

147

something like this. Can you not think of somebody who has a really good reason to dislike you enough to want to harm you?'

Mma Soleti looked up at the ceiling. 'Maybe,' she said, rather distantly.

Mma Ramotswe waited.

'There is that woman,' she said eventually.

'Which woman?' asked Mma Ramotswe.

Mma Soleti assumed an expression of disgust. 'The one who says that I stole her husband.'

'Ah,' said Mma Ramotswe. 'And where did she get that idea from, Mma?'

'It was what happened,' said Mma Soleti. 'But he was ready to be stolen, Mma.'

Chapter Eleven

The Nothing Vacuum Cleaner

That evening Mr J. L. B. Matekoni, *garagiste* saviour of countless marginal vehicles, husband, foster father and citizen of Botswana, enrolled at a community improvement course hosted by the University of Botswana. The course was not at the forefront of the university's offerings to the people of Gaborone; more prominent on that list were popular courses in the History of Post-Independence Botswana, in the Flora and Fauna of the Kalahari, and in the Management of the Domestic Budget. Those were in the top rank in terms of popularity and acclaim; below that were second-ranking courses in Personal Self-Presentation, Managing the Small Business, and First Aid. Finally came the course on which Mr J. L. B. Matekoni had embarked: How to Be a Modern Husband (Level 1). There was no Level 2 of that course, although it had been talked about and the organisers had promised that it would be offered if demand was there.

The Modern Husband course was held in one of the old classrooms, away from the large buildings that had sprung up in the later phases of the university's development. The old buildings were redolent of the city in its more comfortable days, when structures tended to grow outwards rather than upwards. Low squat buildings, painted uniformly white and shaded by wide eaves, were linked to one another by walkways shielded from the sun and, more rarely, from downpours of rain by arched tin roofs. Now the students sat through their lectures in the greater comfort of new lecture theatres, leaving the old classrooms for the occasional use of less popular subjects and, as in this case, outside courses.

Mr J. L. B. Matekoni felt slightly awkward as he parked his aged green truck in the parking lot outside the classrooms. He had every right to be there – as a taxpayer, and a scrupulously conscientious one at that, he paid for at least some of all this, and as a prospective member of a university-hosted evening class he was, in a sense, a student. In spite of this, though, he felt that this was not his world. This was the world of the new Botswana, of the young people who would go on to do things that he would never have dreamed of doing – to be lawyers and accountants, and even doctors, now that the medical school had been opened. In his day, such things had seemed hopelessly remote – the preserve of those who could go off on government scholarships over the border or even overseas. They had not been for somebody like him, the young man from Molepolole who had never dreamed of being anything other than a mechanic.

But now, as he turned off the ignition and the truck's engine coughed into silence, he considered how far he had come. He had his own business, a house, a wife, two foster children who gave him joy, and a reasonable balance in a savings account with the Standard Bank. Of these assets, there was no doubt in his mind that the one he valued most was his wife, Precious Ramotswe, daughter of the late Obed Ramotswe of Mochudi, and owner of her own, perhaps somewhat shakier business, the No. 1 Ladies' Detective Agency. He was so proud of her, and he would willingly sacrifice everything – everything – if he were ever required to choose between Mma Ramotswe and all that he possessed. Although they had been married for some years now, he could hardly believe his luck in finding somebody like her; he could hardly believe that she had agreed to marry him, Mr J. L. B. Matekoni, when he felt that she could have married virtually anybody else in Botswana, had she wanted to. But somehow she had said yes to him, and as a result he had found a happiness that he had never thought was attainable on this side of the great divide that separated those of us who were still alive from those who, being late, were now in a much better place, wherever that was. It was not for him, he thought, to speculate on that location, or even to talk about it. It was somewhere above Botswana, perhaps, or even in Botswana, in those places that you found were special because they somehow felt special: places where you sensed the presence of those who had gone before; some hill with granite rock smoothed by countless rainy seasons; some place of trees and shade where the cattle liked to cluster; some place where there was human silence and you imagined, for some odd reason, that you could actually hear the air.

It was because he valued Mma Ramotswe so highly that he had now taken this step, encouraged, it must be admitted, by Mma Potokwani – who had always pushed him about for various purposes. It was because he wanted to please the wife he loved and to make her life easier that he sought this advice on how to be a modern husband. And now, looking out of his dusty truck window, he saw that there were several other husbands in need of modernisation sitting in their vehicles, all sent there, no doubt, by their wives, or by friends of their wives, all waiting the ten minutes or so before the class was due to start. It was understandable embarrassment, perhaps, that kept them sitting in their cars rather than standing outside in one of the loose groups that men like to stand about in. Going to a course of this nature was in a way an admission that one needed help, and not everybody wanted to be seen in a throng of the needy.

Mr J. L. B. Matekoni glanced furtively at the man in the car parked beside his truck. This man, who looked a few years younger than he was, seemed vaguely familiar and he wondered whether he knew him. The problem with Gaborone was that there were so many people you recognised but could not name. These were people you saw going about their business in the same place and at the same time as you went about yours. After a couple of such encounters you felt that you knew them, even if you did not. Then there were the people whom you did not *quite* know, but who were known to people you did know. You almost knew these people, and indeed you might end up waving to them or greeting them in the street because you knew – and they knew too – some other person who linked you to them and them to you. These people you might subsequently meet at weddings and funerals, when they were united with you in joy or in grief, and then you might talk to them as if they were old friends.

Mr J. L. B. Matekoni got out of his truck at the same time as the man next to him emerged from his vehicle. They both looked at one another sheepishly before the other man spoke.

'I am only here because I have been told to be here,' he announced.

Mr J. L. B. Matekoni laughed. 'It will be very good for us, Rra. It'll be like going to the dentist.'

This exchange gave rise to a warm flow of fellow feeling.

Misfortune, shared even with a stranger, or with somebody who was a stranger until he could remember where he met him, made things easier as they walked the short distance to the classroom. On the door in front of them, which was half-open, was a large sign saying simply: *Husband Course.* Through the door they saw a small group of earlier arrivals – twelve or so – seated behind individual desks. Nobody was speaking.

Mr J. L. B. Matekoni sat down at the back, his new friend preferring the front row. Glances were exchanged with the others present: quick glances of assessment followed by conspiracy. It was, thought Mr J. L. B. Matekoni, rather like one of those groups where people with a problem – drinking or gambling or something of that sort – came together for mutual help and support. What united these men was presumably a failure on their part to understand that marriage had changed; that women were no longer prepared to do everything for husbands who took their wives, and all the work they did, for granted.

After a few minutes the course leader came into the room. She was a tall woman with a high, prominent forehead, and she was dressed in a sombre trouser suit. On the lapel of her jacket she wore a large brooch that Mr J. L. B. Matekoni could make out as a hovering bird of some sort – an eagle, perhaps, or a buzzard.

The woman told them that her name was Keitumeste. 'As you know, men,' she said, 'that name means something in Setswana. Can anyone tell me, please?'

Mr J. L. B. Matekoni noticed that she addressed them, unusually, as *men*. The correct plural term, in Setswana, was *borra*, or in English, *gentlemen*. But *men*? He would never address a group of women as *women*, but then, he suddenly thought, *I am not modern* . . .

'It means *I am happy*,' said a man near the front. 'And I am happy that you are happy, Mma.'

There was a ripple of nervous laughter. Keitumeste, though, did not join in.

'But I am not happy,' she said forcefully, causing the laughter to die out. 'I am far from happy.'

There was complete silence.

'You see,' she went on, glaring at the man who had spoken, 'the reason why I am so unhappy is because I do not think I can be happy as long as there are so many men who are causing unhappiness among the women of Botswana.' She paused. 'At all levels. Up in Francistown. Over in Maun. In Lobatse. In Gaborone. Everywhere.'

The silence continued. One or two of the men shifted uncomfortably in their seats; others remained quite still, as one stays still in the presence of great danger, hoping that the source of the danger will not notice one.

'And who are these men?' Keitumeste asked.

Very tentatively a hand was raised at the front. Keitumeste's gaze fixed on a man slouched in his chair.

'People like us?' he said, with a snigger.

The sheer effrontery of this remark – a risky attempt to defuse the tension – brought a sharp intake of breath from the rest of those present. Mr J. L. B. Matekoni's mouth opened in horror.

For a few moments Keitumeste said nothing. Then she said, 'I see.' Her tone was icy.

The man who had made the suggestion looked over his shoulder for support. When he saw it was not forthcoming, he changed his posture slightly. The slouch became less pronounced.

'Sorry,' he said. 'I wasn't trying to be funny.'

Fixed with an even more intense gaze, he corrected his posture even further.

'And you weren't funny, Rra,' she said, her tone still icy. 'You'll see that I am not laughing. And neither is anybody else in the class laughing.' She scanned the rows of faces. Mr J. L. B. Matekoni looked down at the floor, wondering whether he could slip out unnoticed. Being at the back of the class, he was close to the door, but Keitumeste had closed it when she entered and he thought it would be impossible to leave without being spotted and challenged.

The course began. There was a short introductory lecture from Keitumeste on how she had been brought up in a patriarchal household but had freed herself from all that and made a marriage in which everything was shared equally with her husband. He, however, was an unusual man and she realised shortly after she married him that there were very few men like him in Botswana. At this, she looked sternly at the class members once again. Several nodded their heads in enthusiastic assent.

'My mission,' she went on, 'is to help the men of Botswana to change. That is what God has called me to do, and that is what I shall do.'

The mention of God made Mr J. L. B. Matekoni frown. In his experience, people were always claiming that God agreed with them even when there was little or no evidence that this was the case. And anybody could say that God had called him to do what he did – even burglars. 'God has called me to break into houses,' such a man might say. 'That is the work He planned for me.' Of course, if he said that to a judge, then the judge might say, 'And He has called me to send you to prison.'

No, thought Mr J. L. B. Matekoni – people should be careful about claiming authority that they did not have. It was the same with Mma Ramotswe and Seretse Khama, he reflected – not disloyally, of course. She was always claiming that Seretse Khama believed this, that and the next thing, whether or not there was any indication that he had ever even considered the matter on which she was pronouncing. But that was such a small fault, and rather an endearing one at that . . .

'Now, before we go any further,' continued Keitumeste, 'I should like to carry out a little test. May I have a show of hands, please, on the following: firstly, how many of you consider yourselves to be modern men?'

She looked about her. A hand went up in the front – very tentatively – and then another one in the second row, and a few more in the third. Men looked around and, seeing hands go up, followed suit. Mr J. L. B. Matekoni did not consider himself to be a modern man – not yet – and so he felt he simply could not make the claim.

Keitumeste was smirking. 'Hands down!' she commanded. 'You are all wrong – all except that man at the back. You, Rra, you did not put your hand up.'

Mr J. L. B. Matekoni shook his head. He wished he had not drawn attention to himself in this way, but he could not make an untrue claim. It would be as bad as describing a car as being in good condition when it patently was not; he had never done that sort of thing before, and he had no intention of doing it now.

'Well, then,' said Keitumeste, 'this shows us a very important thing: a really modern man does not pretend to be something that he is not. All of you – all, except our friend at the back – are therefore old-fashioned.'

The other men turned to stare at Mr J. L. B. Matekoni. Their expressions were reproachful – as if he stood accused of trying to curry favour with the teacher. He looked away in embarrassment.

'There are more questions,' announced Keitumeste. 'The first of these is this: when did you last vacuum-clean the house?'

Mr J. L. B. Matekoni bit his lip as he tried to decide on the answer he would give if attention were suddenly to be focused on him. At one level the answer was simple – he had never vacuumed the house – but there was an even more profound issue to be resolved: did they even have a vacuum cleaner? If there was no vacuum cleaner, then it would look less bad for him that he had never used one in the house. Mind you, he had never swept the house either – and they did have a broom.

A forest of hands went up, but it did not include his.

Keitumeste pointed at a man in the middle. 'Yes, Rra? When did you do that?'

The man answered in a clear, confident voice. 'Yesterday, Mma. I vacuumed the living room and the dining room, too. I would have done more if I had not been so tired.'

Keitumeste nodded. 'And what sort of vacuum cleaner is it, Rra?'

The question, so innocently put, found its target. The man opened his mouth to speak, and then closed it.

'You don't know, do you?' said Keitumeste scornfully. 'I can tell you then. Perhaps it was a *Nothing Vacuum Cleaner*. That is a very popular make of vacuum cleaner with men, because it does not exist – that is why!'

Again she looked over the heads of the front two rows to focus on Mr J. L. B. Matekoni. 'You have never vacuumed, have you, Rra?'

Conscious of the eyes of the class upon him, he muttered a response that did not consist of any words – just a few self deprecatory sounds.

'Once again, I must commend you, Rra,' said Keitumeste. 'A truly modern husband does not make up information to please people.' She paused. 'And here is another question: hands up those who have given their wife a present this month?'

Now no hands went up. Mr J. L. B. Matekoni looked around; honesty, it seemed, was beginning to prevail. And then he remembered: two weeks ago he had bought Mma Ramotswe a new plant for her garden. It was not a plant that she had asked for – it was a completely out-of-the-blue present.

Very slowly he raised his hand.

'Ah!' exclaimed Keitumeste. 'What was this present, Rra?'

'It was a plant,' mumbled Mr J. L. B. Matekoni. 'She is a very keen gardener and she likes to get plants.'

Keitumeste smiled broadly. 'You see!' she exclaimed. 'You see what a truly modern, sympathetic husband does? He gives his wife a present of something that he knows *she* wants. He does not choose something that *he* would like to receive himself; he gets something for *her*.'

Mr J. L. B. Matekoni squirmed in his seat. If he had known that the course would involve this ... this humiliation, then he would never have signed up for it. He looked at his watch. Ten minutes had passed. They had another half hour ahead of them. And it was a long half hour – one that moved with all the slowness of time spent in circumstances of social embarrassment.

At the end of it, in spite of Keitumeste's offer to stay and answer any personal questions that the class might have, he slipped away quickly and returned at a fast pace – almost a run – to his truck. He was not made for courses of that sort, he thought. It might be a good thing to be a more modern husband but there were other ways, he felt, of reaching that desired goal – if indeed Mma Potokwani was right in her view that it was a desirable goal. There had been plenty of men in the past who had not been modern husbands, and their wives had seemed pleased enough with them. Perhaps women like Keitumeste should leave men alone for a while, rather than making them uneasy. And then he thought: what would it be like to be married to somebody like her? How unhappy that poor man must be; how uneasily he must sleep, if he slept at all. That was another thing: modern people always appeared to be rushing about doing things, having no time, it seemed, for looking at the sky, or counting the cattle they had already counted, or waiting for somebody to walk by and pass the time of day with them. They missed so much in all their anxiety and anger, and in their determination to stop other people doing things of which they happened to disapprove. Perhaps he should stay more or less as he was: Mr J. L. B. Matekoni, mechanic, not-very-good cook, but nonetheless devoted husband of Precious Ramotswe, the woman he loved and admired above all others and for whom he would do anything – anything at all – in his own not-very-modern way.

While Mr J. L. B. Matekoni was attending his first class on how to be a modern husband, Mma Ramotswe was on her way to visit Mma Makutsi. She had telephoned her assistant to arrange the visit and had been surprised that the telephone had been answered by Mma Makutsi herself, rather than by Phuti's aunt. Had the aunt answered, she had no doubt at all that reasons would have been given for the visit not to take place, but Mma Makutsi, by contrast, was keen that she should come.

'My baby is making a lot of progress,' she said. 'He's taken very great strides, Mma.'

'He's not walking already, Mma?' said Mma Ramotswe. 'Surely it is a bit early for that.'

Mma Makutsi laughed. 'No, I do not mean that, Mma. He will walk in good time, but not yet.'

Mma Ramotswe continued the joke. 'I thought that perhaps up in Bobonong babies walked earlier than down here. I thought maybe they walked back from the hospital with their mother – holding her hand, of course.'

A shriek of laughter came down the line. 'Mma Ramotswe!

You are very funny. You are making my stomach hurt with laughter.'

A time was agreed, and now Mma Ramotswe had closed the Radiphuti gate behind her and was driving her tiny white van cautiously up the rough driveway to the house. The painters who had been working on the outside had made great strides too and had almost finished with the guttering, which was being painted purple. That, thought Mma Ramotswe, was a Makutsi touch, as she had always had a liking for purple shoes. It was something to do with Bobonong, perhaps, where there were whole fields of those strange rocks which, when broken open, revealed purple crystals. Mma Makutsi had brought one into the office to use as a paperweight, and it caught the light sometimes, sending dancing specks of light on to the walls, as if a colourful hand had touched them and left its purple fingerprints.

Mma Ramotswe had hoped that Phuti's aunt would not be in, but it was she who opened the front door.

'It is you,' said the aunt abruptly. 'Yes?'

Mma Ramotswe made an effort to control herself. The rudeness of this woman was almost beyond belief. 'Yes, it is me, Mma. I'm sorry, but it's me.'

'And?' snapped the aunt.

'I am here to see Mma Makutsi.'

'Mma Radiphuti,' shot back the aunt. 'What is this nonsense about keeping names. She is a Radiphuti now.'

Mma Ramotswe took a deep breath. 'And a Makutsi. I am a Ramotswe and a Matekoni. We can use both names, Mma, if that is what we want to do.'

The aunt wrinkled her nose. 'She is very tired. You should come back some other time.'

Mma Ramotswe ignored this. 'Thank you, Mma. You are very kind, but I can show myself in. Thank you very much.'

As on her previous visit, she pushed past the aunt and started to make her way into the house when Mma Makutsi appeared. 'You can get on with your rest now, Auntie,' she said respectfully. 'We shall go to the kitchen.'

The aunt sniffed and retreated, leaving the two women by themselves.

'Your house is looking so good,' said Mma Ramotswe. 'It's many years since we painted Zebra Drive. Mr J. L. B. Matekoni has been promising to do it for a long time, but he has not started yet.'

'He is very busy, Mma. You will need to get our painter. He works very quickly and very well.'

Mma Ramotswe thought of their last painter. 'They are always going off to funerals, Mma. Don't you find that?'

Mma Makutsi smiled. 'He was off this week, but he came back.'

'I think that it is not really funerals they are going to,' said Mma Ramotswe. 'They go off to paint other houses. They have more than one job at a time.'

'Like us,' said Mma Makutsi. 'We do that. We have more than one case going at any time, do we not?'

It was true, and it reminded Mma Ramotswe of the reason for her visit. 'I need to talk to you, Mma,' she said. 'We have some very difficult cases at the moment.'

They went into the kitchen. The baby, Mma Makutsi explained, was sleeping but he would wake up before long and make his presence known. 'He has a very loud voice,' she said. 'And he sounds just like Phuti.'

Mma Ramotswe was puzzled by this remark, but said nothing. How could a baby sound like his father? Babies said nothing, they cried, and Phuti ... The awful thought occurred to her: did the baby have a stammer, as Phuti had? Could one stutter as one cried? It was an absurd idea, and she stopped herself from thinking it, as she had stopped herself envisaging the baby making great strides around the nursery . . .

Mma Makutsi made tea. Mma Ramotswe saw that she had a special supply of redbush tea specially for her, and was touched; that one woman should keep something in the house for the visit of another woman was a nice example of what friendship might be.

'Now, Mma,' said Mma Makutsi as she sipped at her own cup of Tanganda Tea. 'What is all this?'

Mma Ramotswe began with the Molapo case. Mma Makutsi had been there for the visit of Mma Sheba, of course, but Mma Ramotswe brought her up to date with what had happened since, including the visit to the farm and the encounter with Liso.

'I didn't like the look of him to begin with,' she said. 'He was wearing one of those ridiculous hats that young men wear. I know it means nothing, but it put me against him.'

'It is a sign,' said Mma Makutsi. 'A hat can be a sign.'

'Yes, but you have to be careful. Remember what Clovis Andersen says in the book? Remember how he says that the shirt a man wears is not always the shirt he would like to wear?'

Mma Makutsi remembered that. 'Have you heard from him?' she asked.

'From?'

'From Mr Andersen? I thought that perhaps he might have written again.'

'No, he has not, Mma. He has many important things to do.'

There had been one letter since Clovis Andersen had returned to Muncie, Indiana. It had arrived shortly after his trip to Botswana had come to an end and it had been read and reread by both Mma Ramotswe and Mma Makutsi before being filed away in a file specially devoted to it.

Dear ladies,

There are some letters that are easy to write and some that are hard. This is a hard letter, not because I have anything unpleasant to say – as some hard letters require – but because I am not sure that I can find the words to express what I feel I need to say. And that is to thank you not merely for all your kindness to me when I was in your wonderful country, but to thank you for helping me come to terms with what has happened to me and with who I am. I could say so much more about that, but I know that it would make you embarrassed. We Americans can sometimes say too much about how we are feeling when other people keep those things to themselves. So I will not say much more than I have said because I know that you will understand. Here may be a wide sea between us, and many thousand of miles of it, but that sea and those miles are nothing to true friends, which is what I hope you will allow me to call you.

Yours truly,
Clovis Andersen

Now Mma Makutsi mused, 'I might write to him and tell him about my baby.'

In Mma Ramotswe's view this was a good idea. 'He would be very interested, Mma.'

'Especially in the name,' said Mma Makutsi.

Mma Ramotswe looked up. 'You have chosen it now?'

Mma Makutsi nodded. 'Phuti and I have agreed.'

Mma Ramotswe took a sip of her tea, glancing at Mma Makutsi over the rim of her cup. 'And, Mma?'

'Itumelang,' said Mma Makutsi.

It was a reasonably common name in a country where names were highly individual and there were many thousands from which to choose.

'It is a good name,' said Mma Ramotswe. 'Itumelang Radiphuti sounds very good to my ear, Mma.' She paused. 'Have there been many Itumelangs in Phuti's family?'

'His father's brother,' said Mma Makutsi. 'But that is not the reason we have chosen it. We like the name for its own sake.'

'Of course.'

'But he has other names too,' said Mma Makutsi. 'His full name will be Itumelang Clovis Radiphuti.'

Mma Ramotswe clapped her hands in pleasure. 'That is wonderful, Mma! That is a very good name. Phuti told me you might do that.'

Mma Makutsi smiled demurely. 'I am glad that you like it, Mma. It is a tribute to Clovis Andersen.'

'Of course it is. Of course it is. And Rra Andersen will be very pleased when he hears it, I think. You must write to him. Send him a photograph and tell him that this baby has been given his name. People like that.'

'I will do that, Mma.'

They reverted to the subject of Liso. 'I was not sure of him at first, Mma,' continued Mma Ramotswe, 'but then I ended up liking him. You know how that can happen – you start off being wary of somebody and then you realise that your suspicions are wrong.'

Mma Makutsi had experienced that, but it was possible, she pointed out, that exactly the opposite might happen. 'You may meet people who you think are all right and then you realise that they are not. That happens too, Mma.'

Mma Ramotswe moved on to describe the anxiety that Liso's aunt had felt about leaving him alone with her. 'And every time

I asked him a question, she answered. It was as if she was worried that he would say something that would give him away.'

Mma Makutsi looked thoughtful. 'Sometimes people are like that,' she said. 'They feel anxious about what their relatives will say. I have an aunt in Bobonong who replies for her husband all the time. Now he never opens his mouth at all when anybody speaks to him – he just looks at her and she tells that other person what he is thinking.'

'Yes,' said Mma Ramotswe. 'That can happen. But there is something more, Mma.'

'Yes?'

Mma Ramotswe lifted her teacup and tilted it to make sure that she got the last few drops. Mma Makutsi saw this; it was a signal that they had both used many times and was picked up immediately.

'I shall get you more tea,' she said. 'Then you can tell me.'

Their cups refreshed, Mma Makutsi listened while Mma Ramotswe related what Gwithie had told her about Liso calling his aunt his mother. Mma Makutsi weighed this for some time before she gave her response.

'There is something that Clovis Andersen says,' she began. 'He says that you should always ask who has an interest in something. Remember that, Mma? Remember how he said: find out who has a stake?'

She did remember.

'So, Mma,' continued Mma Makutsi, 'you must ask yourself: who has a stake in all this?'

Mma Ramotswe thought it was obvious. 'The aunt. The nephew.' She paused as she tried to imagine who else had an interest in the outcome of the Molapo succession. Eventually she said, 'And the lawyer too, I suppose.' She had her suspicions about Mma Sheba, and perhaps it was now time to spell them out.

Mma Makutsi looked thoughtful. 'Her? Why would a lawyer be interested?'

'She is a lawyer who is giving us opinions. And if anybody gives you an opinion, then you have to ask what they want to achieve by that opinion.'

Mma Ramotswe reached out to touch the tablecloth on the table at which they were sitting. It had been embroidered round the edges with brightly coloured images of Botswana flowers. She touched a motif of a jacaranda blossom – more purple.

'I suppose,' she said, 'that lawyers may want a case to work out in a particular way. If you are defending somebody and you think he is innocent, then . . .'

Mma Makutsi became animated. 'Exactly. Or if you are looking after an inheritance and you think that the person who stands to get it is not a good person, then you might want to do all you can—'

'To prevent that happening,' supplied Mma Ramotswe.

They stared at one another.

'So you need to look at the will, Mma,' said Mma Makutsi. 'Anybody can do that, you know.'

It was Mma Ramotswe who had first told Mma Makutsi about the government registry where wills, and all sorts of other documents, could be seen – for a fee.

'I do know that, Mma,' she said. 'In fact, I think I may have told you about it a few years ago.'

Mma Makutsi shrugged. 'Maybe. But have you looked at the will, Mma?'

'No, I haven't. Not yet.'

'Because it will show who stands to gain if Liso is not Liso,' said Mma Makutsi. 'And that is what we really need to know.'

Mma Ramotswe was thoughtful. 'I shall do this,' she said.

'Yes,' said Mma Makutsi. 'There is a man. Phuti told me about him. He bought a sofa.'

Mma Ramotswe waited for her to continue. Since she had married Phuti Radiphuti, sofas and chairs and all sorts of furniture regularly entered Mma Makutsi's conversation, and people were described in terms of the furniture they had bought. Thus a prominent politician had been identified as a man who had a large dining room table made of Zambian *mukwa* wood; or a rising businesswomen had been referred to as having recently acquired a set of expensive office chairs.

'This man with the sofa,' Mma Makutsi went on, ' is called the Master of the High Court. He keeps all the wills.'

'A big filing task,' said Mma Ramotswe.

Mma Makutsi rolled her eyes heavenward as she contemplated the immensity of filing all the wills made in Botswana. She would have no trouble in coping with it herself, of course, but the Master of the High Court, whatever else his training, would not have had the benefit of studying at the Botswana Secretarial College. Had he done that, then he would have studied filing under the tutorship of the legendary teacher who had taught Mma Makutsi, a woman who was now living in retirement in one of the western suburbs but whom she saw occasionally doing her grocery shopping. It pleased Mma Makutsi that her tutor remembered her name. It can be difficult for teachers, through whose hands pass so many students every year, but she had remembered, saying, 'My goodness, Grace Makutsi, you are the one who did so well. And now I hear that you are a very senior investigator. We are proud of you, you know.'

Mma Makutsi agreed with Mma Ramotswe. 'I am sure, though, that they have it under control, Mma. It may take them some time to find it, but they will have it.'

They moved on to discuss Mma Soleti. Mma Ramotswe told

Mma Makutsi about the whispering campaign and the identification of the potential enemy. Her assistant listened with interest.

'It may be that woman,' she said once Mma Ramotswe had finished. 'It may be that she is angry because Mma Soleti has stolen her husband. You should go and see her.'

'I am intending to do that,' said Mma Ramotswe.

Mma Makutsi bit her lip. 'May I ask you something, Mma?'

'Of course.'

'May I come with you? You see, I want to get back to work as soon as possible, and if I can do the occasional small thing then that will help me so much. It is not that I do not like being here with my baby – with Itumelang – but it's just that ... well, Mma Ramotswe, I know I've only been away for a few days, but I'm missing our office, I'm missing the conversations we have, the discussions. I miss making tea for you. I even miss filing.'

Mma Ramotswe was taken aback to learn that, even with a new baby to care for, her assistant shared the same feelings she had experienced, but then she knew that, were we suddenly separated from them, we all would miss the things that made up our daily lives – even if these things were mundane and inconsequential.

'Your filing is exceptional,' said Mma Ramotswe. And the compliment was received with all the gravity accorded to those compliments that are fully intended – and fully justified.

'I think I'll come back very soon,' said Mma Makutsi. 'The baby is small, but—'

Mma Ramotswe interrupted her. 'The baby is very, very small, Mma.'

'Yes, but that makes him easier to carry. And I think it's good for babies to get out and about; I am a modern person in that respect, Mma Ramotswe.' She paused. 'So, if you have no objection, Mma ...'

Mma Ramotswe smiled. 'I have no objection, Mma.'

'I'll come in for a few hours at a time.'

'As you wish, Mma Makutsi.'

They remained silent after that, sitting in the silence of a friendship that was the greatest and deepest and most valuable friendship that either of them had ever had, or ever would have. Then it was time for a further cup of tea and the conversation shifted to the subject of husbands, on which they both declared themselves to be most fortunate.

'I would not want Phuti to change,' said Mma Makutsi. 'He is perfect just as he is.'

'And I would not like Mr J. L. B. Matekoni to change either,' said Mma Ramotswe. 'For the same reason.'

This was not strictly speaking true. Neither husband was perfect – as both wives knew – but then who among us is perfect? Nobody, thought Mma Ramotswe. And Mma Makutsi thought much the same thing, but perhaps slightly more forcefully.

Chapter Twelve

Shoes Are Wasted on Men

Mma Soleti had given Mma Ramotswe the name of her enemy and Mma Ramotswe had written it down on a scrap of paper. The following day, sitting in the office of the No. 1 Ladies' Detective Agency, she examined what she had written. *Daisy Manchwe, runs a photocopy shop in town.* That was all that Mma Soleti had said about her; she clearly found the subject distasteful. That did not surprise Mma Ramotswe a great deal: we do not, in general, like to discuss those we have wronged, and it seemed to her that whatever Mma Soleti said about Daisy Manchwe's husband being ready to leave, it was likely that this was a simple case of husband-grabbing. In her experience, those who took the husbands or wives of others could rewrite history – not always, but often – and the marriage they had broken up would be portrayed as being in much worse condition than it really was.

She had no real idea what she would find when she went to see Daisy Manchwe, but she felt the likelihood was she would find that Daisy had done nothing to justify her husband's departure and would, indeed, be nurturing antagonism towards Mma Soleti. One could never really understand other people's marriages. Mma Ramotswe was as well aware of that as anybody – perhaps even more so, given that her work often required her to investigate the conjugal arrangements of others. A marriage, she had learned, is seldom what it seems to be on the surface; what appears to be the most equable, well settled of arrangements might be a seething mass of discontent and resentment underneath. And conversely, chaotic and noisy relationships, littered with conflict and infidelity, might prove to be the most durable of unions. There was simply no telling, she felt, and you had to be prepared to find anything.

This did not mean, though, that she thought Mma Soleti was wrong about the enmity of Mma Manchwe. You could be mistaken about many things in this life, thought Mma Ramotswe, but one thing that you were very rarely wrong about was whether somebody disliked you – that you could always tell. If Mma Soleti thought that Daisy Manchwe nursed an undying hatred towards her for stealing her husband, then she was probably right. She would have seen the daggers in the other woman's eyes; daggers in the eyes were always visible, sometimes even through sunglasses.

It was not difficult to locate Daisy Manchwe's details in the Gaborone Trade Directory. This was a publication heavily relied upon by Mma Makutsi, who believed that most tasks of identification could be completed by the simple expedient of looking through the telephone book or any of the other public directories she kept in the top drawer of her desk.

'It's all there,' she said to Mma Ramotswe. 'You just have to know where to look – which I do, Mma. I know my way around these things.'

The trade directory revealed that there were three photocopying businesses in the town. Daisy Manchwe's, known as Clear Image Copies, was located in the new cluster of shops that had been set up near Kgale Hill. It was not a place that Mma Ramotswe liked to go, as she was loyal to the older and more sedate Riverwalk shopping centre. She also liked small, local shops; places where you were able to buy pins and candles and tins of syrup – the sort of *real* things that you needed, rather than the insubstantial clothes and flashy electrical goods that newer, louder shops sold.

The directory entry for Clear Image Copies put the matter of ownership beyond doubt. *Founded and under the management of Daisy Manchwe*, it read, before going on to reveal that the prices at which copies could be made could not be bettered elsewhere in Gaborone. *From one to one thousand copies*, came the claim, *we are the cheapest and the clearest in town.*

The directory entry provided even more interesting information than these advertising puffs. At the bottom of the entry was a picture of Daisy Manchwe herself, standing proudly in front of a large photocopying machine. Mma Ramotswe studied the picture with interest. It was not very clearly printed – a sorry thing for a company that boasted of clear images – but then they had not printed the directory and would presumably have done a much better job themselves. What struck Mma Ramotswe about the picture was the cheerful look of Daisy Manchwc. People smiled when having their photographs taken, of course, but if you were heartbroken inside, your camera smile would always be unconvincing. Daisy Manchwe did not look like the abandoned spouse; far from it – she appeared happy with the world.

It was a passing reflection and did not amount to much, but it was something that she mentioned to Mma Makutsi when she picked her up from her house. She felt extremely cheerful herself when they set off in the van together. This was just like it used to be – the two of them heading off on some investigation, going over the details of the case together in the cab of the tiny white van as they watched Botswana pass by.

'There was no trouble leaving Itumelang?' she asked, as Mma Makutsi settled herself in the van on their departure.

Mma Makutsi shook her head. 'He is sleeping, and the girl I have helping me is very good. There is his bottle in the fridge and he will be given that. It is personal milk.'

Mma Ramotswe had not heard the expression *personal milk* before, but she rather liked it. 'Personal milk is very good,' she said.

'Yes, it is. And I am having no trouble with that side of things, Mma, so I will soon be able to come back to work more or less full-time.'

'I will be very happy when that happens,' said Mma Ramotswe. 'Of course, you have Phuti's aunt to help with running the house. I suppose that will make it easier.'

Mma Makutsi shook her head. 'I do not, Mma. The aunt has gone.'

Mma Ramotswe looked at her companion, a lapse in attention that caused the van to swerve towards the side of the road. She corrected quickly.

'Well, Mma, that's an interesting piece of news. Was there a ... ' There must have been a fight, she thought, and for a moment she imagined Mma Makutsi and the aunt locked in battle, the aunt perhaps clutching at Mma Makutsi's large glasses and Mma Makutsi struggling to hold on to them.

'An argument?' supplied Mma Makutsi. 'Yes, there were arguments, but I did not antagonise her. I felt too weak and tired to do that. I thought that I would have it out with her later on, once I was stronger.'

'That is wise,' said Mma Ramotswe. 'They say that it is very important to choose your moment.' She paused. 'Some people never find their moment. You see them waiting and waiting, but never finding it.'

'That's as may· be,' said Mma Makutsi. 'What happened, though, had nothing to do with me. It was a snake.'

Mma Ramotswe recalled that Mma Makutsi had said something about Phuti having killed a cobra in the house. Had that upset the aunt?

Mma Makutsi grinned. Victory over the aunt had clearly been sweet. 'It was not that, Mma,' she said. 'What happened was that Phuti had only dealt with one of the snakes. Then I went into labour and we forgot all about the fact that there was another one around somewhere. While I was in hospital, he searched the house from top to bottom but did not find it, and so he concluded that it had gone away. But it had not.'

Mma Ramotswe gave an involuntary shiver. Like most of her fellow Batswana, she did not like snakes, although she had come round to the more tolerant view that they should be left alone as much as possible. In that, she was a minority; people still killed them on sight, not bothering to distinguish between the non-venomous and the venomous ones – the cobras, the mambas, the puff adders – that one could not allow to be around the house. The puff adders were the most dangerous, even if their venom was not as powerful as that of the black mambas. The *lebolobolo*, as the puff adder was known in Setswana, was a lazy snake, not given to moving very fast – except when striking – and the danger was that it would not get out of your way. Cobras and mambas generally avoided contact with people, although the mamba could be aggressive and might pursue an intruder on its territory.

Puff adders did not stir themselves; they could lie in sluggish inactivity halfway across a path and then respond with furious and fatal indignation if trodden upon.

The thought occurred to her that the aunt had been bitten. Mma Makutsi had said that the aunt had 'gone'; surely that could not mean that the aunt was late? Surely she would not have dropped this fact into the conversation so casually. Mma Makutsi might be prickly from time to time, but she was not as cold-hearted as that.

Mma Makutsi explained what had happened. 'The aunt complained about noises in the ceiling above her bed,' she said. 'Phuti said that he thought she was imagining things, which made her very angry. So he eventually got a ladder and went up into the roof. That is where he found the snake's skin. But he also found something else, which he didn't tell us about when he came down.

'The aunt was very frightened. She started to shout and weep and say that now that the snake had shed its skin it would be very hungry and would be looking for something to bite. Phuti tried to calm her down. He said, "Oh no, Auntie, there is no danger. I promise you there is no danger."

'The aunt did not like this,' Mma Makutsi continued. 'She carried on shouting and pointing at the empty snakeskin. Phuti kept telling her that he was sure that there was no danger. Nobody was going to be bitten by a snake, he said.'

Mma Ramotswe smiled at the thought of the two Radiphutis – nephew and aunt – at odds with one another, with the snakeskin, the vital evidence, in front of them.

'Eventually,' said Mma Makutsi, 'the aunt said that she could not stay in a house that was crawling with snakes and she was better off in her own place.'

'She left?'

'She left, Mma. And then, after she had gone, Phuti did not say anything, but he climbed back up into the roof. I heard him moving about up there and I was worried that he would fall through the ceiling – he did not. Then he came down, Mma Ramotswe, and he was carrying a dead cobra. He had not killed this snake – it had died because it had choked on a rat that was too big for it. You could see the shape of the rat in its throat.'

Mma Ramotswe chuckled. 'Phuti did not lie to his aunt. He told her that there was no danger, and there was not. There was no longer any snake.'

'That is right,' said Mma Makutsi. 'Sometimes saying what is true may not be altogether true but is still not a lie.'

'That is so, Mma,' said Mma Ramotswe. 'That is entirely true, I think.'

Mma Makutsi now changed the subject. 'This woman we are going to see,' she said. 'This Daisy Manchwe.'

'Yes?'

'What are you going to say to her?'

Mma Ramotswe hesitated for a few moments before replying. 'We shall need to be careful.'

'Of course.'

'We will tell her that we have been looking into threats against Mma Soleti. Then we watch her reaction. Guilty people give themselves away, Mma.'

Mma Makutsi agreed. 'And then? What if she gives herself away – what then?'

'Then we ... Then we ...' Mma Ramotswe faltered.

'Yes, Mma?'

'We remind her that this is a country in which the law says that you cannot intimidate people. We mention a lawyer.'

'Which lawyer, Mma?'

Mma Ramotswe shrugged. 'Any lawyer, Mma. There are

176

plenty of them. And anyway, people who tell other people about their lawyers rarely have a lawyer. Just mentioning a lawyer is usually enough, even if you don't have one, which we don't.'

'Mma Sheba?'

Mma Ramotswe had not thought of her. It was useful to have a name of a lawyer, even if the lawyer had not agreed to act for you. 'A very good idea, Mma,' she said. 'Now we have a lawyer.'

The premises of Clear Image Copies were sandwiched between a takeaway food place and a shop selling fashionable men's shoes. Mma Makutsi stopped outside the men's shoe shop; she had never been able to walk past a shoe shop without pausing to admire the display, and Mma Ramotswe waited patiently as her assistant examined the offerings in the window.

'Shoes are wasted on men,' said Mma Makutsi. 'They don't appreciate them, Mma.'

Mma Ramotswe made a non-committal sound. Mr J. L. B. Matekoni possessed two pairs of shoes: one was his working pair, made of ancient suede and covered in grease to the extent that their original colour could not be discerned, and the other was a black leather pair that he donned on those occasions when he wore his one and only suit. 'I do not need more shoes than that,' he said to Mma Ramotswe. 'I have only got one pair of feet.'

'Those shoes over there,' said Mma Makutsi, pointing to a pair of white shoes with narrow, pointed toes. 'Those are very good shoes, Mma – very fashionable, I think – but there would be no point my buying those for Phuti. No point at all. He would not appreciate them. Men never do.' She paused. 'And he has that problem with his foot after that accident. He can't use any old shoes.'

She reluctantly tore herself away from the shoe shop window and joined Mma Ramotswe, who was now standing outside the door of Clear Image Copies. It was not a large store, and much of the space within was occupied by a photocopying machine that was in action when they arrived, spitting out paper into a receiving tray at the side. Operating this machine was a woman in a red dress, who looked out through the shop window when Mma Ramotswe and Mma Makutsi appeared. She nodded to the two women, and then continued with her task of duplication.

Mma Ramotswe entered first.

'One moment, Mma,' the woman said. 'One moment and I will be finished.'

The machine cast a leaked band of light across the wall with each pass. Mma Ramotswe noticed how the light caught Mma Makutsi's glasses and was reflected for a second time. Their eyes met briefly and she thought: she has decided; her mind is made up.

The machine gave a final whirr and then settled into silence. 'There you are,' said the woman. 'Another job done.' She flicked a switch. 'Now then, ladies, what can I do for you?'

Mma Ramotswe did not approve of the sudden launch into business. She felt that even if you had things to do, there was no reason not to introduce yourself and enquire after the other person. That was the way it had always been done in Botswana, and she saw no reason to change. So she greeted the woman in the traditional way and introduced herself.

'I am Mma Ramotswe,' she said, offering her hand. 'And this is Mma Makutsi, my assistant.'

'Associate,' corrected Mma Makutsi.

'My associate.'

They shook hands.

'You are Mma Manchwe?' asked Mma Ramotswe.

The woman nodded. 'I am. That is me. I am the owner of this business and I shall be very pleased to do some copying for you ladies, if that is what you need. You'll find that my charges are competitive.'

'I'm sure they are,' said Mma Ramotswe. 'But that, Mma, is not why we are here.'

Mma Manchwe's eyes narrowed, but only slightly. Mma Makutsi noticed, though, and glanced at Mma Ramotswe: proof – if it were still needed.

'We are from the No. 1 Ladies' Detective Agency,' Mma Ramotswe said.

It seemed to take Mma Manchwe a few moments to absorb this information. Then her head went back and she laughed. 'That place! The ladies' detective place? I've seen that sign of yours, Mma – that funny sign.'

Mma Ramotswe sensed Mma Makutsi stiffen beside her. 'I do not see why the sign is funny, Mma,' she said mildly. 'You have a sign too. A business needs a sign.'

Mma Manchwe was unapologetic. 'But it says something about the problems of ladies, doesn't it? It says something like: *For the problems of ladies and others.*' She paused, looking almost incredulously at her visitors. 'Don't you think that sounds a little bit ... a little bit *gynaecological*?'

Mma Makutsi drew in her breath sharply. 'I do not think that, Mma. I do not think that any reasonable person would think that at all. In fact, I think only a person with a very crude mind would think that, Mma.'

Mma Ramotswe reached out to touch Mma Makutsi's forearm. 'I do not think that she meant it unkindly, Mma,' she said.

Mma Manchwe was placatory. 'Of course not, Mma,' she said, looking anxiously at Mma Makutsi. 'I was just saying.'

Mma Makutsi was not to be so easily pacified. 'There are many people who just say things, Mma,' she said icily. 'There are fewer people who think before they open their mouths. That is something I have observed, you know. I have seen it many, many times.'

Mma Ramotswe touched Mma Makuti's arm again. 'We all understand that, Mma.' She turned to face Mma Manchwe again. 'We are working on behalf of Mma Soleti, Mma. I believe you know this lady.'

Mma Manchwe did not flinch. As she replied, her voice was even, and she held Mma Ramotswe's gaze without that falling away of eyes that can signify fear or distrust. 'That lady, Mma? Do I know her? I do. And I am very thankful to her. She may not know that, but I am.'

Mma Makutsi shot a puzzled glance at Mma Ramotswe. 'You are thankful, Mma? Why?'

Mma Manchwe shrugged. 'Why should I not be thankful to the lady who took a great load off my shoulders? If you were walking along carrying a big heavy burden on your shoulders, Mma, and somebody came along and took it off you, would you not be thankful? Would you not want to shake her hand and say: "Thank you very much for taking this great weight off my back"?'

For a while there was silence, to be broken at last by Mma Makutsi. 'You are not her enemy, Mma?'

Mma Manchwe laughed again. It was a loud, irritating laugh – one that was impossible to ignore. 'Enemy? I have no enemies in this world, Mma – not one. I am a Christian, you see, and a Christian does not have enemies. If you have enemies, then your biggest enemy is yourself. Do you know that, Mma?'

'But that lady went off with your husband, Mma,' protested Mma Makutsi. 'Any woman would feel very angry about that. It is human nature to feel that way.'

'Not if you had a husband like mine,' Mma Manchwe countered. 'Do you know him? I don't think you do. He is a man who is very kind to ladies – many ladies. Ten, twelve, maybe more. Oh yes, he is a very kind man.'

Mma Ramotswe sighed. 'A philanderer?'

'A very big philanderer. The biggest in the country. Head of the No. 1 Men's Philandering Agency.' She shook her head. 'That poor woman learned about that very quickly. Two months, I think, and then, bang, he is gone. On to the next lady. Goodbye Mma Soleti. Ha!'

Mma Ramotswe sighed again.

Yes,' said Mma Manchwe, 'you may sigh, Mma. But you will notice that I am not sighing. And that is because I am pleased that Mma Soleti came and took that man away. I am grateful to her, you know. She is a very big heroine as far as I am concerned.'

Mma Ramotswe glanced at Mma Makutsi, who was pursing her lips. She turned to address Mma Manchwe. 'So, Mma,' she said, 'you would never wish to harm that lady?'

Mma Manchwe seemed genuinely surprised. 'Harm her? Why should I want to harm her?' She stopped. She was looking at Mma Ramotswe with some distrust now. 'Why are you asking me, Mma? Are you wanting to get somebody to help *you* harm her? Is that what's happening?'

Mma Makutsi intervened. 'Certainly not,' she exploded. 'We would never do that sort of thing, Mma.'

'I am only asking,' said Mma Manchwe. 'You never know these days.' She looked at her watch before she continued. 'I'm sorry, Mma Ramotswe and Mma ... '

'Makutsi. Makutsi.'

'Yes, I'm sorry, Mma Makutsi, but I am going to have to get on with my work. Let me give you my leaflet here, though, as it explains my charges. If you can get a lower per copy price any-where in Gaborone – and I mean anywhere – then I will do your copying free. How about that? You take that leaflet, Mma, and get back to me if you have any copying to be done. You will get very good service from me – I promise you that.'

Mma Manchwe smiled as she gave them the leaflet. It was not the smile of one who would send a ground hornbill feather to another, nor was it the smile of one who would spread false rumours aimed at destroying somebody's business. But there was something odd about the smile, thought Mma Ramotswe. Although you could say what it was not, you could not necessarily say what it was.

Chapter Thirteen

Bless You, and Your Shoes

Mma Ramotswe was late home that evening. The school that Motholeli and Puso attended had arranged for parents – including, of course, foster parents – to visit their children's classrooms and speak to their teachers. Since most of the parents worked, these meetings took place after five-thirty, which gave time for everybody to reach the school through the after-work traffic. After a chat with the teachers, the school choirs, of which there were four, were due to entertain the parents before they went home. Both Motholeli and Puso were in a choir, but in different ones. Puso was in a choir of boys whose voices were yet to break, which sang traditional Botswana songs; Motholeli was in a mixed choir – boys and girls – which sang gospel music and occasional jazz.

Motholeli's teacher was happy with the progress that she had made over the year. 'She is very good with her hands,' she said. 'She is one of those children who will be able to make anything.'

'She wants to be a mechanic,' said Mma Ramotswe. 'She has always wanted that.'

The teacher nodded. 'Your husband ... '

'Yes, he is a mechanic. But it is not because of that. He has never tried to persuade her. She is naturally good at it.'

The teacher smiled. 'And she is brave too.'

Mma Ramotswe lowered her eyes. 'It is not always easy for her.'

They sat in silence. The teacher knew.

'I hope that she is able to follow her heart,' said Mma Ramotswe quietly. 'I hope that she will be able to be a mechanic, but ... ' She did not like to spell it out, and anyway, the doctors had said that they could not tell; the course of the young girl's illness was unpredictable, even if they could say with certainty that she would always need the wheelchair. 'But we do not know. There are many things that we do not know about life.'

The teacher fiddled with a piece of paper. Looking after thirty children meant that you gave thirty hostages to fortune. A parent's heart may be broken once, maybe twice or thrice; as a teacher your heart could be broken thirty times.

'That she is happy is the main thing, Mma Ramotswe. She is happy in the home you have given her. That is a good thing.'

Puso's teacher had a more mixed message for Mma Ramotswe. The boy's schoolwork was good enough, he said, but he had a tendency to daydream.

'He has always been like that,' said Mma Ramotswe. 'I try to snap him out of it, but it is a very big thing for him. I have asked him what he is thinking about and he says *nothing*. That is what all children say, I think. You ask them what they have been doing, and the answer is nothing. You ask them what they are talking about on the telephone and they tell you it is nothing. They are very busy with this nothing of theirs.'

The teacher nodded. He knew all about that.

'You cannot get inside their minds,' Mma Ramotswe continued. 'I can also see that he is daydreaming, but he will never admit it. He just sits there and smiles at you.'

'That is better than those children who sit there and frown at you, Mma,' mused the teacher. 'We have more and more of those, I'm afraid.'

After the meetings with the teachers, Mma Ramotswe made her way into the school hall, where the choirs were to perform. Puso's was on first, and she listened intently as they sang one of the songs that she remembered being taught as a girl, all those years ago, in Mochudi. Then Motholeli's choir came on and sang 'Shall We Gather By the River?' She knew that song, and liked it. *Soon we'll reach the shining river.* She closed her eyes. The voices of the children were pure; their hearts were pure. Some of them had already discovered how hard life could be; others had yet to do so and probably did not fully understand what the world could be. We wanted to protect them, she thought, of course we did, but we knew that we could not and they would have to deal with the disappointments and shocks of life as best they could. All we could do was to give them that one thing that they could use to protect themselves from all of that. At least we could do that. That thing was love, of course.

She stayed to the end, although some of the parents slipped out early. Then they travelled back to the house together, where they saw that Mr J. L. B. Matekoni was already at home and in the kitchen. Leaving the children to do their homework, Mma Ramotswe joined her husband. She was surprised to find him standing over the sink, a pot before him.

'What are you doing, Rra?'

He turned round almost guiltily.

'I am cooking the potatoes, Mma Ramotswe. I am helping you with the evening meal.'

She looked over his shoulder and into the pot. It was tricky to work out exactly what he was doing. 'What is happening inside this pot, Mr J. L. B. Matekoni?'

He shot her a puzzled glance. 'I thought we might have mashed potatoes. I know you like those.'

'I do. So you are mashing them now?'

He nodded. 'And it's rather hard work, Mma.'

'You're mashing them even before you have cooked them, Rra?'

He frowned. 'You cook them first?'

Mma Ramotswe reached around him and took the pan from his hands. It was half-filled with water in which fragments of raw potato floated morosely, like a soup. Very gently she poured the mixture down the drain. 'I will show you how to start with new ones,' she said. 'You cook the potatoes first and then you take them out and mash them up with butter and salt. That is how mashed potatoes are made, Rra.'

He turned away sheepishly. 'I was only trying to help, Mma.'

She felt a warm rush of affection for the man beside her. 'But of course you were, Rra. But I am quite happy to cook mashed potatoes. I do not mind.'

'I want to be a more modern husband, Mma.'

She nodded. 'That is a very good thing to want. I think you are quite modern enough, but even if that were not true, I think that you are something even better than that. You are a kind husband, Rra. That is the most important thing, I think. A husband may be very modern, but not kind. That is no good.'

He looked embarrassed. 'I actually went on a course,' he said. 'It was for husbands.'

Mma Ramotswe smiled. 'I know about that course, Rra. Everybody has been talking about it. But I didn't know you were going.'

'It was very ... very ...' He searched for the word. 'Frightening. It was frightening, Mma.'

'You don't have to go, Rra,' she said.

'No?'

'No. Not if you don't want to.'

'Then maybe I won't go any more. I will still try to be more modern, though.'

He sat down while she attended to the cooking of the potatoes. She poured him a beer from the fridge and they talked of what had happened to each of them that day. There was much to discuss. There was the story of the snake and Phuti's aunt. There was the account of the meeting with Mma Manchwe, an enemy who was not an enemy. There were the comments that the teachers had made and the songs that the choirs had sung. For his part, there were events at the garage: a gearbox restored, a braking system replaced, an invoice issued and a bill paid in full.

She sought his views on Mma Manchwe. Could she be lying? Mma Ramotswe wondered.

'No,' he said. 'She is innocent.'

'Why, Rra?'

'Because, in general, people are, Mma, unless there is good reason to suspect otherwise. Only in books and films are they not, Mma. In real life it is different, I think.'

The children ate first, so then, because the business of the potatoes had made it run late, husband and wife ate dinner alone. After they had finished, they went out into the garden as it was hot in the house and they wanted fresh air.

There was a wind coming up. They felt it on their skin; it was cooler than the air it replaced, and it bore on it the smell that they had been longing for so intensely – the smell of rain.

'It will be here soon,' he said. 'Later tonight, or maybe tomorrow morning.'

The rain came the following morning. The cool breeze of the previous evening had dropped away and the night had become almost unbearably hot as the humidity built up. By breakfast time both Mr J. L. B. Matekoni and Mma Ramotswe felt quite exhausted, although the day was just beginning.

'I think we should buy a bigger fridge,' said Mr J. L. B. Matekoni. 'Then you and I could sit in it, Mma Ramotswe. We could sit in it and drink iced tea all day.'

Mma Ramotswe fanned herself with an old copy of the *Botswana Daily News*. She imagined herself lying in the vegetable tray, perhaps, while Mr J. L. B. Matekoni leaned against the icebox. It would be a refreshing alternative to the heat.

'I know I'm going to have to work today,' she said. 'But I don't know how I shall manage it. And you in your garage ...'
She had given him a large electric fan, and that helped a bit, but the roof of Tlokweng Road Speedy Motors was made of tin and there was no insulation from the sun's rays. People talked about frying eggs on roofs like that. They were right – you could do it – but she thought that today the eggs would burn.

'I'll cope,' said Mr J. L. B. Matekoni. 'And the rains will definitely come. It'll cool down.'

By nine o'clock the first clouds had appeared in the sky. At first there was a darkening band of grey on the horizon, which became rapidly larger, filling the lower half of the sky and developing into great rounded masses, stacked high and angry. Grey became purple, and purple shaded into black, to be obscured suddenly by white veils of rain descending, fold upon fold, like great muslin curtains. There was thunder and distant forks of lightning joining sky to earth, the patter of the first drops, and then the steady roar of the downpour. There came the smell of laid dust, and then of lightning – the smell of electricity, if electricity had a smell. And finally the smell of rain, that watery scent that so lifted the heart of anybody who lived in a dry land.

All work stopped at the garage and in the agency. As the rain pelted down, thunderous on the tin roof of Tlokweng Road Speedy Motors, Mr J. L. B. Matekoni, along with Charlie and Fanwell, joined Mma Ramotswe in her office. She made tea earlier than usual, in case the storm led to a power cut that would prevent the kettle from being boiled.

Charlie was excited by the rain. 'You'll get more work coming in, boss,' he said. 'All those cars with water in the wrong place and refusing to start. Nice busy time for us!'

Mr J. L. B. Matekoni shook his head. 'The misfortunes of others are no cause for satisfaction, Charlie,' he said. 'You should never take pleasure in the mechanical problems of other people. I've told you that before.'

'Come on, boss,' said Charlie. 'If it weren't for people wrecking their cars, there wouldn't be enough work for us. Everybody knows that.'

Mr J. L. B. Matekoni stared at him in reproach, but Charlie, unrepentant, continued. 'Especially women, boss. If it weren't for all those women breaking their engines, then we wouldn't have much to do. We'd go hungry, boss – we really would.'

Mr J. L. B. Matekoni shook his head. 'That's nonsense, Charlie. Women drivers are more careful than men. Men wreck their cars more often than women do, I'm afraid.'

Charlie laughed. 'Good try, boss! But don't worry, you can tell it like it is now that Miss Ninety-seven Per Cent is off having babies.'

Fanwell looked awkward. 'I don't know, Charlie. Maybe—'

'And you don't have to worry either,' said Charlie. 'She can't hear you. You don't have to be frightened of somebody who can't hear you.' He paused, his face breaking into a broad, mischievous smile. 'I'm not afraid to say it: put me in the cab with a woman driver at the wheel and you'll see me hop out pretty smartly.'

It was at that moment, within a second or two of his finishing, that the lightning struck. It did not hit the roof of Tlokweng Road Speedy Motors, even though its corrugated tin must have been a tempting target; it came to earth a short distance away, striking a small acacia tree and splitting its trunk neatly in two. The impact of the bolt shook the walls of the office, rattling the metal filing cabinet and causing a pane of glass in the window above Mma Ramotswe's desk to crack. The clap of thunder that accompanied the strike rose briefly above the sound of the rain, and then died away. Now the steady sound of the falling rain asserted itself again.

Charlie stood quite still. He had dropped his mug of tea, and it lay shattered on the floor at his feet, steam rising from the spilled liquid.

Fanwell was staring at him. 'You see,' he said, half under his breath. 'You see.'

Charlie opened his mouth but no intelligible sound emerged. Mma Ramotswe watched him, amused; it was costing her a great effort not to laugh.

'Perhaps you should be a bit more careful of what you say, Charlie,' she said at last. 'You never know who's listening, do you?'

Again Charlie started to say something, but again no words came. Mma Ramotswe reflected that it would be a very good story to relay to Mma Makutsi, but now there was a broken mug to be picked up off the floor, a pool of tea to be mopped up, and a trip to be made to the office of the Master of the High Court, the custodian and enforcer of the wills of Botswana.

The storm lasted forty minutes or so, stopping even more abruptly than it had started with the sudden cessation of the rain. One moment the air was white with the dense curtains of falling water; the next the curtains had parted, revealing a transformed world. The earth and the objects upon it seemed to shine – as if polished. The shimmering heat was gone; the soil, once hard, was soft again, and breathed; the heat-exhausted leaves on the trees were revived, instantly restored to dark green by the water that had fallen upon them.

The mechanics returned to work, Mr J. L. B. Matekoni saying, 'Well, that's the rains arrived, but the cars are still waiting.'

And Mma Ramotswe, gathering up her keys and her notebook, said, 'Time for us to get back to work too.' She stopped. The others, leaving the room, did not notice, but she did. She had spoken as if Mma Makutsi were still there.

She looked at the desk that she had tidied herself when Mma Makutsi had first gone off. And she thought, I must do something. There is something I can do for her, and I must do it.

She went outside. The tiny white van had been washed by the downpour, and now stood sparkling and resplendent, as if some passing evangelist had chosen to baptise it, had sought to make it without sin. She smiled at the unexpected thought. It was the sort of thing that Mr J. L. B. Matekoni, with his tendency to speak of cars in human terms, might appreciate. He had once said cars had souls; well, perhaps he was right. Perhaps everything had a soul of sorts, which is what some people still believed – that the world all about us was endowed with life and with the very same spirit we saw within ourselves. It was only now, she thought, when we were finishing with the earth, using it up, that we were beginning to understand how right they were. Even Botswana, with all its air and its grasslands and its thorn trees and its brown-red earth, did not go on for ever.

They were big thoughts, and she knew that people had to think them. But for the moment, there was a more immediate task – the one of looking at Rra Edgar's will. It might not tell her much that she did not already know from Mma Sheba's account of the document, but Mma Makutsi was right in suggesting that she should look at it. Bless you, Mma Makutsi, she said to herself as she started the van and began to drive away. Bless you, and your shoes, and your baby, Itumelang Clovis Radiphuti, and that good husband of yours, and your ninety-seven per cent . . .

The woman who greeted her at the registry office was business-like.

'That name, Mma,' she said. 'Molapo. That is a common name. There are many people who die and are called that.'

Mma Ramotswe frowned. 'But do they all make wills?' she asked.

The official hesitated. 'There are many people who do not make wills. They are very foolish people, Mma.'

Mma Ramotswe was aware of the fact that the woman was staring at her in a way that was almost accusatory. She had no will herself; nor did Mr J. L. B. Matekoni. Most people, she thought, had no will. But did it really matter? Everything she had, such as it was, would go to Mr J. L. B. Matekoni, and everything he had would go to her – or so she assumed. And then she thought of the children. Motholeli and Puso were not related to her – as foster children they presumably had no legal claim, and yet surely they had every other sort of claim. Of course they did.

'I shall make a will,' she muttered.

The woman behind the desk looked pleased. 'That is a very good idea, Mma.' And then added hurriedly, 'Not that I am hoping that you will become late for a long time yet. But it is a very good idea and we always recommend it.'

Mma Ramotswe's positive attitude to wills seemed to clear the obstructions that she felt officials could naturally, almost instinctively, place before those who wanted help or information.

'Of course there are not many people called Molapo who become late and have wills,' the woman said. 'I shall be able to find it very quickly if you give me the year when this late person became late.'

'He has been late for less than a year,' said Mma Ramotswe. 'And, as I said, he is called Molapo. Edgar Molapo, although he might have had another Setswana first name – I do not know, Mma.'

The official thought this would not be a problem. 'And you are sure that the late Rra Molapo made a will?'

'I am sure of that, Mma. There is a lawyer, Mma Sheba, who has consulted me about some problem in the estate. She is handling all this.'

Mma Ramotswe might easily have missed the official's reaction to this had she not been looking directly at her when she spoke. As it was, she saw the tensing of muscles around the jaw and lips; sudden and transient, but enough to tell her that this woman did not like Mma Sheba.

'You must know her, Mma,' said Mma Ramotswe, keeping her voice even but watching closely.

The signs of animosity were still there, but the other woman was more guarded now, and that, thought Mma Ramotswe, may be because she thinks that I am an ally of Mma Sheba and she must be careful.

'Yes, I know her, Mma.' She rose from her chair. 'I shall get you that will now.'

It did not take long for her to return with the document,

bound with other documents into a large blue-backed binder. The front page of the deed had been stamped by the Master's office, and a series of dates and figures had been added to it in blue ink.

'You may have a copy,' said the official. 'Or you can read it here, Mma – also for a fee.'

Mma Ramotswe decided to read it where she stood, on the public side of a large government desk. It was not a long document – two and a half pages, most of which was in formal legal prose and of no interest to her. There was the instruction that the farm should go to Liso – described as 'my nephew, the son of my late brother' – and there was a generous financial legacy to 'my dear sister, who has been a support for me over the years'. But then, at the end of the document, was a clause she had not expected. The residue of the estate was to go to 'my good friend, Mma Sheba Kutso'.

Mma Ramotswe read this provision carefully, and then read it again. She looked at the official behind the desk, who was now watching her. 'What does "residue" mean in these documents?' she asked.

The official seemed pleased to be consulted. 'It means what is left over,' she said.

Mma Ramotswe pondered this. 'And if, let's say, somebody who is left something in a legacy becomes late before the person who makes the will—'

'The testator,' interjected the official. 'We call the person who makes the will the *testator.*'

'Yes, so let me get this right, Mma: if the person who has been left something in a will dies before the testator dies, then what happens to that thing?'

The other woman shrugged. 'It goes into the residue of the estate,' she said.

'I see,' said Mma Ramotswe. 'And the person who gets the residue in the will – that person gets the thing that couldn't go to the other person mentioned in the will because that other person—'

'Is late,' the official supplied. 'Yes. That is right, Mma. It is quite simple, you see. If you know what you are talking about, that is.' She paused, reaching for the folder of documents. 'Have you found out what you wanted to find out?'

'Maybe,' said Mma Ramotswe.

Chapter Fourteen

Washing the Feet of Another

She could not contain herself. Now that her vague suspicions about Mma Sheba had turned into actual knowledge – the proven fact that the lawyer stood to benefit from the Molapo estate – everything was changed. She wanted – she *needed* – to talk to somebody about this and, as she drove back to the office, she realised that the only person with whom she could discuss the afternoon's discovery, the only person who would truly understand the implications, was Mma Makutsi. She could talk to Mr J. L. B. Matekoni about it, of course, and he would listen courteously, as he always did; but for all his attentiveness, Mr J. L. B. Matekoni looked at situations as a man, and men, for all their merits, thought about things differently from the way women thought about them. And without wishing to belittle men whatsoever, Mma Ramotswe felt that on balance, just on balance, women often saw things that men might miss. So a man, considering this matter, might say, 'That Mma Sheba is simply accepting a gift from an old friend'; while a woman was far more likely to say, 'Well, well, she may be a lawyer but she's clearly used her female wiles to get that poor late man to leave her this so-called residue'. And what a residue it was: not merely a few scraps of otherwise unwanted property, bits and pieces left over when relatives had taken their pickings – as the term *residue* might imply – but the most valuable asset that Rra Edgar had possessed: his farm.

Halfway back to the office, while driving through a pool of storm water that had suddenly appeared at the edge of the road, she decided that she would not go back to the No. 1 Ladies' Detective Agency after all and would go instead to the Radiphuti house. Mma Makutsi would be bound to be in and would surely welcome a visit. She had confessed to Mma Ramotswe that staying at home with nobody to talk to could be tedious, and so the chance to discuss the Molapo case would be a welcome break. There was no doubt that motherhood was a great privilege, Mma Makutsi had said, but it could bring loneliness too.

Mma Ramotswe turned the van on to the track that led from the Radiphuti gate to the house some six hundred yards into the plot. Had she given the matter more thought, the possibility might have occurred to her that this track, recently created from the virgin bush and not properly flattened by grader and steamroller, might not be in a good condition to receive the heavy rain that had fallen a few hours ago. As it was, with her mind full of residues and legacies and the questions to which such matters gave rise, she did not think about mud at all until she had already encountered it and she felt the tiny white van sinking beneath her. For a few moments she allowed the wheels to turn as they sought purchase in the glutinous mass, but then she removed her foot from the accelerator lest the van should dig itself further in, perhaps even disappear altogether as vans were said to do in quicksand. There was no point in racing the engine of a mud-engulfed vehicle; she would have to be pulled out by a stronger, four-wheel-drive vehicle – Mr J. L. B. Matekoni's rescue truck, for example, or a friendly tractor.

She prepared to step out of the van. This was not the simple operation it normally was; as a traditionally built woman, Mma Ramotswe was accustomed to occasional issues of manoeuvrability in awkward spaces, but what greeted her now was something more daunting than that. What had been a track was now a river, a spreading delta indeed, of shimmering mud, stretching almost as far as the house itself. Here and there, tufts of grass and small shrubs made for tiny islands, but for the rest there was only a red-brown sea. She looked up at the sky. The Israelites had received help in crossing the Red Sea, she recalled, when an unseen hand had parted the waves; no such help would be forthcoming here.

She sighed again and removed her shoes. Then, holding one shoe in each hand as a tightrope walker might use weights to balance himself, she stepped into the mud.

From the veranda Mma Makutsi waved and shouted. Mma Ramotswe tried to make out what she was saying but could not hear her very well. So, taking a deep breath, she made her viscous way along the mud-locked path and into the yard. Her traditional build did not help, and she felt herself sinking deeper with every step. The mud was between her toes, and that was a strange sensation but not unpleasant.

Mma Makutsi came out to meet her. 'Mma, I was worried,' she said. 'I was going to phone Phuti to come and rescue you.'

'That would not have been necessary,' said Mma Ramotswe, surveying her mud-covered feet and ankles. 'There is nothing wrong with a little mud. Some people say it is very good for the skin, Mma.'

Mma Makutsi looked with concern at her employer's feet. 'It is good for the face,' she said. 'I have not heard it is good for the feet.' She frowned. 'But there are different views, Mma. There are always different views on these things.'

She invited Mma Ramotswe to sit on the parapet of the veranda while she went to collect a basin for her to wash her feet. When she returned, she was carrying a small towel, a bar of soap and a plastic basin filled with warm water.

'Let me wash them, Mma,' she said. 'You sit there, I'll wash your feet for you.'

Mma Ramotswe felt the warm embrace of the water and the slippery caress of the soap. The intimacy of the situation impressed itself upon her; that an old friend – and that was how she looked at Mma Makutsi – should do this for you was strangely moving. *Washing the feet of another*, she thought. She tried to remember whether any other friend had done this for her. She thought not; and she had not done it for another. People were used to doing these things for children – washing them, changing them, tending to their physicals needs – but one so easily forgot what it was to do this for another adult, or to have it done for you.

Over a cup of tea, Mma Ramotswe told Mma Makutsi what she had learned from the will. Mma Makutsi listened gravely, interrupting her guest only to fetch the baby, who had awoken from a sleep. The rest of the story was heard with Itumelang Clovis Radiphuti clasped to his mother's breast. Mma Ramotswe looked at the little head – so perfect, so untroubled by the world, so tiny. It was for this, exactly this, that people sought advantage over others, denied themselves, risked everything, and would, if pressed, even give their lives.

The baby finished his feed. 'So,' said Mma Makutsi. 'You know what I think, Mma?'

Mma Ramotswe said that she would very much like to find out. 'I have some ideas, Mma, but if you tell me yours, I shall have some more, I think.'

Mma Makutsi smiled. 'It is as if we were in the office,' she said.

Mma Ramotswe tried not to look sad. 'Yes.'

'The lawyer is using you,' said Mma Makutsi. 'She does not want to find out the truth about that young man on the farm.'

'That is what I thought,' said Mma Ramotswe.

'She is determined that he will not inherit the farm.'

Mma Ramotswe nodded. 'I think you are right.'

Mma Makutsi was silent for a few moments. 'The aunt knows about her brother's affair with the lawyer and does not approve.'

Mma Ramotswe was surprised that Mma Makutsi had drawn the same conclusion as she had. 'I thought exactly that, Mma,' she said. 'There is no evidence that they were having an affair, but I thought that.'

'It is the only thing one can think,' said Mma Makutsi. 'People don't leave legacies to their lawyers unless they are very friendly, Mma. I think we can assume that they were lovers.'

'And so?'

Mma Makutsi gently brushed away a fly that had settled on her baby's brow. 'The original Liso, the real Liso, can't be traced, for whatever reason. Or she did not bother to trace him. So she has substituted her own son. Every mother would like her son to inherit a farm. That hardly needs any discussion.'

'No.'

Mma Makutsi looked at Mma Ramotswe. 'We need to confirm that the boy who claims to be Liso is, in fact, the aunt's son. How should we do that, Mma?'

Mma Ramotswe noticed the use of the word *we*. Mma Makutsi was back. 'We go and see her, I suppose. We confront her with the truth and see how she reacts. People reveal themselves, Mma.'

'They do, Mma Ramotswe. You have always said that, and I have always thought you were right. You are right most of the time.'

'Thank you, Mma Makutsi – that is very kind of you. But sometimes I am wrong.'

'This is not one of those times, Mma. This is a very simple case, and you have solved it without any difficulty. This is what Mr Andersen would call an *open-and-shut case*, I believe.'

Mma Ramotswe now spoke hesitantly. 'When shall we go, Mma?'

Mma Makutsi seemed to take some time to prepare her answer. 'I have reached a decision,' she said eventually. 'I am coming back to work tomorrow morning.'

'Oh, Mma—'

Mma Makutsi raised a hand. 'No, Mma. It is the right decision. Perhaps I can bring Itumelang in for the first few days. We shall stay just a few hours for the first little while, and then we can work out a regime. I have my young woman here who is helping with the cooking and with the baby. She used to work for Phuti's parents before they became late. She looked after Phuti when he was a boy, you know.'

Mma Ramotswe could not stop herself imagining Phuti as a boy: she saw an ungainly little boy with spindly legs and a perplexed expression on his face. Beside him there appeared another child, a little girl with ribbons tied into her hair and childish, round glasses. It was the young Mma Makutsi. So that was what she looked like.

'I am sure that woman is very good, Mma,' said Mma Ramotswe. She wanted to rise from her chair and embrace her assistant. She wanted to say to her: We are back again in the team that has always worked so well. She wanted to say to her: You were only away for a very short time, Mma, but I've missed you so much; I've missed your odd remarks; I've missed your talking shoes; I've missed your going on and on about the Botswana Secretarial College; I've missed everything, Mma, everything. But she did not – she simply said what she said and smiled. For once again she sensed that our heart is not always able to say what it wants to say and frequently has to content itself with less.

The extraction of the tiny white van, now spattered brown with mud, was arranged by Mma Makutsi, who telephoned one of Phuti's men. He came round with a four-wheel-drive truck that pulled the van out of the mud with ease while the two women shouted encouragement from the veranda. After that, Mma Ramotswe decided not to go back to the office. She had left the *Back Sometime* notice on the door – the notice that she displayed when there was a chance that she might return that day but when there was also a chance that she would decide to do something impulsive. That often turned out to be a drive out to Mochudi, for no reason other than a desire to get back to the village where she had been brought up and which was, in a sense, her real home.

But it was not the prospect of a drive to Mochudi that made her choose not to go back to the No. 1 Ladies' Detective Agency that afternoon; rather, it was a sense of excitement and antici-pation, a feeling bordering on joy, about Mma Makutsi's return to work. Admittedly there was an aspect of this return that gave cause for concern – the bringing of Itumelang Clovis Radiphuti into the office might prove to be awkward – but any difficulties would no doubt be sorted out. People took babies everywhere, and babies seemed to be happy enough with such arrangements. And Mma Makutsi, surely, would be reasonably flexible if the baby proved to be too much of a distraction in the office. The important thing was that she would be around for at least a couple of hours each day, and that would make all the difference.

Mma Ramotswe wondered where Itumelang would be put. Mma Makutsi had mentioned a portable crib that could be brought in and set up near her desk. It was a good spot, as the light from the window was blocked by Mma Makutsi's own desk and so the baby would not get too hot. Of course, one of the drawers in the filing cabinet could be cleared out and he could be placed there on folded blankets ... It would be entirely appropriate if such a devotee of filing as Mma Makutsi were to place her baby there, under *BABIES* perhaps, or some other suitable category. She smiled. It was an absurd thought, but one never knew with Mma Makutsi, and stranger things had happened.

Determined not to return to the office, she was briefly tempted to drive over to see Mma Potokwani. She had not seen the matron for some time, and it would be pleasant to spend half an hour or so with her over a cup of tea and a slice of fruitcake. But then she remembered that she had to call in at the bank to deposit a cheque. She was not far from the Riverwalk now, where there was a branch of the bank, and she could go there before heading home and indulging in the luxury of a rest. The children would not be home until shortly after four and the house would be quiet. There were three or four magazines that had been passed on to her by her friend Mma Moffat, and she could page through these while lying on her bed, until sleep caught up with her and the magazines fell from her hand. It was exactly the sort of afternoon to which she liked to treat herself, and this was a perfect day for it. After her rest she could spend some time working in the garden now that the ground had been refreshed by the rain and was soft and receptive.

She parked the tiny white van at Riverwalk. A shopping cart had been left in a parking place, where an unwary driver might easily reverse into it. She started to wheel this cart out of harm's way, but what she saw lying on the bottom of the cart made her stop: there were several leaflets, the usual bright detritus – money-off coupons, a loud listing of cut-price tinned foods – and, strangely, what looked like a homemade notice with *Be Warned!* printed across the top in large letters.

Her curiosity was aroused. It is not easy to ignore a notice headed: *Be Warned!* Be warned about what? There were so many dangers in the world and always plenty of people warning you about them. It was difficult, she felt, to do anything without being warned by somebody about the dangers of whatever it was that you were about to do. Even walking was risky, especially while wearing the sort of high-heel shoes favoured by Mma Makutsi. It would be easy to find that a heel had become trapped – in a grid, for example, or a hole in the ground – and then you might be felled as surely as if somebody had come and chopped you down. And breathing had its dangers too: she remembered all those years ago in Mochudi being told by one of her classmates that she had almost lost a brother when he had breathed in a number of flying ants that had blocked his air passages. An unlikely story, perhaps, but one that lingered in the back of the mind.

She peered closer at the leaflet.

BE WARNED!

Yes, that means you! On no account venture into that place they call the Minor Adjustment Beauty Salon. Minor Adjustment? The major adjustment they make is to your purse – it will be much lighter after only a few minutes in that place. And what about your face? Bad news for your face. Many people are now having expensive medical treatment to undo the damage that this so-called beauty salon has caused. Be warned! Be careful! Don't let vanity lead you into something you will always regret!

Mma Ramotswe read this text with horror. She looked for a signature, some sign of authorship, but there was none. All that was written at the bottom of the leaflet was: *This message is brought to you by one who cares.*

She felt her heart racing with outrage. *One who cares* was clearly one and the same person who had been spreading the rumour about somebody's face coming off in the salon. This had all the signs of an organised campaign, and a vituperative one at that.

Abandoning the shopping cart in a safe corner, Mma Ramotswe made her way as quickly as she could to the Minor Adjustment Beauty Salon. The door was open and she saw Mma Soleti inside with another woman. When Mma Ramotswe entered the salon, Mma Soleti turned round. Mma Ramotswe could tell immediately that she knew about the leaflet and its contents.

'Mma,' said Mma Ramotswe. 'This is very bad.'

'Yes,' said Mma Soleti. 'It is the end, Mma. The end.'

The woman who was with her, an older woman, reached out and took Mma Soleti's hand. 'No, Mma. You must not give up.'

Mma Soleti introduced her companion. 'This is my cousin,' she said. 'She found one of those leaflets on the windscreen of her car. She had parked it in the car park and when she came back she found the leaflet there.'

'This person is a criminal,' said the cousin. 'There is only one word for it: criminal.' She paused. 'You must find her.'

Mma Ramotswe assured her that she would do her best. 'But it is difficult, Mma. Anonymous letters and anonymous leaflets are often very hard to deal with. They are written by cowards who hide away under rocks. It is not easy to find them.'

'I am finished now,' said Mma Soleti. 'Nobody is coming to my salon. How will I pay the rent? This place is expensive.'

The cousin looked expectantly at Mma Ramotswe. 'You must find these wicked people, Mma. Please.'

Mma Ramotswe inclined her head slightly – a tiny gesture, but one that signified that she accepted responsibility. If there was any point to being a private detective, then surely it was to sort out cases of this sort, to protect people from bullying and malice, to put a stop to the coursing of poison through the veins of the community. She would do it.

Chapter Fifteen

Like a Tiny Spark Plug

Itumelang Clovis Radiphuti behaved impeccably on his first morning in the No. 1 Ladies' Detective Agency.

'He is not a colicky baby,' said Mma Makutsi as she settled him in his portable crib. 'He is happy lying there and thinking. He will not disturb us, Mma.'

Mma Ramotswe smiled. 'I am not sure if they think very much at that age, Mma. Later, maybe, but not when they are very young.'

Mma Makutsi disagreed. 'No, Mma. Itumelang is always thinking. I can see it in his eyes. He does this with his eyes. This sort of thing. See? Thinking, thinking.'

Mma Makutsi demonstrated, opening her eyes wide as if in astonishment.

Mma Ramotswe raised an eyebrow. 'I think that he is probably trying to focus,' she ventured. 'Tiny babies don't see far—'

Her suggestion was cut short by Mma Makutsi. 'He is definitely thinking, Mma,' she said severely. 'There is no doubt in my mind about that.'

Mma Ramotswe knew better than to argue with Mma Makutsi when her assistant was sure of something, as she manifestly was now. 'Well, there you are,' she said. 'It is much better for a baby to be thinking than crying.' She did not want any arguments on this most auspicious of days: the day of Mma Makutsi's return to work.

'What has been happening just lately?' asked Mma Makutsi, settling herself down at her desk.

Mma Ramotswe had made a list of matters on which she needed to brief her assistant. There were a number of enquiries from potential new clients. Mma Makutsi usually wrote those replies, as she had a persuasive turn of phrase that often translated a tentative approach into a firm contract. There were also bills to be paid – another task that Mma Makutsi always coordinated and Mma Ramotswe had let slip a little in her absence.

But whatever background tasks awaited her, the two issues that most interested Mma Makutsi were the Soleti and Molapo affairs. These were both investigations with an intense human-interest dimension, and that aspect always intrigued Mma Makutsi.

As Mma Ramotswe told her about the leaflet, Mma Makutsi's expression clouded over. 'Where is the leaflet in question?' she asked.

Mma Ramotswe reached into her bag and withdrew the copy she had picked up at Riverwalk the day before. Mma Makutsi unfolded it and read the message in silence. After she had finished, she put it down on her desk and stared at it.

'There is no clue as to who wrote it,' said Mma Ramotswe from behind her own desk. 'That bit at the bottom of the page about a concerned person is nonsense, don't you think?'

Mma Makutsi did not reply. She was still staring intently at the page.

'And there is nothing else,' said Mma Ramotswe after a while. 'I cannot see that we have anything else to go on.'

Mma Makutsi now looked up. 'This is not printed, Mma,' she said, holding up the piece of paper as one might a soiled rag. 'This is photocopied.'

Mma Ramotswe nodded. 'It is very easy to photocopy these things.'

'If you have a machine,' said Mma Makutsi. 'And many people do not have one.'

'No ...'

'So,' Mma Makutsi went on, 'if you do not have a machine, you go to one of those places where they photocopy things cheaply. Such as ...'

'Clear Image Copies,' said Mma Ramotswe.

Mma Makutsi adjusted her glasses. 'Do you have that leaflet that woman at Clear Image gave us, Mma? Daisy Something-or-other.'

'Daisy Manchwe.'

Mma Ramotswe rifled through the papers on her desk and extracted Mma Manchwe's price sheet. Rising from her desk, she passed it to Mma Makutsi. She could see where this was going, and it excited her. The first step from having nothing to having something, even if not much, was always thrilling.

Mma Makutsi laid the two pieces of paper out beside one another. Then, reaching into her desk drawer, she fished out a large magnifying glass. Mma Ramotswe remembered when she had bought this, on the recommendation of Clovis Andersen in a chapter entitled: 'What the investigator must always have by his side'. This glass, though, had never had occasion to be used – before this occasion.

Mma Makutsi bent forward to get a closer view. Then, lifting her head very slowly, she addressed Mma Ramotswe. Her tone was perfectly even. 'They were copied on the same machine, Mma.'

Mma Ramotswe crossed to her desk and peered over her shoulder.

'You see, Mma,' explained Mma Makutsi. 'Down the side of this leaflet there is that wavy black mark. And down the side of this one here – exactly the same wavy black line. I believe these things are caused by some impurity on the ink cartridge, or on the mirror inside the machine, or something like that.'

Mma Ramotswe saw what she meant. 'That is amazing, Mma,' she said. 'That is detective work of the highest order.'

Mma Makutsi gave a modest shrug. 'It is knowing what to look for,' she said. 'That is all. I'm sure you would have seen the same thing when you started to look for it.'

'*If* I started to look for it,' Mma Ramotswe corrected. 'I'm not sure that I would have thought of that, Mma.'

'You would,' said Mma Makutsi. 'You have always thought of these things, Mma. So I am sure you would have thought of doing this.'

Mma Ramotswe returned to her desk. 'What now, Mma?'

'We go to see our friend, Daisy Manchwe, and we present her with the evidence. That is what we must do, Mma Ramotswe.'

'And then?'

'That is for you to decide, Mma,' said Mma Makutsi. 'Remember: I am only an associate detective.' She smiled sweetly. 'If I were a *principal* detective, then no doubt I would be able to suggest what we should do. But . . . ' The smile changed to a look of slight reproach. 'But I am not that, of course.'

And what about us, boss?

They both gave a start. Mma Ramotswe imagined that she had heard something, a high-pitched, thin voice, rather what one would imagine a bird would sound like if a bird were to talk. But she was not sure. And nor was Mma Makutsi, although she looked down furtively and shifted her feet.

They decided not to go immediately, but to make the trip after lunch. This would enable Mma Makutsi to accompany Mma Ramotswe, having first taken the baby back to the house to be looked after by the nurse. It would also enable Mma Makutsi to attend to the filing that she felt had been badly overlooked. As papers were unearthed, quickly read to assess their content and then placed in carefully separated pending files, Mma Makutsi uttered the occasional *tut, tut!* accompanied by a shake of the head that was at the same time both approving and disapproving.

By the time they were ready to have morning tea – the second (official) cup of morning tea – the office was looking distinctly more organised. It was not that Mma Ramotswe was untidy – she was not – it was just that Mma Makutsi's standards were so high. She had a habit of expressing these standards in terms of an aphorism: *An unfiled piece of paper is a lost piece of paper*, or *Dust settles thickest on unfinished work*, or *Never leave your desk at night with a sheet of paper on it: sheets are for beds, not for desks*.

Mr J. L. B. Matekoni came in for tea first. He noticed the difference and smiled. He knew that Mma Ramotswe had been missing Mma Makutsi, and he was pleased to see them together again. Somehow, he thought, the No. 1 Ladies' Detective Agency without Mma Makutsi was like ... He searched his mind for a suitable comparison, and came up with *like a car with only one gear*. It was a mechanical analogy, but so were all of his analogies and they served him well.

Mma Makutsi was back in charge of tea. Within a few minutes she had prepared a steaming mug for Mr J. L. B. Matekoni, of precisely the right strength (halfway between weak and strong, but slightly tilted towards the strong), and with precisely the right amount of sugar (one and two-thirds spoonfuls, stirred, but not too much). For Mma Ramotswe she made the usual redbush tea, which, again, she made according to a method that she knew would please the other woman. This involved leaving the tea to infuse until the aroma of the tea reached the nose when it was placed a hand's-breadth-and-a-half above the open teapot.

When Charlie and Fanwell came in, they were both surprised to see Mma Makutsi.

'So!' exclaimed Charlie. 'So you're back, Mma! Nice holiday then?'

Mma Makutsi flashed him a warning glance. 'I'd like to see you in a maternity ward,' she said. 'If that's your idea of a holiday ...'

'I'm sure it isn't,' said Mma Ramotswe pleasantly. 'And have you met Itumelang Clovis Radiphuti, Charlie?'

Charlie made a face. He had not yet seen the crib behind Mma Makutsi's desk. 'Itumelang What's-his-face?' he asked.

'He is Mma Makutsi's baby – and he is in that crib.'

Charlie took a step to the side and craned his neck. He gave a start. 'Your baby, Mma Makutsi?'

'Yes, you can look at him,' said Mma Makutsi. 'But don't touch him. I don't want him covered in greasy fingerprints. And I don't want him to pick up any of your language, Charlie – so watch your tongue.'

Charlie crept forward, followed by Fanwell. 'Ow!' he muttered under his breath. 'Look at him!'

Fanwell smiled at Mma Makutsi. 'It is a very fine baby, Mma. Well done!'

Mma Makutsi acknowledged the compliment. 'Thank you, Fanwell,' she said, and glanced at Charlie.

'Oh yes, Mma,' whispered Charlie. 'This is a wonderful baby. Look at his head.'

'What's wrong with his head?' snapped Mma Makutsi.

'But there is nothing wrong with his head, Mma,' replied Charlie. 'It's perfect. And look at his nose. It's like a tiny ... a tiny spark plug!'

Mma Makutsi hesitated, but decided that this was a compliment. 'Thank you, Charlie.'

Charlie got closer. 'Oh, he is so handsome, Mma Makutsi. He's a very nice baby.'

Now pride crept into Mma Makutsi's voice. 'Yes, Charlie, he is.'

'Not ninety-seven per cent, Mma – one hundred per cent!'

'That's very kind, Charlie. Phuti thinks so too. He said exactly that, for some reason.'

Charlie, who had been peering closely at the sleeping baby, now turned to Mma Makutsi. 'I think he's waking up, Mma,' he whispered. 'His little eyes are opening. See. Just like that. Tiny eyes.'

'He's due to wake up,' said Mma Makutsi.

Charlie looked at her pleadingly. 'Do you think, Mma ... Do you think ...'

'Think what, Charlie?'

He looked at his hands. 'Do you think that if I washed my hands – washed them properly – I could hold him? Not for long. Just a little bit.'

Mma Ramotswe thought that she had witnessed something important. 'I think you should let him, Mma,' she said to Mma Makutsi. 'And Fanwell too.'

Fanwell shook his head, and made a self-deprecatory gesture with his hands. 'Oh, not me, Mma. I'm always worried about dropping babies if somebody passes one to me. Not me.'

'I'm not,' said Charlie quickly. 'I won't drop him.'

Mma Makutsi thought for a moment before she said, 'Go and wash your hands, Charlie. Not a couple of seconds under the tap – wash them properly. Then you can pick him up.'

Charlie gave a low whoop of delight and left the room.

'I think he likes him,' said Fanwell.

A few minutes later, Charlie returned. 'See,' he said, showing his hands to Mma Makutsi. 'Totally clean.'

She nodded and rose from her chair. Itumelang was now quite awake, but silent, staring with interest at the ceiling. Very gently, Mma Makutsi picked him up. 'You hold him like this,' she said as she handed him to Charlie.

'Oh look, Mma,' said Charlie. 'Look at him!'

They all watched as the young man walked up and down the office, cooing to the baby in his arms. Mma Ramotswe caught Mr J. L. B. Matekoni's eye and she could tell that he was as surprised as any of them.

'I want to get married,' said Charlie when he handed Itumelang back to his mother. 'Then maybe I can have a baby as fine as yours, Mma.'

'Maybe,' said Mma Makutsi. 'But you'll have to find a nice girl first, Charlie. And that means a girl with the right sort of figure to have nice babies. Not one of your fashionable girls. Not one of those girls I've seen you with – they're not interested in babies, you know.'

Charlie was quick to agree. 'That is true, Mma. Those girls are . . . they're useless for these things.'

Mma Ramotswe laughed. 'Think very carefully about fatherhood, Charlie,' she said. 'You have to be sure that you are ready.'

'Oh, I'm ready, Mma,' said Charlie. 'When I see a baby like that, I know I'm ready.'

Mma Ramotswe was both amused and puzzled. She was amused by the young man's evident pleasure in holding the baby, and puzzled by the apparent change in his attitude. Not all that long ago, when he was suspected – wrongly, as it turned out – of being the father of a girlfriend's twins, he had been horrified by

213

the thought of being a father. Now, it seemed, the idea had become appealing. We change, she thought. A year or so can make a very big difference, especially if you are a young man.

Mma Makutsi looked at her watch. 'That's enough now,' she said. 'Itumelang needs his feed, and then Mma Ramotswe and I have some important work to do.' She clapped her hands peremptorily. 'Tea break over.'

Mma Ramotswe lowered her eyes. It had always been for her to say when the tea break started and when it ended; now it seemed that Mma Makutsi had taken that role upon herself. For a moment – the briefest of moments – she felt resentment, but it did not last, for of all the emotions and attitudes of which she was composed, resentment or envy surely had the smallest place. So rather than dwell on Mma Makutsi's assumptions, she reminded herself of her good fortune in having her assistant back. And with that, she felt that most exquisite, and regrettably rare, of pleasures – that of welcoming back one who has left your life. We cannot do that with late people, Mma Ramotswe thought, much as we would love to be able to do so, but we can do it with the living.

Mma Ramotswe spoke suddenly. The mechanics had left the room, and it was just Mma Makutsi, Itumelang and herself. She said, 'Mma Makutsi, thank you. Thank you for coming back.'

'That is quite all right, Mma,' said Mma Makutsi. 'I am very happy to be back at work.'

'And thank you for everything you have done for me – and for the No. 1 Ladies' Detective Agency. I don't know if I have ever thanked you for that – thanked you enough, that is.'

Mma Makutsi stared at Mma Ramotswe. 'You don't have to thank me, Mma. I'm the one who should thank you. You took me – a nothing girl from Bobonong – and gave me a job. You taught me everything. You showed me how to be ... myself.'

'You were always yourself,' said Mma Ramotswe. 'Right from the word go, you were yourself.'

Mma Makutsi shook her head. 'No, Mma, you showed me. So I should be thanking you.'

'Well, then,' said Mma Ramotswe. 'You're thanking me and I'm thanking you. We are both thanking one another.'

'Good,' said Mma Makutsi. 'But now, Mma, I think we should stop putting things off. We need to go to see Mma Manchwe.'

Mma Ramotswe thought, I'm not putting things off. But she did not say that. Instead, she said, 'Yes. Right now. Let's go, Mma.'

Mma Manchwe was behind her desk when they entered the premises of Clear Image Copies. She greeted them warmly.

'You've looked at my price list?' she said. 'What did I tell you? Nobody beats my prices.'

'Well, we did . . . ' began Mma Ramotswe.

She was interrupted by Mma Manchwe. 'So what did you want me to do? I can have documents designed, you know. I have a young man who designs for me.'

Mma Ramotswe reached into her bag and took out the leaflet headed *Be warned!* 'I suppose he designed this, did he?' she asked, handing it to her.

Mma Manchwe took a pair of reading glasses out of her pocket and put them on the end of her nose. 'What have we here?' she said, beginning to read. 'Be warned. Warned about what?'

As she read further down the document, her frown deepened. When she had finished, she handed the piece of paper back to Mma Ramotswe. 'I most certainly did not design that – or give it to anybody to be designed. That is what I call poison, Mma, and I will have nothing to do with it.'

Mma Ramotswe knew immediately that she was telling the truth. She might not have been able to say *why* she thought this;

it was one of those things one knew in a way that could not be explained. It was something to do with the voice; or to do with the voice and the face combined; or perhaps to do with the eyes.

Mma Makutsi stepped forward. 'Then why, Mma,' she began, 'was it copied on your machine?'

Mma Manchwe looked indignant. 'On my machine? I did not do that. And anyway, how can you possibly tell?'

Mma Makutsi was ready. 'This is the way we tell, Mma,' she said, producing the price list. 'I take it that you copied your own price list?'

She put the two pieces of paper on the table and pointed out the telltale mark. While Mma Manchwe studied it sullenly, Mma Ramotswe made a suggestion.

'I think that it might have been done by somebody else,' she said. 'Can you think of who else might have used your machine?'

Mma Manchwe looked up at the ceiling. 'I have an assistant who covers for me a few times a week. She might have done it for somebody. But then it would be entered in the book. We enter all our copying jobs in the book. I don't think I've seen the names of any new clients – just the usual ones.'

'Unless your assistant did it for somebody without entering it – for a friend, perhaps.'

'She is not allowed to do that,' said Mma Manchwe. 'I would fire her if she used the machine for private purposes.'

'But everybody does that,' said Mma Makutsi. 'Everybody uses their office photocopier for private copies.'

Mma Ramotswe asked who the assistant was.

'Most of the time she works in one of the shops at Riverwalk,' said Mma Manchwe. 'But she has two afternoons off a week, and that is when she works for me – and for a few other people too.'

Mma Ramotswe glanced at Mma Makutsi, and she returned the glance. Riverwalk was the vital clue, she felt.

'Which shop at Riverwalk, Mma?' Mma Ramotswe asked.

'There is a dress shop. I forget what it is called.'

'Botswana Elegance?' prompted Mma Makutsi.

'That's the one,' said Mma Manchwe. 'It belongs to that Sephotho woman.'

There was complete silence, which lasted a good two minutes. Then Mma Ramotswe spoke. 'Violet Sephotho?'

'That's the one,' said Mma Manchwe. 'I don't know her, but they say she's quite something.'

'There are many words for Violet Sephotho,' said Mma Makutsi. 'Something may be one of them, but there are many others.' She glared at Mma Manchwe. 'I shall not tell you what the other words are, Mma – I shall leave it up to your imagination.'

As they left, Mma Ramotswe heard Mma Makutsi muttering under her breath. 'Something, something. Fifty per cent – if that. Fifty per cent and there she is with her own dress shop. Fifty per cent.'

Mma Ramotswe suppressed a smile. 'You don't like that Violet Sephotho, do you?' she said.

It was enough to trigger the response. 'I do *not* like her,' Mma Makutsi said between clenched teeth. 'And here, once again, we find her behind a piece of despicable character assassination. It's typical of her, Mma. Absolutely typical.' She paused. 'But why would she do it – other than out of pure malice?'

Mma Ramotswe had been mulling over possibilities in her mind. 'I wonder if her lease is coming up for renewal,' she said. 'That would give her a reason to want that shop – the one that Mma Soleti managed to get hold of.'

'But how can we find out about it?'

'We phone one of the big property management agents. They always know what's happening. We ask them if they know of any suitable shops coming up on the market, preferably in Riverwalk. We tell them that we can pay very competitively.' She looked at Mma Makutsi and smiled. 'They, being eager to make a profit – as everybody is – will say, "As it happens, Mma, there is a shop coming up for renewal in Riverwalk and, if you're prepared to pay a bit of a premium, we might be able to ..."'

Which is exactly what they did say when Mma Ramotswe telephoned them later that day.

'Mma Makutsi,' she said, as she replaced the telephone in its cradle. 'We have our culprit. Violet Sephotho. We have her motive. I think that is clear enough.'

Mma Makutsi punched the air in delight. 'This time we have her!' she exclaimed. 'I've been waiting for this, Mma Ramotswe. Ever since those days at the Botswana Secretarial College when she laughed at me – mocked me, Mma Ramotswe, and said I would never get anywhere because I had difficult skin and came from Bobonong – ever since those days I have been waiting to expose her for what she is – a fifty per cent, if that, useless person—'

Mma Ramotswe held up a hand. 'Wait a moment, Mma Makutsi. We have not yet brought Violet Sephotho to justice. All we have done is discovered the person we think is behind the campaign against Mma Soleti.'

'But she can't wriggle out of it,' said Mma Makutsi. 'Not even Violet Sephotho can get away with this.'

Mma Ramotswe shook her head. 'Unfortunately, Mma, the world is full of people who have wriggled out of things. It is a very, very wriggly place.' She paused before adding, 'That is well known, Mma, I'm sorry to say.'

Chapter Sixteen

That is Not How You
Treat a Sausage

Mma Makutsi did not appear in the offices of the No. 1
Ladies' Detective Agency on Monday, as she had to take
Itumelang to the baby clinic. 'There is nothing wrong with him,
Mma,' she reassured Mma Ramotswe over the telephone. 'They
want to check that he is putting on weight. And he is, Mma. He
is getting heavier and heavier.'

'That is good,' said Mma Ramotswe. 'A fat baby is a happy
baby.'

There was silence at the other end of the line. 'I did not say
that he is *fat*, Mma. I said that he is putting on weight. That is
different.'

Mma Ramotswe was quick to assure her assistant that she did
not think of Itumelang as being fat; she had merely pointed out

that there were at least *some* fat babies, and these fat babies tended to be happy.

This conversation was overheard by Mr J. L. B. Matekoni, who was in the room at the time. 'But he is definitely a fat child,' he said. 'I saw her pick him up and I saw how fat he is. He's a very fat baby, Mma.'

Mma Ramotswe put her finger to her lips in the universal gesture of silence, and of tact. 'Perhaps it would be best if we did not mention that,' she said. 'You know how Mma Makutsi is, Rra. I think, though, he seems a bit greedy. And when she says that he's thinking . . . '

'He's thinking of food?' said Mr J. L. B. Matekoni.

They left the matter at that, and Mma Ramotswe, now faced with a clear desk – thanks to Mma Makutsi's filing blitz of the previous day – contemplated how she would spend that morning. Although they had made great strides in the resolution of Mma Soleti's problem, she still had the Molapo case to sort out, and she felt that this was going to be rather more challenging. She had, of course, discussed the matter with Mma Makutsi, but that discussion, helpful though it had been in terms of clarifying the issues, had far from solved them.

She looked out of the window. Sometimes it was important simply to get out. It did not matter where you went, as long as you got out of the office, or the kitchen, or any other place where duty required you to be, and went to some place that you did not *have* to be. So she did not *have* to be in Mochudi, or in her garden, or on the veranda of the President Hotel. If she were in any of these places it would be because she had chosen to be standing at the top of the hill in Mochudi looking down over the village and hearing the sound of the cattle bells; or tending a plant that needed moving from one spot to another so as to get the benefit of a patch of shade; or simply drinking tea in the presence of others who were doing the same thing. The thought of tea quite naturally led to the thought of cake, and that in turn led to a mental picture of Mma Potokwani standing on the step of her office, smiling and calling out, 'Well, Mma Ramotswe, this is a well-timed visit! I have just baked a new cake and I was wondering whether you might like a piece.' And she would reply, 'Well, Mma Potokwani, it is funny that you should mention cake when I happened to be thinking of exactly that thing.'

The decision was made. Since she was not making much progress on the Molapo case by sitting in the office, she might as well pay a visit to the orphan farm to see how the matron was doing. This could count as work – just – if she viewed the visit as an opportunity to get from Mma Potokwani those little snippets of news – inconsequential in isolation, but when put together providing a useful overall picture of what was happening in the town. Or, perhaps more honestly, it could count as a purely social pleasure, an hour or two of simple friendship and chat of the sort that we all needed from time to time. And being a detective did not mean that you were above all those simple human needs. Indeed, there were occasions when you needed them more than people in jobs did, where things were somehow simpler. Most jobs, thought Mma Ramotswe.

Before she left, she went into the garage to tell Mr J. L. B. Matekoni where she was going and to ask him what he favoured for his dinner that night. The question about dinner seemed to trouble him, and he took some time to answer.

'I am always happy with whatever you give me, Mma – you know that.'

She smiled at him. 'That is very kind, Rra, but it is still possible for you to say I like this thing rather than that thing. Or I like potatoes a bit more than I like rice. That sort of comment does not make a cook feel bad. It is not the same as saying "I do not like your rice". It is simply saying that you like potatoes a bit more.'

He put down the spanner he was holding. 'Perhaps I should cook for you, Mma. I could cook something like ... '

It was not her visible astonishment that made him falter; it was more the realisation that he had no idea at all as to what he could make for a meal. But then, after a pause, he blurted out, 'Sausages, Mma. I could cook sausages. And make some beans to go with them. Those red beans that grow in tins ... '

She laughed. 'Baked beans? The ones with tomato sauce?'

'Yes, those beans.'

She did not want to discourage him. 'The children would like those,' she said. 'Especially Puso. He could live on those beans.'

He looked relieved that his suggestion had met with approval. 'I could cook for all of us,' he said.

She said that this would be a very good idea; but did he have time?

'There is no problem with time,' he said. And then, rather anxiously, asked, 'How long does a sausage take to cook, Mma? Half an hour?'

'No, Rra. A sausage cooks in a shorter time than that. Half an hour would burn most sausages.'

'You boil them for fifteen minutes? Is that it?'

She was gentle. 'You do not boil sausages, Rra. That is not how you treat a sausage. You put it in a frying pan and you fry it. Or you can put it under the grill and grill it. These are both very good things to do to a sausage.' She paused. 'But why don't you let me show you, Rra? We can cook sausages together and then you will know next time.'

Charlie, half under a car, had been listening to this. 'They'll be offering you a job at the Grand Palm Hotel, boss. Guest chef this week: Mr J. L. B. Matekoni, formerly of Tlokweng Road Speedy

Motors, now cooking full-time. Try his famous signature dish, everybody: sausages and baked beans. They're talking about this new dish over in Johannesburg, Cape Town, everywhere. Talking about it, maybe, but not eating it.'

Mma Ramotswe peered under the car. 'And you, Charlie, can you cook anything at all?'

Charlie chuckled. 'That is women's work, Mma. I do not want to take work from women. That would not be kind.'

Mma Ramotswe shook her finger at him playfully. 'I shall tell Mma Makutsi that, Charlie. She will be speaking to you when she comes in tomorrow.'

She turned to Mr J. L. B. Matekoni. 'I shall get the sausages on the way back from Mma Potokwani's. I am going to visit her now.'

He looked at her with interest. 'Could you tell her something, Mma?'

'Of course.'

'Tell her that I'm going to be learning how to cook sausages. Please tell her that.'

'And beans, boss,' Charlie called out from beneath the car. 'Don't forget the beans.'

Mma Potokwani had spotted Mma Ramotswe's arrival and, as her friend got out of her van to stretch her legs, she called out, 'Well, Mma Ramotswe, this is well timed! I've just baked a cake, as it happens, and I wondered . . .'

'Whether I would like a piece? I think I would, Mma Potokwani.'

It was an exchange they had had countless times before – one of those rituals between friends that never change very much yet never seem to grow stale. And these words, of course, were a prelude to others that had been uttered many times and yet were equally valued, as much for their familiarity as for anything else:

enquiries about health; remarks about the rain, or lack of rain; observations on the state of the roads, of the country, of Africa, of the world. Among old friends the agenda can be a wide one, even if we know what they are likely to say and have heard it all before.

Mma Ramotswe accompanied Mma Potokwani into the office. It was a room that she particularly liked because of its clear association with children. There were children's drawings on the wall alongside group photographs; there were boxes of battered toys donated by schools for more fortunate children; there were recipe books and accounts and bottles of those curious iron tonics that Mma Potokwani thought of as a panacea for all the ills of childhood.

Cake was produced. 'A new recipe,' Mma Potokwani announced. 'More sultanas.'

Mma Ramotswe loved sultanas and was urged to take two large pieces so that the tin need not be opened again. 'I like to keep air out,' said Mma Potokwani. 'Air can make a cake go stale very quickly.'

As they set about the serious business of tackling the cake, they exchanged day-to-day news. Mma Potokwani's husband had developed a frozen shoulder and was finding it difficult to drive. Mma Ramotswe remembered having this problem herself many years previously and said it had taken a long time to get better. Mma Potokwani then asked after Mma Makutsi's baby and was told about the disagreement with the aunt about the proper time at which to expose a baby to visits from others.

'I am very much in favour of the modern approach,' she said. 'One or two of the housemothers here, though, are very conservative about these things.'

They moved on to the latest price increases, and from there they went on to the issue of traffic jams. There would have to be more roads, they concluded, but roads cost money.

'Everything costs money,' said Mma Potokwani. 'That's why people borrow so much.'

Mma Ramotswe agreed that this was a problem. 'And yet there are people who say that we shouldn't worry about borrowing,' she said. 'I do not understand how you can borrow to get out of debt.'

'You cannot,' said Mma Potokwani. 'You cannot get uphill by walking downhill.'

'Or downhill by walking uphill,' suggested Mma Ramotswe.

Mma Potokwani, whose mouth was full of cake at the time that this observation was made, simply nodded. There are times when it is better to concentrate on the cake in one's mouth than to contribute to a debate.

There was then a short silence before Mma Ramotswe spoke again. 'I have been to see some people called Molapo,' she said. 'Do you know that family, Mma?'

Mma Potokwani brushed a few fragments of cake from her lips. 'It is a common name, Mma. I have known some people called that. There are some Molapos at Kanye, I think. I met them a long time ago.'

'This family has a farm not far from the Gaborone Dam,' Mma Ramotswe said. 'They have been there for a long time.'

Mma Potokwani gave a nod of recognition. 'Oh yes, I have heard of those people. The old man was a politician, I think.'

'He was. Yes, that's the family.'

'I have never met them,' said Mma Potokwani. She took a small fragment of fruitcake from her plate – she was down to crumbs now. 'But one of the housemothers here worked for them, I believe. She was with them for years before she came here.'

Mma Ramotswe was instantly alert. 'Worked in the house?'

'Yes. She was the cook at the farmhouse. I seem to remember

her saying that they were good employers, but she wanted to move closer to town because her daughter and her grandchildren are in Gaborone.'

Mma Ramotswe replied that this was understandable, but her mind was elsewhere. She wanted to talk to this woman; would that be possible?

'We can go and see her,' said Mma Potokwani. 'The house-mothers are usually in the houses doing some cooking or keeping the place tidy. If she isn't there, she won't be far away.'

They finished their tea. The cake, Mma Ramotswe pronounced, was very much better for the additional sultanas and she ventured to suggest that even more might be added to good effect. Mma Potokwani considered this possibility and said that she would try. 'There will be a limit, though,' she pointed out. 'A fruitcake must have some other fruit, not just sultanas, otherwise it becomes a sultana cake.'

They left the office and walked a short distance to one of the ten small houses that made up the children's home. These houses were dotted about under the shade of large jacaranda trees from the limbs of which here and there hung a child's swing. The lower boughs, bending under their own weight towards the ground, were clearly accustomed to being climbed upon by children, their bark scuffed here, polished there, by the limbs of young climbers. I used to climb trees, thought Mma Ramotswe. I used to climb trees and sit there for hours, watching. She smiled as the memory came back of the tree behind the school that they had all climbed until somebody fell out and broke a leg and the practice was banned. They had moved to other trees.

Mma Potokwani called out as they approached the small, well-swept veranda of the house: '*Ko, ko! Ko, ko!*'

The main door of the house was invitingly open; inside, another door slammed and the housemother emerged, a kitchen cloth in her hand. She greeted the matron respectfully before turning to Mma Ramotswe and greeting her too.

'This is Mmamodise,' said Mma Potokwani. 'She is the house-mother I told you about.'

Mmamodise gestured for them to go inside. 'I have been cooking for the children,' she said. 'But everything is in the oven now.'

'It smells very good,' said Mma Ramotswe. And she suddenly remembered the sausages for Mr J. L. B. Matekoni. She must buy those on the way home.

'The children in this house eat well,' said Mma Potokwani with a smile. 'They do not know how lucky they are, having one of the best cooks in Botswana as their housemother. They are all ... well-built children.'

Mmamodise turned to Mma Ramotswe. 'They are always hungry, Mma. Children, and men too, are always hungry.'

'That is true,' said Mma Ramotswe, looking about the room into which Mmamodise had led them. She noticed the red concrete floor, so highly polished that it shone; she noticed the yellow curtains that looked as if they had been ironed; she saw the framed portrait high on the wall (almost too high, she thought, for the children to see it), of a young President Khama with the coat of arms of Botswana, that lovely emblem with its zebra supporter, reminding one of what it meant to be part of this country they all loved so much – a country that had tried to lead a good life and, she thought, had succeeded.

The picture gave her an idea. 'You used to work with the Molapo family, I hear, Mma,' she began. She looked up at the picture. 'I believe that the old man, the father of Rra Edgar, worked in the government with Seretse Khama.'

Mmamodise nodded. 'That is so, Mma. He was a good friend of Seretse Khama. I saw him come to the house many times. They would talk and talk.'

Mma Ramotswe encouraged her. 'I saw him too – in Mochudi. My father did not know him, but he met him once and he talked to him about cattle.'

At first, Mmamodise had nothing to add to this, but then, appearing to realise that some comment was required from her, she said, 'Those days are in the past now, Mma.'

'Yes, of course,' said Mma Ramotswe. 'We live in the present day, but the past ... the past is still there, I think, Mma.' She paused. Mma Potokwani was staring at the ceiling thoughtfully. 'You know that Rra Edgar is now late, Mma? You know that, I assume?'

Mmamodise did know that. 'I was at the funeral, Mma. There were many, many people. He was well known throughout the country; maybe because of his father, but still well known.'

'And now the sister is living on the farm,' prompted Mma Ramotswe.

'Yes, she has been there for some time. Rra Edgar built her a house. I don't think that she liked it very much. She always said it was too hot.'

'That might be the country, not the house.'

The two of them laughed. Mma Potokwani was still gazing at the ceiling, apparently lost in her own thoughts.

Mma Ramotswe clasped her hands together. 'Now the farm is going to go to the nephew – to Liso.'

She watched Mmamodise as she spoke and saw immediately that what she said triggered a response. It was almost imperceptible, but it was there. A tiny electric wire, a filament, had touched a nerve and made a connection.

'That is good,' said Mmamodise. 'I have not seen that boy for many years, but I remember him. He was a very good boy.'

'He spent his holidays on the farm?'

'Yes, he did. He was there a lot. He was very helpful with the

228

farm work, and he used to help me, too. He was very keen on peeling potatoes. He had a penknife that he used for everything, including for peeling potatoes.'

'So you're pleased that he is getting the farm?'

There was a slight hesitation, so Mma Ramotswe decided to probe. 'You feel a bit doubtful, Mma?'

Mmamodise reacted quickly and defensively. 'I am not doubtful, Mma. He is a good boy – I told you that.'

Mma Ramotswe decided that if Mmamodise knew anything, she was not going to reveal it in the course of an informal conversation.

'Mmamodise, I'll tell you why I'm interested in this. It is because there is somebody – a lawyer – who thinks that Liso is not who he claims to be. She thinks he is another boy altogether.'

The effect of this showed even before Mma Ramotswe had finished speaking. Mmamodise clapped a hand to her mouth. 'Oh,' she said. 'Oh! So they know.'

Now it was Mma Ramotswe who hesitated. *Let somebody think you know what you don't know*, Clovis Andersen had written. *Then it will all come out.* But should she apply that technique – that trick – to this good woman, this kind and conscientious housemother?

She did not have to answer her own question, as Mmamodise continued of her own accord. 'I knew all about it, Mma. I knew because I was living in that house, and you hear things. But I never spoke to anybody about it – never.'

'That is very good of you, Mma. But now ...'

'Now everybody is talking about it, you say.'

'I didn't say that, Mma. I said that a lawyer had asked me to look into it.'

Mmamodise was anguished. 'It is not his fault. How can it be a child's fault?'

'It is never the child's fault,' said Mma Ramotswe, wondering what fault was being talked about. 'It is always the fault of the adults.'

'But sometimes it isn't the mother's fault,' said Mmamodise.

'No, that is true. The mother is not always to blame.'

'She was very young.'

Mma Ramotswe wondered who: the aunt? 'Rra Edgar's sister?'

The answer Mmamodise gave was crucial, and it was a single word. 'Yes.'

'She is the mother of Liso.'

A nod of the head confirmed that. 'When they discovered that she was pregnant,' Mmamodise continued, 'they sent her up to Francistown to get her as far away as possible. They did not want the child to be born on the farm.'

Mma Ramotswe thought quickly. 'And then they sent the boy to Swaziland?'

Mmamodise shook her head. 'No, he stayed in Botswana. He never went to Swaziland. There was a boy in Swaziland – he was the son of Rra Edgar's brother, the one he had fought with. Nobody here ever met that boy. He was killed in the accident that killed his father, but nobody ever told Rra Edgar that. His sister kept it from him. He thought his nephew in Swaziland was still alive.'

'Of course.'

'Later on, Rra Edgar's sister told Rra Edgar that she had heard from the mother of that boy, their nephew, in Swaziland and he was coming to visit them. He was very pleased with that, and he was happy when a boy called Liso arrived. But it was not the son of his brother he was meeting. Although he did not know it, he was meeting the son of his sister.'

'So where had this boy been?'

'After the old man – the father of Rra Edgar and his sister – had sent the sister away, her little boy had been kept up north with some people the old man knew. He paid them to look after this boy, because he was so ashamed of him. He never saw his grandson – not once.'

Mma Ramotswe now felt that she understood. She imagined the situation: the old man – the one who had been in politics – discovered that his teenage daughter was pregnant. Feeling ashamed and angry, he sent her up to the north of the country to have the baby, and the baby remained there in the care of others. After the old man's death, the daughter wanted to bring her little boy down to the farm but did not want, for whatever reason, to let her brother Edgar know that she had had a child; perhaps, once again, it was shame over the very early pregnancy. When she learned that the nephew in Swaziland, the second brother's child and the real nephew of both siblings, had died, she saw her chance and brought her own son down from the north, passing him off as the nephew, Liso. Because Rra Edgar had never met his nephew in Swaziland, he had no reason to doubt the identity of this Liso who came to stay. As far as he was concerned, this was the son of his brother.

Mma Ramotswe looked at Mmamodise. 'So this boy who is on the farm now – this Liso – came down to the farm because his mother was there? His real mother?'

'Yes. And his father.'

Mma Ramotswe was silent. She knew nothing of the father, but said, 'Of course.'

Mmamodise's expression suddenly became one of distaste. 'I am not saying that I approve of what happened. It was very bad. But you should not punish the boy.'

'The father ...'

'Rra Edgar.'

231

Mma Ramotswe stared at her. 'No, the father ... '

'Yes, that's right: Rra Edgar, the father.'

Mma Ramotswe gasped. Mma Potokwani, who had stopped looking at the ceiling, was staring incredulously at the house-mother.

'His sister,' muttered Mma Ramotswe.

'It was very shameful,' said Mmamodise. She frowned. 'But you knew this, Mma. This lawyer you mentioned knows all this?'

'We suspected something,' said Mma Ramotswe. 'I did not expect that.'

Mmamodise turned away. Her voice was trembling. 'I am very ashamed of myself. I thought you knew. Now I have told you something that should be kept very secret, Mma. I have spoiled that.'

'No, Mma,' said Mma Ramotswe. 'You did not do that deliberately. And I promise you, I shall not speak of this to anybody.' She turned to Mma Potokwani. 'And you will say the same, won't you, Mma Potokwani?'

Mma Potokwani nodded. 'I shall not speak of this either.'

Mmamodise seemed reassured. 'It was a terrible thing. I know about it because I was there when it happened. I was in the house and I heard the voices and all the crying. The old man was still alive and he said that this would kill him. I think it made his death come earlier.'

'Does the boy know?' asked Mma Ramotswe.

'He does not know. He thinks that his father is a man who worked on the farm and then left.'

There was another question for Mma Ramotswe to ask. 'And Rra Edgar? He knew?'

Mmamodise shook her head. She spoke with some embarrassment now and Mma Ramotswe understood; people like Mmamodise did not like talking about such matters. And she would not press her. Why should people not have their realms of privacy and reticence?

'When it happened, the old man did not want his son Edgar to know that he was becoming a father. It was too shameful. You see, Mma, what I heard was this: the girl confessed to her father that she had shared a blanket with the brother just once. That was all. I don't think that Rra Edgar ever knew that the consequence of what he had done was the sister's pregnancy. You see, Mma, I don't think any of them could face it.'

Mma Ramotswe nodded. She noticed that Mmamodise had used the old-fashioned expression – to share a blanket. It was how people spoke of these things.

'I see,' she said. She knew now. It was shame, and an understandable shame at that.

They sat in silence for a while; nobody seemed to want to say anything. The disclosure had been so powerful that Mma Ramotswe and Mma Potokwani were shocked into speechlessness. And for her part, Mmamodise was wrestling with guilt over having revealed the painful secret. Mma Ramotswe could tell that, and she reached over and touched the housemother on the arm.

'Do not be upset, Mma,' she whispered. 'What has happened has happened. The boy is not to blame. And now he will be getting something that will make up for it. That can happen in life, Mma, can't it? Things start badly – very badly – and then they change for the better and those who have nothing, or who are unhappy, or who live in fear, suddenly find that these things that were bad for them have gone.'

'It's like rain,' said Mma Potokwani, who had not said much but had clearly been affected by the story. 'The rains come and they wash everything away. The dryness, the thirst, the dust on your skin – these are washed away, Mma, all washed away.'

Chapter Seventeen

The Best Woman in Botswana

When he arrived in his carrycot at the No. 1 Ladies' Detective Agency the following morning, Itumelang Clovis Radiphuti was wearing a red baby outfit with a jaunty matching cap. Charlie wriggled out from under a car to greet him.

'I see you, my brother!' he shouted. 'I see you, Itumelang Cl . . .' He turned to Mma Makutsi. 'What's the rest of it, Mma?'

'Itumelang Clovis Radiphuti,' said Mma Makutsi obligingly. She usually addressed Charlie with a note of irritation in her voice, but now that he was showing such attachment to her son her tone was more forgiving.

'Itumelang Clovis Radiphuti,' repeated Charlie, reaching out to stroke him. 'A big, important name for a big, important young man!'

'Don't touch him, Charlie,' said Mma Makutsi, pointing at his hands. 'You're covered in grease.'

Charlie looked down at his hands, as if he would be surprised at the suggestion of grease. 'I have been thinking about him, Mma,' he said. 'I've been thinking that he could be a mechanic when he grows up. He could be my apprentice.'

Mma Makutsi's eyes widened. 'Your apprentice? But ...' She did not finish her sentence. She had been about to say that Charlie might not have finished his own apprenticeship in sixteen years' time. But she decided not to.

'Lovely boy,' Charlie crooned, looking admiringly at the baby. 'Who's the most handsome baby in Gaborone – in all Botswana? You are! Yes, you!'

Mma Makutsi smiled as she went into the office to put Itumelang into his office cot. This enthusiasm for babies on Charlie's part was most unexpected but very welcome. Of course, if it got out that Charlie was looking for a wife and was prepared to have a baby and *stay*, then there would be no shortage of suitable young women. Charlie might be trampled in the rush and go to the altar covered in sticking plasters where the girls had tried to grab hold of him. She smiled at the thought.

'Something funny, Mma Makutsi?'

Mma Ramotswe was already behind her desk, the day's newspaper spread out in front of her.

'I was thinking of Charlie,' said Mma Makutsi. 'He is very keen on Itumelang. I was thinking of how quickly Charlie would be snapped up if the girls heard that he was interested in marriage.'

'Very quickly, I'd say,' said Mma Ramotswe. 'For all his faults, Charlie is a very good-looking young man. And he's good fun to be with.'

'Within reason,' said Mma Makutsi.

Once Itumelang was settled, Mma Makutsi took her place at her desk and looked over the room towards Mma Ramotswe. They had business to discuss, and they launched straight into it. Mma Ramotswe, somewhat breathlessly, told Mma Makutsi about the events of the previous day and the unexpected breakthrough in the Molapo enquiry. She was shocked, just as Mma Ramotswe and Mma Potokwani had been, but saw how the whole thing now made sense.

'That is a dreadful story,' she said at the end of Mma Ramotswe's account. 'To think that such things happen.'

'Everything happens,' said Mma Ramotswe. 'Sooner or later, just about everything happens.'

'And that boy not knowing the truth,' said Mma Makutsi. 'There he is going through life not knowing who he really is.'

'He thinks he knows,' said Mma Ramotswe. 'And surely that's what counts. We need a story about ourselves, but does it really matter whether it is the true one or it has been made up? I wonder.'

'You mean, as long as we believe it ourselves?'

She had not thought it through, but she imagined that this was so. 'At the end of the day, Mma Makutsi, aren't we all the same? Aren't we simply people? Aren't we all distant cousins from long, long ago?'

'We all came from Africa,' said Mma Makutsi. 'It doesn't matter what the colour of our skin is; we're all from Africa originally. I have read that, Mma Ramotswe. There was an article about it in the paper. East Africa. That's where everyone comes from. Me, you, the King of Sweden.'

'The King of Sweden?'

'I choose him as an example,' said Mma Makutsi. 'I'm not saying that he had an African grandmother, but a long, long time ago his people would have been from Africa, same as everybody.'

Mma Ramotswe grinned. 'So there were these Swedens in Kenya – just ordinary farmers . . . '

'Cattle,' said Mma Makutsi. 'They had many cattle, those people over there. They wore long red cloaks and looked after their cattle. I have seen photographs.'

'And that Sweden family?'

'They were there too. And the Arabs. And the Jews. Everyone. No enemies in those days.'

Mma Ramotswe looked doubtful. 'I'm not so sure, Mma. I don't think human nature has changed. We have always been unkind to one another.'

'And good sometimes.'

'Yes, and good sometimes.'

Mma Ramotswe returned to the topic of Liso. 'The truth, Mma Makutsi, is that it doesn't matter in the slightest that that boy has a father who is also his uncle. We do not like things like that, but once it has happened it makes no difference to that boy himself. We must love him the same as we love everybody else. That is all there is to it.'

Mma Makutsi agreed. But she asked what this meant in practical terms. What were they going to say to Mma Sheba, who had asked them to investigate in the first place?

Mma Ramotswe took a deep breath. There were moments when one knew that a few words uttered could change somebody's life.

'We tell her that the boy on the farm is the boy Rra Edgar had in mind when he made the will. He is the person whom he wanted to inherit. That is very clear.'

'The will says that the farm must go to his nephew . . . '

'Who is late.'

Mma Makutsi was still concerned. 'Yes, but if the real Liso is late, then the farm goes to Mma Sheba. That is what the will says.

It says that the farm is to go to his nephew, Liso. We know that nephew is dead, and so the legacy cannot be executed. It goes into the residue.'

'Yes, but when he said "my nephew", he didn't mean his real nephew Liso, he meant his son, Liso,' said Mma Ramotswe. 'He meant the Liso he knew. The Liso who was his son, but who he thought was his nephew. That's what he wanted.'

'But would the courts agree with that?'

Mma Ramotswe was not sure. She wondered whether a court would try to work out what Rra Edgar had wanted. If they did that, then Liso – the Liso on the farm – would inherit. But the law was not always reasonable, and there might be reasons why a court might not try to work it out. It was best not to risk it, she thought.

'The right thing,' she said, 'is for Liso to get the farm. It is what Rra Edgar intended.'

Mma Makutsi was ready to be persuaded. 'And it's only fair too, don't you think, Mma? The farm is going to his child, as is right. We should do nothing to change that.'

'So we will not be lying to Mma Sheba if we tell her what I suggested,' said Mma Ramotswe. 'We tell her that Liso is the young man Rra Edgar was thinking of when he made the will. That is absolutely true, Mma Makutsi. One hundred per cent true. We don't have to tell her anything else we happen to have found out. She will have to do what the will says.'

'She won't like that, Mma.'

'That doesn't matter. We all have to do things we don't like. You had to be polite to that aunt of Phuti's. You did it. You put up with her.'

'That snake, Mma, it did us a big favour. Maybe it knew all about difficult aunts. Maybe it had a very nasty snake aunt who was always hissing.'

Mma Ramotswe laughed. 'Yes, maybe.' She became serious again. 'It's sad, isn't it, Mma, that a person can feel so ashamed of something that they can never talk about it. That woman on the farm – the mother – she has spent her life being frightened that her secret will be found out. That cannot be easy.'

'She is frightened more for the boy than for herself, I think,' said Mma Makutsi. 'But it is equally sad.'

'That is why I am pleased that they will get the farm. He will be a good farmer and she will be there watching him look after his father's place. That is a good result, Mma.'

'And Mma Sheba?' asked Mma Makutsi.

'She has enough money, I think – she does not need more. And she has her sadness, too, like the rest of us.'

'Because Rra Edgar is late?'

Mma Ramotswe nodded. 'She has lost him. But she does not need his farm to be able to remember him. She does not need that.'

And now they had to tell Mma Soleti that they had identified the person who was waging the campaign against her: Violet Sephotho. Mma Makutsi was looking forward to this and to the subsequent denunciation – to Violet's face – that she had been taking great pleasure in planning. Mma Ramotswe was more hesitant. She was prepared to be firm when firmness was required, but she did not like confrontation if she could possibly avoid it.

They left the office with Itumelang Clovis Radiphuti sound asleep in the small baby-seat that Phuti had bought and that strapped neatly into the passenger seat of the tiny white van, with Mma Makutsi herself travelling in the back. When they arrived, the infant was removed from the seat and tied firmly into a traditional African baby sling on his mother's back. Some mothers, Mma Ramotswe had noticed, were beginning to use front slings, but this seemed to her to be all wrong. Babies had always been carried on their mothers' backs in Africa, and it would be very confusing for everybody if they were to be carried in the front. What if the mother fell? She would fall on top of the baby. What if she were hit by one of those thorny branches while walking along a path through the bush? The baby would feel the thorns first. There were many arguments for the traditional approach, and she was pleased that she did not have to raise any of them with Mma Makutsi.

They went straight to the Minor Adjustment Beauty Salon. Mma Soleti was there, together with a young woman whom she introduced as her cousin's daughter, whom she had agreed to train as a beautician. Both looked despondent. When they saw Mma Makutsi's baby, however, they cheered up immediately and spent some time cuddling him and exchanging baby gossip with Mma Makutsi. There were tips to be given on the care of the delicate skin that babies had, and several special creams were produced and demonstrated on Itumelang, with the result that his face was soon quite pale with all the creams and potions applied.

It was Mma Ramotswe who broached the subject of the campaign. 'I think we have found out who is responsible for your troubles,' she said. She glanced at the young woman, uncertain as to whether she was aware of what had been happening.

Mma Soleti intercepted the look and reassured her. 'Angela knows all about it,' she said. 'You can talk freely.'

Mma Soleti handed Itumelang back to his mother and wiped her hands clean of the creams she had been applying. 'That is very good news,' she continued. 'Who is this person?'

'It is Violet Sephotho,' said Mma Makutsi. There was a note of triumph in her voice.

'Her!' hissed Mma Soleti.

'Yes,' said Mma Makutsi with relish. 'Her!'

'We think it's her,' said Mma Ramotswe. 'We know that it is

somebody Violet Sephotho employs who probably photocopied that leaflet. This suggests that Violet is behind it.'

'It is the sort of thing that woman would do,' said Mma Soleti. 'We all know about her.'

'I have known about her for many years,' said Mma Makutsi. 'Ever since those early days at the Botswana Secretarial College, I have known all about her and her . . . her machinations.'

'So what now?' asked Mma Soleti.

Mma Ramotswe explained that they would go to see her and reveal that they knew she was responsible. 'That should stop it,' she said. 'Which is what you want, isn't it?'

'And what about her punishment?' asked Mma Soleti.

'That will be more difficult,' said Mma Ramotswe. 'If we go to the police, they will ask where is our proof? And we don't really have much proof. We might be able to get her assistant to confess to having done the photocopying, but if she keeps her mouth shut then we will have nothing concrete to give the police.'

'So she may go unpunished?' The disappointment in Mma Soleti's voice was evident.

Angela was also dismayed. 'There is no justice,' she said. 'Maybe somewhere else there is justice, but not here.'

'For a person like that, to be stopped in her tracks might be punishment enough,' said Mma Ramotswe. 'She will not like being thwarted.'

This was clearly less than what Mma Soleti wanted, but at least it would set her mind at rest. To be persecuted by a known person was bad enough; to be persecuted by an unknown one was perhaps more terrifying.

Mma Soleti began to smile. 'I'm very happy, Mma Ramotswe. Now that I know who my enemy is, and that her campaign against me will come to an end, I feel much happier.'

'I'm glad,' said Mma Ramotswe.

'Let us give you free face treatments,' said Mma Soleti. 'Both of you. I will do you, Mma Makutsi, as you are a challenge. Angela will do Mma Ramotswe.'

Fortunately, Mma Makutsi did not seem to take offence at Mma Soleti's tactless remark. Itumelang had dropped off to sleep and she held him gently as she lay down on the couch. Angela took Mma Ramotswe into the back room, where there was a chair for her to sit in while she had her facial treatment.

'I am very glad that you have sorted this out, Mma,' said Angela as she began to apply cold cream. 'Mma Soleti is a very kind lady, and I have been very angry that she has been frightened. It is very bad.'

'Well, I think it is over now,' said Mma Ramotswe. 'Or it will be, soon enough.'

'That Violet Sephotho,' said Angela. 'Even I have heard of her, Mma. She is a very wicked woman.'

'I'm afraid she is,' said Mma Ramotswe. 'I think it must be because she is unhappy. People who behave badly are often unhappy with themselves – and with the world.'

Angela rubbed the cream into Mma Ramotswe's cheeks. She worked gently, and Mma Ramotswe decided that she would be good at her craft.

'Mind you,' said the young woman, 'I thought it was somebody else.'

'Did you?'

'Yes. I thought it was the person who wanted this shop.'

'Violet Sephotho wants this shop,' said Mma Ramotswe. 'That's why we knew it was her.'

'Yes,' said Angela. 'Maybe she does want it, but somebody else wants it even more. I heard about another person altogether but I didn't want to say anything to Mma Soleti because I wasn't sure and I knew that there had been a lot of trouble with that person.'

Mma Ramotswe was listening carefully. 'How did you hear all this?' she asked.

'Because I met the agent who lets these places,' said Angela. 'He lives near my parents. He said to me that he hoped that Mma Soleti was pleased with this place because he could have let it to somebody else. He said that there was somebody who tried to bribe him to let it to her, even after Mma Soleti had signed the agreement. He said she offered him money because she was desperate to get this shop. She wanted to open a branch of her printing business here and she thought this was the best place for that. He refused.'

Mma Ramotswe sat motionless, holding her breath. 'Did he say who it was, Mma?'

'It was that woman whose husband went off with Mma Soleti.'

'Daisy Manchwe?'

'Yes. He said it was her. So I thought that she must be the person who was trying to get us out. But now I know that I am wrong and it was really Violet Sephotho, I'm glad that I didn't say anything.'

Mma Ramotswe held up a hand. 'Can you wipe the cream off?' she said. 'I need to go.'

'But I've hardly started,' Angela complained.

'I'm sorry,' said Mma Ramotswe. 'There are things that are more important than beauty.'

Angela removed the cream and Mma Ramotswe stood up. Returning to the main treatment room, she addressed Mma Soleti, who was applying a thick layer of cream to Mma Makutsi's face.

'I think,' she began, 'that it might not be Violet Sephotho after all.'

Mma Soleti put down the jar of cream with a thump. 'Not her?'

'No. I think it is somebody else.' Mma Ramotswe glanced at Mma Makutsi. 'I . . . we both probably jumped to a conclusion. It was not an unreasonable conclusion, but it was perhaps a little bit too early to decide what we decided. I'm sorry, Mma.'

Mma Soleti frowned. 'It is not one person, but you say it is another. Who is this other person, Mma?'

'I think it is Daisy Manchwe. Angela has just told me that she tried to get hold of this shop. She is the one who copied that notice – and I think she probably wrote it too.'

Mma Soleti gasped. 'Her! I told you, Mma Ramotswe! You asked me for a list of enemies and I put her name at the top. Remember?'

'You did tell me, Mma,' agreed Mma Ramotswe. 'And I went to see her. She told me that she bore you no ill will. She said that she was pleased that you had taken her husband from her because . . .'

'Because of what, Mma?' Mma Soleti exploded.

Mma Ramotswe made an effort to summon every reserve of tact. 'Because she felt perhaps the two of them were not very well suited. It was something like that.'

Mma Soleti gave a crowing laugh. 'I rescued him from that big liar, Mma. She is a very big, famous liar.'

'Yes,' said Angela loyally. 'That is what she is. A big, big liar. There are many liars in this country, Mma, and her name is up at the top of the list. If the government published a list of liars, whose name would be at the top? Daisy Manchwe.'

Mma Ramotswe turned to Mma Makutsi. 'I'm sorry it wasn't Violet,' said Mma Ramotswe. 'I know you were looking forward to denouncing her.'

'There will always be another time,' said Mma Makutsi philosophically. 'When there are many bad ladies around, Mma, it is best to deal with them one by one, I think.'

'That's all very well,' interjected Angela. 'But what are you going to do with this Manchwe person? Is she going to get away with it, like Violet Sephotho would have done?'

Mma Ramotswe turned to Angela. 'There are ways of handling these things, Mma.'

'What are they?' challenged Angela.

Mma Ramotswe was tolerant of the younger woman's impatience. 'Mma Makutsi and I will go to speak to her. We will tell her that we know that it was her who has done these things.' She paused. 'Have you ever confronted a person who has done something really bad, Mma?'

Angela said nothing.

'Well,' continued Mma Ramotswe, 'sometimes you don't have to say very much to them. You look at them and you must not blink. You look at them, and you watch them, thinking about what they have done. It doesn't always work – there are some people who are without shame, but most people have some shame inside them, Mma. And you let that shame do its work. And . . . ' Now she raised a finger. 'You may tell them that they are forgiven. That can be very, very powerful, Mma. Don't forget it. Forgiveness works.'

Angela looked down at the floor. 'I'm sorry, Mma. I was a bit rude.'

'No, you weren't,' said Mma Ramotswe. 'What you said was understandable. There are times when it is necessary to punish people to make them face up to their actions – and to make others feel that justice has been done. So we might come up with something that will bring it home to Daisy Manchwe that what she did was wrong. I've thought of something, in fact.'

Mma Makutsi looked interested. 'What is that, Mma?'

'Could you use some advertising leaflets, Mma Soleti?'

Mma Makutsi let out a chuckle. 'Free, of course.'

But then Mma Ramotswe took Mma Soleti aside and whispered to her so that the others did not hear what she said. 'Mma, it may be that you need to think a bit about what happened between you and Daisy Manchwe. When there is something like this, it may be that there are two people at fault. It may be that you need to ask for forgiveness too. She may not feel entirely happy about her husband leaving her, you know – whatever she says about him.'

When Mma Soleti began to protest, Mma Ramotswe quietened her. 'No, Mma, you must think too. That is all I'm saying.'

Mma Soleti took a deep breath. 'All right, Mma, I'll think.'

'Good,' said Mma Ramotswe. 'Thinking is a good thing.' She smiled. 'Not always, but certainly most of the time.'

At lunchtime Mma Ramotswe drove Mma Makutsi and Itumelang Clovis Radiphuti back to the Radiphuti house as Phuti was delayed in a business meeting and could not collect them. Mma Makutsi, her face glowing from the creams that Mma Soleti had applied, invited Mma Ramotswe to return later on, after work, to share a cup of tea with her.

'I have some new chairs, Mma,' she said. 'And I would like you to see them.'

So Mma Ramotswe returned shortly after five that evening. They sat together on the veranda, watching the sun sink beneath the canopy of acacia that made the horizon. The sun was copperred, a great ball, and it floated down so gently, as if to nudge us into night, to let us take the garments of the dark about us slowly and deliberately, without haste and without fear.

Mma Ramotswe reflected on the events of the last few days. Matters that she had thought would not be easily settled had been resolved in ways that were quite unexpected.

'Isn't it odd,' she said to Mma Makutsi, 'how things work out in ways that you would never expect?'

'It is very odd,' said Mma Makutsi. 'Or maybe not. If it always happens, then maybe it isn't odd.'

'Perhaps not,' agreed Mma Ramotswe. 'Perhaps we should learn to expect the unexpected.'

'Then it would not be unexpected, Mma,' pointed out Mma Makutsi.

'No, you're right.'

Mma Ramotswe leaned back in her chair. The new chairs were very comfortable, but that was to be expected, surely, in the household of the man who owned the Double Comfort Furniture Store.

'I'm very grateful to you, Mma Makutsi,' she said. 'I think I may already have told you that I'm very grateful to you for coming back to work.'

'You have told me before, Mma,' said Mma Makutsi. 'But it does not matter if one says something more than once – if it is a good thing to begin with.'

Mma Ramotswe studied the glow in the sky where the sun had been. The glow left by the sun is like a good act done, she thought; or like love, which left the same warm signature behind it.

'Mma Makutsi,' she said. 'I have been thinking.'

'About what, Mma?'

'I have been thinking about this little business of ours.'

Ours, thought Mma Makutsi. *Ours*.

'And what I have decided,' Mma Ramotswe continued, 'is that you should be a partner in this business. Not an associate but a partner, sharing the profit, which may be nothing at the moment and may never be more than nothing, but may be more one day – who knows?'

247

Mma Makutsi looked at Mma Ramotswe and thought: This is the best woman in Botswana.

'Mma Ramotswe,' she said, 'half of nothing is better than nothing of nothing. And even if we made a big loss, I would be honoured to share that loss with you.' She paused. 'You are a very kind lady, Mma. I have always known that.'

Mma Ramotswe was quiet for a moment, but then she said, 'Well, Mma Makutsi, I think that's settled.'

They sat in silence. Nothing further needed to be said. As night embraced Botswana, the red glow in the sky faded, yet still seemed to be there, somehow, well after it had gone.

Read the next in the series . . .

Even the arrival of her baby can't hold Mma Makutsi back from success in the workplace, and so no sooner than she becomes a full partner in the No. 1 Ladies' Detective Agency (in spite of Mma Ramotswe's belated claims that she is only 'an assistant full partner'), she also launches a new enterprise of her own, the Handsome Man's De Luxe Café. Grace Makutsi is a lady with a business plan, but who could predict temperamental chefs, drunken waiters and more? Luckily, help is at hand, from the only person in Gaborone more gently determined than Mma Makutsi . . . Mma Ramotswe, of course.

The Handsome Man's De Luxe Café

Coming soon from Little, Brown

Alexander McCall Smith is the author of over eighty books on a wide array of subjects. For many years he was Professor of Medical Law at the University of Edinburgh and served on national and international bioethics bodies. Then in 1999 he achieved global recognition for his award-winning series The No. 1 Ladies' Detective Agency, and thereafter has devoted his time to the writing of fiction, including the 44 Scotland Street and Corduroy Mansions series. His books have been translated into forty-six languages. He lives in Edinburgh with his wife, Elizabeth, a doctor.